THE KIDNAPPER'S ACCOMPLICE

GLASS AND STEELE, #10

C.J. ARCHER

WWW.CJARCHER.COM

CHAPTER 1

LONDON, WINTER 1890

or all her whining about not being invited, Willie would have hated Lord Coyle and Hope Glass's wedding. The vicar's monotone set the scene for a staid affair that continued at the breakfast reception held at the bride's London home. Although Lord Coyle's townhouse was bigger, tradition dictated that Lord and Lady Rycroft host the event and, as Matt stated in a muttered breath as he steered me to a corner away from the beaming mother-of-the-bride, tradition was the glue that kept the upper-classes from falling off the top shelf.

"There are very few young people here," I whispered to Matt as I surveyed the small number of guests in the drawing room. "Where are all of Hope's friends?"

"She probably doesn't have any."

"Don't be unkind. Besides, she can be quite charming when she wants to be."

Hope's charms were on full display at the reception. She smiled prettily, as each guest congratulated her, and clung to her new husband's arm as if she adored him. It was a rather point-less show. Not a single person in that room would believe she'd married the grotesque Lord Coyle for love. The lifelong bachelor was one of the wealthiest men in the country, and his power and influence were extensive. Matthew's cousin had made a very good match, albeit a loveless one. Yet I didn't envy her at all.

I rested my hand on Matt's arm and smiled up at him.

He smiled back. "I hope the food is good. I need something to rub Willie's nose in."

"Now *that* is unkind."

"She deserves it after saying I look fat in this suit." He pressed a hand to his stomach. His very flat stomach. There was hardly an ounce of fat on Matt's body.

"She didn't say fat, she said you look as though married life is agreeing with you."

"That's a euphemism for getting fat."

I rolled my eyes. I never suspected he'd be so sensitive about his looks. "You know Willie is incapable of giving compliments so they're usually shrouded in sarcastic setdowns. She was really being quite sweet when she said marriage agrees with you."

An elderly lady passed by and smiled at Matt.

He gave her a shallow bow. "Don't let Willie hear you calling her sweet," he said through his smile. "She'll shoot something just to prove you wrong."

Aunt Letitia broke away from the clutch of ladies she'd been chatting to and joined us. Her face bore an earnest look, and I steeled myself for what I suspected would be a lecture. "What are you both doing hiding in the corner?"

"Hiding," Matt said.

"You should be mingling. There are people here who haven't met India and are put out that you didn't invite them to your wedding."

"Even now?" I asked.

"The older we get, the longer our memories are. And our grudges." She took my hand. "Let me introduce you to Matthew's second cousins."

"I have second cousins?" Matt asked.

His aunt gave him a narrow glare. "You met them at Patience's wedding to Lord Cox."

"You can't call him that anymore," I reminded her as she tugged me towards Matt's second cousins. "He lost the barony when the real heir was—er—found."

I glanced at Lord Coyle, conversing with his guests alongside his new wife. He'd been the one to set in motion the events that upturned Patience and Byron's life by informing the elder half-brother that he was, in fact, the true heir. It was no surprise that the couple hadn't attended the wedding of the youngest Glass sister to the man who'd orchestrated their downfall. They'd taken Byron's children on a holiday to Scotland, using the excuse of escaping the London gossip after the news became public, but I suspected it was also to avoid facing Lord Coyle today.

They would have to do it at some point, however.

"He was Lord Cox when she married him, so that's how I will refer to him," Aunt Letitia said. "Come along, India, Matthew. Duty calls. You must meet every single guest before the breakfast is over."

"Thank goodness they have so few friends," Matt said.

"Many are in the country for Christmas and the winter."

"England is covered in railways, Aunt. They could have come if they wanted to."

"Don't be impertinent, Matthew. Lord Coyle wanted to keep the wedding to a small number of intimates. That's why most of the guests are from the Glass side and only a few influential friends of his lordship."

I wasn't sure if I classed Lady Louisa Hollingbroke or Lord Farnsworth friends. As members of the magical collector's club, along with Coyle, they were acquaintances at best. He had not invited other members of the club, only those with a noble title. Not even Sir Charles Whittaker was among the guests, and certainly not the Delanceys, who were extraordinarily wealthy but not titled.

"Oh, look," I said as a procession of footmen entered carrying silver trays. "The food has arrived."

Aunt Letitia pulled me hard alongside her. "No eating until after you've met the second cousins."

Matt and I performed our duty and spoke to every Glass family member, most of whom were of Aunt Letitia's vintage. We even spoke briefly to the middle Glass sister, Charity, and with civility too, even though she didn't deserve it after claiming Cyclops had behaved abominably toward her when he'd done nothing of the sort. When she asked if Cyclops had mentioned her recently, Matt gave her a tight smile, said, "No," and steered me away.

I plucked a tasty looking French pastry off the tray carried by a footman and shot a glance towards the bride and groom, seated on the sofa. While Hope smiled as she chatted to the woman beside her, Lord Coyle alternately gazed longingly at the door then at his wife. When Lord Rycroft tried to engage him in conversation, Coyle gave him a curt response that stole the smile from Rycroft's eyes. He bowed and moved away.

The dining room wasn't large enough to seat everyone, so the guests congregated in the drawing room where some had to stand. Upon a signal given by her mother, Hope rose from the sofa like a delicate butterfly, clad in white silk and lace, and exited the room. With a strained smile, Lady Rycroft urged Charity to assist her sister. Charity scooped up Hope's long bridal train and flung it over her forearm like a butler carrying a freshly ironed newspaper. She dawdled behind her sister until Hope hissed something at her over her shoulder that made Charity quicken her pace. The two of them exited the drawing room with Lady Rycroft at their heels.

"Oddest wedding I've ever been to," came the laconic voice of Lord Farnsworth behind me. "The groom looks like

THE KIDNAPPER'S ACCOMPLICE

he's ready for a nap and the bride doesn't look like she minds that her new husband's as old and dull as dirt."

Lord Farnsworth was dashing in a tailcoat and white bowtie, his burnished blond hair parted down the middle. His blue eyes would have been piercing if not for the half-closed lids that hooded them. I wondered if he hid his best features on purpose before dismissing the notion. Why would anyone do that? Particularly one who declared himself on the marriage market.

I'd seen Lord Farnsworth quite a number of times since first meeting him, weeks ago, at a collector's club soiree where I'd been the guest of honor. He turned up at our house at the oddest times, such as the evening he'd left the opera during the interval and the morning when he'd joined us for breakfast after clearly having no sleep and far too much to drink. That had been Willie's fault. They'd met at a gambling den and she'd invited him back for breakfast after he complained of losing his cook to an opponent in a game of poker.

"Lord Coyle is not dull," I told him. "He's highly intelligent and plays a deep game."

Lord Farnsworth pouted. "I play a deep game too, you know. Played one just last night, in fact. I won a diamond and an evening in a round of skillful card playing, if I do say so myself."

I arched a brow. "You won an evening?"

Matt cleared his throat in what could only be described as a warning. Lord Farnsworth didn't heed it. "Off a lovely widow of a bold nature. Can't quite recall her name now, but she has long red hair and fine fingers. Don't s'pose you'd know her, Mrs. Glass. You and she don't swim in the same lake, as it were."

I pressed my lips together to stop myself smiling; not because of Lord Farnsworth's chatter but because Matt looked like he wanted to flee. His tolerance for his lordship grew weaker with every meeting.

"Speaking of odd couples, here come Louisa and her newspaperman," Lord Farnsworth said as Oscar and Louisa approached. "What does she see in him, do you think?"

"Magic," Matt said as he extended his hand in greeting to Oscar.

"What about it?" Oscar asked.

Lord Farnsworth waggled his fingers. "It's in the air at weddings, I find. Don't you, Louisa?"

Louisa eyed Lord Coyle on the sofa. A disinterested cross-ness had settled over his brow after Hope left the room. "Marriage has nothing to do with magic and everything to do with practical matters," she said, missing Lord Farnsworth's meaning.

"Some marriages have everything to do with magic," Oscar said with forced cheerfulness that made his fiancée glance sharply at him. "India, you look very elegant today."

"Thank you."

"No Mr. and Mrs. Swinsbury?" Oscar asked, referring to Patience and Byron, the former Lord and Lady Cox.

Matt's spine stiffened ever so slightly. "Looking for fodder for an article?"

"I'm not that much of a blackguard, Glass. I simply wanted to talk to the fellow, one ordinary man to another. I don't relish in his downfall."

"It's not a downfall."

Wisely, Oscar kept his mouth shut. Lord Farnsworth did not.

"I agree with the newspaperman. Going from a baron to a nobody is definitely a downfall. I say that with the utmost respect, with no offence intended to those of you who aren't peers."

I could almost hear Willie's voice taking him to task over that comment.

Fortunately neither Matt nor Oscar were the sort who cared what someone like Lord Farnsworth thought, or cared about being noble. Even Oscar, who was marrying a peeress, would admit that he was marrying Louisa for her money and not her title, which he could not adopt for himself anyway when they married, anyway.

"I hear they're enjoying a holiday in Scotland," Lord Farnsworth went on.

"Away from prying eyes," Matt added without taking his gaze off Oscar.

Oscar bristled.

"I'm surprised Sir Charles Whittaker isn't here," I cut in. "I thought he and Lord Coyle were friends, of sorts."

Louisa shook her head, making her blonde curls bounce girlishly and reminding me how young she was. Her confident nature made it easy to forget. "It's only their mutual magical interest that throws them together," she said. "I don't think Coyle likes him."

"Coyle doesn't like anyone," Matt said. "I thought I saw he and Whittaker walking together in Belgrave Square, once. They certainly seemed friendly on that occasion."

"They must have both been walking through the garden at the same time," Louisa said. "I can assure you, Lord Coyle wouldn't think of inviting him to his wedding. He considers himself above Sir Charles."

I squeezed Matt's arm, warning him not to say more. We didn't want to let anyone know that we'd overheard Sir Charles telling Lord Coyle that I'd made inquiries about wool magicians. He could only have received such information from Mrs. Delancey. The wool magician was needed for my experiments with Fabian Charbonneau, my magical mentor and spell collaborator, something which Sir Charles had immediately guessed when Mrs. Delancey informed him.

We'd not confronted either gentleman or Mrs. Delancey about it, and were yet to do anything with our knowledge of their collaboration. Matt wanted to feed them false information about my experiments with Fabian, but I wasn't sure that was a good idea. The most sensible course of action seemed to be inaction. Matt, however, didn't like doing nothing.

A flurry of activity by the door announced the return of Hope, now dressed in a sea-green gown trimmed with jade-green velvet and a leafy design embroidered from collar to hem. With little curls of hair arranged across her forehead, she looked very pretty indeed. From the way she held her head, with her chin slightly out-thrust, I suspected she knew it.

Charity looked cadaverous beside her more glamorous sister. She seemed to have grown paler in recent weeks, and the black gown she wore didn't help. She entered the drawing room with reluctance, as if dragged by the sheer force of her sister's wake.

Lord Coyle rocked until he had enough momentum to push his considerable self up from the sofa. He took his wife's hands. "Shall we depart, my dear?"

Lady Rycroft bustled forward and kissed her daughter's cheek. It was a signal for other family members to wish the couple well on their honeymoon. When it came to my turn, I didn't know what to say. Wishing Hope good luck seemed to imply she was going to need it, and telling them to enjoy their holiday seemed inappropriate. I couldn't imagine either of them enjoying time outside the city. Lord Coyle in particular was hardly the sort to partake in an idyll stroll along a seaside promenade far away from his business affairs here in London.

I simply congratulated them again and said, "Goodbye."

Hope patted my hand. "Perhaps you and Matt can join us for tea upon our return. We won't be gone long."

I smiled and gave what I hoped she took as a non-committal nod.

"We're both very busy," Matt said. He must have realized

how rude that sounded, because he added, "Send us dates and times and we shall see."

"No need for you to attend," Lord Coyle told him. "Just your wife. She can tell me all about her experiments with Charbonneau."

"She won't be telling you anything, Coyle." Matt managed to instill a measure of ice into his otherwise amiable tone.

Hope's smile froze, but Lord Coyle merely grunted acceptance. I suspected he expected the rebuke.

Aunt Letitia bustled over and tilted her head for her niece to kiss her cheek. "You must hold a dinner for his lordship's friends upon your return, Hope. Invite Charity. She needs to mix with good company."

Charity made a sound of disgust in the back of her throat.

Her mother tried to cover it with a laugh that only drew everyone's attention with its falseness. "It's no longer Hope now, Letitia. She's Lady Coyle."

Aunt Letitia sniffed. "She's my niece. She'll always be just Hope to me."

Lady Rycroft looked as though she would protest until her husband raised his glass and called for a toast to the happy couple. Lord and Lady Coyle departed as quickly as his lordship's gait would allow. I let out a breath, thankful I'd managed to get through the event without a bitter word passing between Hope and me, or a threat from her new husband. I hadn't been sure what to expect now that he knew about my search for a wool magician.

I eyed Oscar, making his excuses to our hosts with Louisa.

"No," Matt said, his voice a deep boom in my ear that vibrated through my body.

"No?" I echoed. "Care to elaborate?"

"I know what you're thinking, and I'm expressing my displeasure at you asking Barrett if he can put you in touch with a wool magician."

Sometimes Matt's ability to read my mind was freakish.

"You were expressing more than your displeasure. You were forbidding me."

"I'm offended you think that of me, India. I wouldn't dream of forbidding you anything."

I pressed my lips together.

His fingers lightly brushed mine. "I wouldn't dream of forbidding you, because I know that would have the opposite effect. I am simply *advising* you not to ask him. Barratt already knows too much about the watch flying spell you created with Charbonneau, and while he might be trustworthy, his fiancée isn't."

"You think he'll tell her, even if I ask him not to?"

"I think she'll get the information out of him, one way or another."

We seemed to be surrounded by manipulators at every turn. "Very well. I won't ask him."

Avoiding Louisa altogether proved impossible, however. As soon as Matt left my side to assist his aunt into our waiting carriage, she moved up alongside me.

"I noticed you looking at my fiancé with a curious expression, India," she said smoothly. "Is there something you wanted to discuss with him?"

"I was simply wondering when to expect the happy occasion of your wedding day," I said, equally as smooth. "Today had me thinking about it, that's all."

"We haven't set a date yet." Louisa's gaze followed the retreating figure of Oscar as he walked off, a hand clamped to his hat to stop it blowing away in the stiff breeze. He had somewhere to be and had declined the offer of a ride in our carriage and that of his fiancée.

"He's a fair man," she added, as if she were trying to convince me of his good qualities. "He's earnest about magic, too."

No, she wasn't listing his good qualities to convince *me* of his suitability, she was trying to convince herself. She was not in love with Oscar, and she knew he wasn't in love with her. Theirs would be a marriage of convenience, just as much as Lord Coyle's was to Hope. Except Louisa was marrying Oscar for his magic lineage, not his money and influence.

"How is Fabian?" she suddenly asked.

I blinked, taken aback. "He's very well."

She smiled, but it quickly vanished. She grasped my hands. "Will you tell him something from me?"

"Of course, but surely you can tell him yourself. He'd be happy to see you."

She withdrew her hands. "I doubt it. After he rejected my proposal of marriage, things became awkward between us." Her carriage drew up and she waited for a footman to open the door.

"What did you want me to tell him?" I asked.

She accepted the footman's assistance up the step to the cabin. "Never mind. It doesn't matter." The footman closed the door and signaled to the driver to drive off.

"India?" Matt prompted from where he stood a little further along the pavement near our conveyance. "What did she want?"

"I'm not really sure."

I joined Aunt Letitia inside the cabin where she sat with a blanket over her knees and her chin tucked into the fur collar of her coat. I took her hand as I sat beside her and rubbed it.

She gave a contented sigh. "Two nieces wed and one to go."

"Finding a husband for Charity will prove a difficult task," Matt said with a crooked smile.

"Nonsense. There's someone for everyone. Even Charity. And Willie, too."

I wasn't so sure there was any particular *one* for Willie. She seemed to prefer to have two or more partners at a time, never getting too content with any of them. She was nothing if not unique. Perhaps too unique for Aunt Letitia's sensibilities, however, and it was best not to bring attention to the fact.

Matt suddenly sat forward and thumped the roof. "Stop!"

We ground to a halt that almost sent Aunt Letitia and me sliding off the seat. Matt leaped out of the carriage before it had fully come to a halt.

"Barratt!" he barked. It was indeed Oscar, leaning against a wall near the entrance to a narrow lane, his body bent forward, his breathing ragged as he gulped in large breaths.

He looked up and I gasped. His nose was bloody, his eye red and starting to swell. "I was attacked." He pointed at a figure running away.

Matt set off at a sprint after him. No amount of calling him back had an effect. He turned a corner, several paces behind Oscar's attacker, but gaining fast.

"Be careful!" Oscar called out. "He's got a knife!"

CHAPTER 2

"*Y*ou should have said he had a knife before Matt set off in pursuit," I snapped at Oscar.

He dabbed at his bloody nose with his gloved hand. "Sorry. I wasn't thinking."

A chilly wind nipped my cheeks. I rubbed my arms and stared after Matt, willing him to return unharmed.

"Ma'am," called Woodall, our coachman, from the driver's perch. "I think I should go after him."

I was about to agree when Matt reappeared at the corner. He jogged toward us and took my hand when I went to him.

"Don't run off after villains again," I scolded. "Let the police do it."

"There are no constables nearby," he said.

Oscar dabbed at his nose. "That's because this is a good area. They don't think it's necessary."

"Your eye is almost swollen shut," I said. "You need to see a doctor. We'll take you now."

"Thank you, India."

"You can spend the journey telling us why someone attacked you," Matt said darkly.

I stopped with one foot on the step up to the coach cabin. "You don't think it was a random attack from a thief?"

"In the middle of the day? No, I do not." Matt eyed Oscar.

Oscar sighed. "You're right. It wasn't a random attack. That thug was sent by someone."

I gasped. "Who would do such a thing? And why?"

Matt assisted me up the step. "There'll be a long list, starting with people who don't like magicians."

It was true that Oscar had made no secret of the fact he was a magician. We knew first-hand that there were a number of artless craftsmen in the city and beyond who were worried about magicians using their magic to manufacture products of superior quality. Even though that magic was temporary, and once the magic wore off the product would return to its natural quality, the artless were afraid of losing custom. It had led to tensions in the guilds as suspected magicians were forced out or, at the very least, eyed with suspicion. There had even been violent acts committed by magicians in retaliation, and against them too. It was quite likely Oscar was the latest victim.

He had a different opinion, however. "My attacker demanded I stop writing the book."

Oscar was writing a book about magic, but some people thought it a bad idea and wanted it suppressed. Matt was one of those people. He thought it would only stir up more trouble between the two factions.

Matt wasn't scowling at Oscar, however. Indeed, he wasn't paying Oscar any attention. "Aunt? Are you all right?"

Aunt Letitia said nothing. She simply stared out of the window, a blank look on her face. Matt leaned forward and touched her elbow, rousing her.

"What a cold day," she said. "I don't think we should go for our walk after all, Harry. Father ordered you to stay indoors, anyway. Do try not to vex him today. My nerves can't take another argument."

"I'll do as you ask, if only for the sake of your nerves." Matt smiled gently at her. "We have to make one stop to take my friend somewhere then we'll go home."

We deposited Oscar at the residence of our friend Gabe Seaford, the medical magician, then continued home to Park Street. Matt steered Aunt Letitia up the stairs to her room. I fetched her maid and joined Duke and Willie in the sitting room. Cyclops was out visiting Catherine Mason at her watch and clock shop. He was there quite a lot lately, but they were yet to talk to her parents about their growing affection. They insisted on progressing their relationship slowly. It was most frustrating.

"What set her off this time?" Willie asked. She lounged in an armchair by the fireplace in a most unladylike sprawl, her stockinged feet angled to the warmth, her boots by the chair.

"We stopped on the way home to assist Oscar," I said. "He endured a beating."

Neither Duke nor Willie looked overly concerned by this news. "Did he deserve it?" Duke asked.

"Course he did," Willie said. "It's a wonder he ain't been beat up more."

"He's not that bad," I said, sitting beside Duke on the sofa. "His passion for living freely as a magician simply makes him do foolish things from time to time. He means well."

"Meaning well ain't an excuse for being stupid."

Duke poured a cup of tea from the teapot and handed it to me just as Matt entered. "So how was the wedding?" he asked.

"Dull," Matt said. "We left as soon as the couple departed for their honeymoon."

Willie *humphed* into her teacup which I suspected held a nip of something stronger than tea. "I should have been invited. I'm family."

Duke rolled his eyes. "She's been like this all morning. Wish I'd gone with Cyclops."

"Ain't no one stopped you from going," Willie shot back.

"They don't want me there. Not when Ronnie's out doing deliveries all morning and they can be alone. So why was Barratt beaten up? Did he offend some toff at the wedding?"

"Not that we know of," Matt said. "The attacker demanded Oscar stop writing his book about magic. Oscar refused, so the attacker tried to force him into agreeing with a beating. I chased after him but he jumped into a hansom and got away. I did overhear him direct the driver to Hammersmith but I didn't see his face."

"Will Barratt report it to the police?" Willie asked without looking up from her cup.

"Why?" I asked coyly. "Will you ask Detective Inspector Brockwell to look into the case on Oscar's behalf? I'm sure he'd be appreciative of the personal touch."

Duke snorted. "Who? Brockwell or Barratt?"

"Shut it, both of you." Willie set the cup down on a table beside her chair with a thud. Fortunately it was empty or the impact would have sent the contents sloshing over the sides. "Me and Jasper are finished. He made it clear I disgust him and he doesn't want anything more to do with me."

"You shocked him, Willie, that's all," I said. "Now that he's had time to become used to the idea that you like women as well as men, he might be ready to have another dalliance with you."

She slumped further into the chair, her arms crossed high up on her chest. She scowled at the glowing coals in the fireplace as if they were the cause of her problems with the detective inspector. The real problem was that she hadn't been open with him about her inclinations from the start. She had assumed he wouldn't like her once he knew. I had more faith in Brockwell. He might seem as stodgy as undercooked bread, but he was really quite broad-minded. Despite initial misgivings, he accepted the existence of magic and Willie's restless nature and desire to be intimate with other people. He just hadn't expected her to be intimate with women, and when he'd found out, he'd been taken aback. One could hardly blame him when it was something Willie hadn't mentioned.

"India's right," Matt said. "Give Brockwell another chance."

She made a sound in the back of her throat, but I couldn't decipher its meaning.

Duke seemed to have a better understanding of her grunts. "Don't be so stubborn. You should at least talk to him. I reckon India's right, and he'll be ready to pick up where you left off if you let him."

Willie looked like the idea was beginning to appeal to her when Duke added, "It can't be easy for a man to find a woman who doesn't want to get married."

She pushed to her feet. "Thanks, Duke. There ain't no other reason he'd like me, is there?" She snatched up her boots and stormed out.

Duke twisted his mouth to the side as he watched her go. "I think I know what I said wrong."

"I should hope so," Matt said, trying not to smile. "Your error is as obvious as the lack of Christmas decorations that you three were supposed to put up in our absence."

Duke poured himself another cup of tea then removed the flask from his pocket. "When Cyclops left, me and Willie lost interest." He poured a dash of whiskey into his tea then offered the flask to Matt. Matt shook his head. "We did make a start on a paper garland. It's in the library."

"It's quite all right," I told him. "When Aunt Letitia is feeling better, we can make some together."

In truth, I wanted to decorate the house myself. It was my first Christmas there; my first with Matt and my first as a married woman. While we'd ordered a tree, I'd wanted to get started on paper decorations immediately. I'd only wanted the others to assist me, but they'd said they'd make a start this morning while we were at the wedding. Thankfully Cyclops had better things to do, Willie had the attention span of a small child, and Duke followed where Willie led.

Aunt Letitia awoke from a nap feeling herself again and not like the teenager she imagined she was during one of her memory lapses. We spent the afternoon together in the library planning Christmas decorations and celebrations.

Matt received a note from Oscar thanking him for his assistance earlier and asking us not to tell anyone about the incident, including Louisa. I thought it foolish to keep something so important from his fiancée. Not only did it affect her, but it might make her feel some sympathy toward him and sympathy sometimes led to affection. When I said this to Matt he called me a romantic. The smile on his face as he said it, and the tenderness of his hands as he caressed me, implied he didn't think being a romantic was a bad thing. Quite the opposite.

I spent the following morning with Fabian Charbonneau and a wool magician he'd found. Although he'd only lived in England for a short time, Fabian had quickly become acquainted with several magicians in the city and he'd used those new contacts to locate a wool magician to contribute to our new spell.

Like Oscar, Fabian didn't hide his magic. I hid mine because it was more sought after than theirs. It wasn't the fact I could mend broken watches without even trying, it was my ability to extend the magic of other magicians that made me unique. The time extension spell had been given to me by my grandfather to save Matt's life. Since Chronos and I were the only horology magicians in the country, perhaps the world, our extension spell meant we were valuable indeed. I did not want to live a life where I was constantly pestered to extend the magic of others, particularly in a world where magicians were already feared by the artless. If the artless knew what I could do, what lengths would they go to in order to stop me?

"These words are the same as my watch fixing spell and your iron strengthening spell, Fabian." I said, pointing to the spell Mr. Pyke the wool magician had written down for us. "And these are different. They must be the ones we insert into our spell."

Fabian leaned over my shoulder. He smelled of sandalwood today, a new scent and much more English than his usual French florals. "I agree. Shall we try them?"

Mr. Pyke cleared his throat and emerged from the corner where he'd been standing ever since writing the spell down for us. He was a middle-aged man with slightly protruding teeth and a balding head. According to Fabian, Mr. Pyke didn't use his magic in many of his carpets, only some, so as to avoid detection by his guild.

"Can I ask what your spell will do?" he asked.

Fabian hesitated, but I could see no way in which we could keep it a secret from Mr. Pyke. For one thing, he ought to know since he was contributing to the new spell, and for another, we needed him present while we spoke the spell to ensure we pronounced it correctly.

"We want to make a flying carpet," I said.

Mr. Pyke looked around the room. "That explains why the furniture has been pushed back. How do you create a new spell for that?"

"Mr. Charbonneau can make iron objects fly and control their speed and direction, while I can do the same for timepieces. You cannot do that for woolen things, but your spell does make wool stronger and the carpets quite beautiful."

"Briefly."

"That doesn't matter for this spell. All we need from you are the word or words that represent wool in your spell then we replace the words that mean iron or watches from our spells and *voila*. The new spell should make that rug fly."

Fabian dipped the pen into the ink and added the neces-

19

sary words from the wool spell to our flying spell in the note-book. "Move off the rug please, Mr. Pyke."

Mr. Pyke flattened himself to the wall as Fabian read out the words.

Nothing happened.

"Did I say it right?" Fabian asked Mr. Pyke.

Mr. Pyke shrugged. "Your accent might make a difference."

Fabian placed the notebook in front of me. "You try, India. Your magic is stronger than mine and you have an English accent."

I silently read through the three lines then read them again, out loud, while picturing the rectangular Oriental rug rising.

On the second attempt, the corner fluttered before falling back to the floor.

Mr. Pyke knelt and smoothed out a wrinkle in the carpet. "You have to emphasize the second syllable, not the first." He joined me at the desk and pointed to one of the two words we'd taken from his spell.

I tried it again, and this time the entire rug lifted off the floor. I gasped and it suddenly dropped.

Fabian cheered and Mr. Pyke clapped. "Very good, but it didn't fly."

"I lost concentration in my surprise at our quick success," I said.

Fabian laid a calming hand on my shoulder. "*Your* success, India. Try again. See if you can make it rise to the ceiling."

I steadied my breathing and focused my attention on the rug, on its rich red and gold weave bordered in blue and cream swirls. The rug rose from the floor but this time it kept rising at a steady pace until it touched the chandelier where it hovered for several seconds. I then lowered it, even pausing halfway to see if I could control it to a greater extent. Then I let it drift slowly to the floor where it settled into its original position.

Mr. Pyke stared open-mouthed at me. Fabian grinned and applauded.

"We did it," I murmured.

"*You* did it, India," Fabian said.

I shook my head. "You could have done it too. Your magic is strong and you can imitate the proper accent."

"My magic is not like yours. Yours is special."

He joined Mr. Pyke who placed his hands on the rug. "It's very warm," Mr. Pyke said as he ran his fingers over the weave.

I looked over the spell again then closed the notebook. "That was more successful than I expected."

"What will you do with the new spell?" Mr. Pyke asked.

"Nothing," I said. "We simply wanted to see if it could be done."

"Will you make other things fly now? Other metals, perhaps?"

"I doubt it. There's no point. We'll probably move onto something entirely different."

I looked to Fabian and he smiled back. His eyes shone with wonder at our achievement.

My heart responded with a little flutter in my chest. We *had* achieved something wondrous. We'd created the first new spell in years—perhaps centuries. Not only that, but I had spoken a spell that had nothing to do with timepieces. Magicians had not worked outside their own craft for a very long time and even then only a select few powerful ones could make new spells work using a craft that was not their primary magical one.

I was one of those powerful magicians. It was humbling and rather overwhelming too. The implications could be far-reaching. I passed my hand over the notebook, feeling somewhat giddy.

"I would like my payment please," Mr. Pyke said.

Fabian pulled out some bank notes from his inner jacket pocket. "Of course. Thank you for—"

"I don't want money."

"Pardon?"

"I said I don't want money."

Fabian tilted his head to the side. "But we discussed your fee before you came here today. You agreed to the amount." He tried to hand the bank notes to Mr. Pyke, but the wool magician refused to take them.

Fabian muttered something in French under his breath. "What do you want?"

Mr. Pyke looked to me. "I want you to extend my magic, Mrs. Glass."

I shot to my feet. "No! Absolutely not."

"Your extension spell will make my rugs last a lifetime. Beyond! Imagine owning a rug that never goes threadbare, never frays or fades. My name and reputation will live on in my rugs."

"I do not extend the spells of others, Mr. Pyke. You've agreed to a sum with Mr. Charbonneau; kindly accept the money and leave. Might I also remind you of your promise to keep our achievement to yourself."

Mr. Pyke glanced at Fabian then took a step closer to me. I took one back and Fabian came up alongside me. But Mr. Pyke didn't look like the violent type. He merely huffed in frustration. "It's only fair you do this for me, Mrs. Glass. After all, you make your watches run on time forever. They'll never lose a second when you use your extension spell on them. People will look upon your watches for generations to come and admire their quality and accuracy. Why can't all magicians enjoy the same benefits?"

"For one thing, I don't use the extension spell on my timepieces, and for another, I don't sell watches and clocks. You will make quite a fortune from the sale of your rugs once word got out that that their fine quality lasted."

"I don't care about the money. I want my reputation as a quality rug maker to outlive me." He passed a hand over his mouth and locked his earnest gaze with mine. "Mrs. Pyke and I haven't been blessed with children. My rugs are all I have. I cherish the ones I put my magic into. I weave them with my bare hands and don't sell them to just anyone. The buyer has to be right. They have to appreciate fine quality woolen rugs. If the life of that carpet can be extended by your magic, that'll be my legacy. Do you understand, Mrs. Glass?"

"I do."

I too had an affinity for the timepieces I worked on. I wouldn't say I cherished them, but I did feel a connection to them. For me, it was like a calling, a compulsion, but I could see how other magicians would look upon their magical work and think of it as an extension of themselves.

"But I cannot extend your magic," I went on. "It's not right or fair. I am sorry, but my decision is final."

Mr. Pyke's nostrils flared and his cheeks pinked.

Before the wool magician could utter a word, Fabian stepped between us. "We agreed on a sum and that is what I will pay. No more." He thrust the money into Mr. Pyke's palm. "Leave as a gentleman of your word and not like a vagabond thrown out by my staff."

Mr. Pyke's hand closed around the bank notes. "Can't blame a man for trying."

Fabian barked an order and his footman came running.

"I'm going, I'm going," Mr. Pyke muttered.

I watched him leave and released a breath once his footsteps had receded. "I suppose we should have expected that."

"I am sorry, India. I should have chosen more carefully."

"It's not your fault. He tricked you. At least he didn't dig his heels in and insist."

"It would make no difference. You would still say no and

my man would still throw him out." He shrugged with lazy elegance in what I'd come to think of as his French way. He grinned and indicated the notebook. "Come. Try again. This time I will ride it."

"Ride the carpet! Fabian, are you mad?"

There was that grin again. "Perhaps." He settled cross-legged on the rug and rested his hands on his knees. After a moment's thought, he clutched the edge. "Do it. Speak the spell."

I concentrated on the carpet first, focusing all my attention on picturing it rise. Then I spoke the spell from the book.

The rug lifted as it had done before, but dipped alarmingly beneath Fabian's weight. He slipped off. Fortunately it had risen mere inches off the floor.

"Are you all right?" I asked, assisting him to his feet.

He dusted off his trousers. "I think a little more concentration must be applied to the area beneath me next time."

"I'm not sure it's as simple as that. I wonder if the spell needs to be adjusted."

We both considered this in silence a moment until Fabian shrugged again.

"It did lift," he said. "That is a good sign. I thought it would not with me riding it."

"I'd hardly call it riding, Fabian. It was more like balancing."

He laughed. "Shall we try again?"

We tried three more times, but each attempt ended with the same result. Fabian wanted to try again, but it was time for me to leave. He walked me outside to my waiting carriage and waved me off after declaring he was going to attempt to replicate my success on his own. I ordered him not to ride again without me present.

Matt was home when I arrived. He beckoned me into the library and closed the door. He looked pleased with himself.

"I made a carpet fly!" I blurted out, unable to contain my news.

His brows almost flew off his forehead. "Congratulations."

"You're unhappy about it," I said flatly.

"Just surprised. I didn't think you would make it work so soon." He perched on the edge of the table and took my hand. "I'm pleased for you because I know it's something you've worked hard to achieve, but I reserve the right to remain apprehensive about that spell and all future spells you create."

"The notebook is safely locked away, and Fabian won't let anyone see it." I didn't tell him about Mr. Pyke's demand for payment from me. It had come to naught and wasn't worth worrying Matt over.

He drew me close and kissed me lightly on the lips. "I am immensely proud of you, India. You continue to amaze me."

"Thank you. Now tell me your news. I can see you have something important to say."

"Just after you left, I had word from a civil servant who works at the Home Office. I've been trying to bribe him ever since learning he works for the honors committee."

"The honors committee?"

"They accept nominations and decide who should be put forward for a knighthood."

"Oh," I said, trying to sound like I was following. "Go on."

"Sir Charles Whittaker was not among the candidates in any of the records going back ten years."

I stared at him. "He's not really knighted?"

"He is knighted. I checked."

I frowned. "I'm confused."

He indicated the book on the table. It was a copy of *Debrett's Peerage and Baronetage*, opened to the page listing Sir Charles. "If it's in Debrett's, then his knighthood is authentic.

C.J. ARCHER

He's not just gadding about calling himself a sir for amusement. I wanted to find out what he was knighted for, considering he claims to be nothing more than a civil servant."

"He has never elaborated on what he does for the government," I pointed out.

"Precisely. And I have asked, both directly and indirectly. He won't say, and no one seems to know. So I decided to work backwards from the knighthood, and have discovered through my new friend—"

"Whom you bribed."

"Whom I bribed with a considerable sum, that Whittaker's nomination did not go through the committee, like everyone else's."

"It bypassed the system?"

"Precisely. And that can only mean one thing. He was knighted for work so secretive that no one must know about it, not even the honors committee."

"That seems like a wise decision considering at least one member of the committee can be bribed."

A small crease appeared between his brows. "You're not taking this seriously."

"I am. I'm just not sure what this has to do with Sir Charles telling Lord Coyle about me looking for a wool magician."

"It might have nothing to do with it, but it does point to the fact that he is not who he says he is. At least, he's not who he is *pretending* to be."

"He hasn't lied. He simply hasn't elaborated."

"He doesn't have magical objects in his house despite telling the other club members he does. That's a lie."

"He could keep them somewhere else for protection, as he claims to."

"The mere fact that he is working on some level with Coyle is suspicious enough, let alone that they are sharing secrets about you and magic."

He was right. It was a concern. Sir Charles must be treated with suspicion until we knew more about him. "So how do we find out what he does for the government? Confront him?"

"Not yet." He looked down at the copy of *Debrett's* and began to shake his head, but stopped. His gaze met mine again and a crooked smile touched the corner of his mouth. "We do know he gets information from Mrs. Delancey. I propose we return to our original plan and talk to her."

"You want to feed her false information to throw Sir Charles off the scent?" I wasn't even sure what that scent was. Perhaps I'd been reading too many detective novels lately.

"I just want you to talk to her. Find out what she knows about Whittaker's work, if anything. Don't tell her about the flying carpet."

"Of course not." I circled my arms around his neck. "Are you not coming with me?"

"I'll leave Mrs. Delancey in your capable hands. Take Willie with you."

I drew back with a frown. "Why?"

"She's driving me mad being here all day. She needs to go somewhere that's not a gambling den and be with people who are not Lord Farnsworth. Do you know he regularly takes her to Tattersalls?"

"I thought he didn't like women invading the traditional masculine space of the bloodstock auctions."

"Willie appears to be the exception. I'm worried she's going to purchase a thoroughbred she can't afford based on the advice of a bored aristocrat with nothing better to do than lose money at cards and horses."

"You're being a little harsh on him. Lord Farnsworth treated his lover with a great deal more affection and respect than she deserved. That says much about a man."

He conceded the point with a nod. "I promise I'll try to

think more fairly of him in future, but I can't promise to like him."

"That seems reasonable to me. And I will take Willie with me tomorrow morning when I call on Mrs. Delancey. I quite like watching Mrs. Delancey try to figure Willie out."

I kissed him again and he responded warmly if somewhat absently. I drew away, arched my brow, and said, "What is it, Matt?"

"There's one more thing about Whittaker that occurred to me as I was coming home in a cab. I overheard Barratt's attacker tell the driver to take him to Hammersmith."

"You mentioned it at the time, but I don't see— Oh! Sir Charles lives in Hammersmith! Are you suggesting he sent that thug to threaten Oscar?"

"I am."

"That's an awful thing to insinuate without proof. I can't imagine he'd do such a thing. He might be suspicious, but I don't think he's violent."

"Hiring someone to commit violence is far easier than doing it yourself."

I swallowed heavily. I used to think myself a dreadful judge of character, until Matt convinced me otherwise. But those doubts crept in again. I had liked Sir Charles, on the whole. If I'd been wrong about him, who else had I judged incorrectly?

CHAPTER 3

"**I** heard the bride looked quite sickly," Mrs. Delancey said, handing me a teacup.

"Not at all," I said, accepting it. "She looked as radiant as ever."

"I also heard the ceremony was terribly bland."

"That's true." I didn't feel any guilt for calling the ceremony bland. It had been dull, and I had no reason to protect Lord Coyle or Hope from gossip.

"I also heard the food was awful, and the guests couldn't wait to leave."

"The food was quite delicious." I didn't respond to her comment about wanting to leave. In our case, it had certainly been true.

"I'm glad we didn't go," Mrs. Delancey said as she handed another teacup to Willie, sitting beside me like a washed-out version of herself. "We had another invitation for the same day and I would have been desolated if I'd missed it for a wedding reception that was...how shall I put it...not up to my very particular standards."

I bit the inside of my cheek to stop myself from pointing out that she hadn't been invited to the wedding. Thankfully

Willie was suffering the ill effects of imbibing too much alcohol the previous night to comment. I doubted she'd heard a word over the pounding in her head.

She did not immediately take the offered cup. "Got anything stronger, Mrs. D?"

Mrs. Delancey's polite smile froze. "Coffee?"

Willie screwed up her nose and accepted the teacup.

"Sir Charles wasn't at the wedding either," I said idly. "I wonder why."

Mrs. Delancey sipped her tea.

"Perhaps he wasn't invited," I went on. "Or perhaps he was busy at his place of employment. Tell me, Mrs. Delancey, you are closely acquainted with Sir Charles; where does he work?"

Mrs. Delancey blushed. It would seem she was still mortified at being caught meeting with Sir Charles in secret. We initially suspected they were having an affair, but it turned out she was feeding him information about me and the spells I was creating with Fabian. I didn't feel inclined to alleviate her discomfort.

"We aren't terribly close," she muttered.

"But you must know where he works?" I pressed.

"In one of the government buildings."

"Which one? What department?"

"Why do you want to know?"

"He asked me if an artefact he'd purchased had magic in it, and I wanted to speak to him about it some more." I'd practiced the lie on the way over so it rolled easily off my tongue.

She straightened and her eyes widened. "Oh? What object?"

"He asked me to be discreet. Sorry."

Her face sagged. "Why not speak to him at his place of residence? You know where he lives."

"He never seems to be there when I call on him, so I thought I'd pay him a visit at his office. So, where is that?"

"I don't know."

"What department does he work for?"

"I don't know that either." She lowered her cup to the saucer. "India, why the sudden interest in Sir Charles?"

"I just want to return the artefact to him," I said quickly.

"Is it something important?"

"No. It's nothing." I laughed for good measure to throw her off the scent.

It seemed to have the opposite effect. She leaned forward and held my gaze. "Is the magic in it very strong? Or does it contain a rare magic? Gold, perhaps."

"Nothing like that." I sipped my tea

"But—"

"Have you got any cake?" Willie cut in.

Mrs. Delancey blinked at her then tugged on the bell pull. A footman entered and she asked him to fetch cake. Once he'd gone and shut the door again, she resumed her interrogation.

"It is gold magic, isn't it?" She curled her hand into a fist and struck her knee. "I knew it. How did he get his hands on a magical golden object?"

Lord, how had this escalated so quickly? I scrambled to find a way out of the conversation that wouldn't make things worse, but it was Willie who came to the rescue.

She suddenly turned very green and shot to her feet. She got as far as the closed door when she must have realized she wouldn't make it to the privy, and threw up in a large blue and white vase perched on a pedestal.

"That's a magical piece!" Mrs. Delancey cried. "It cost a fortune."

"Worth every penny." Willie returned the bunch of pink flowers she'd hastily removed to the vase. "I feel better now, thanks."

"I did not ask after your health," Mrs. Delancey quipped. "Clearly you cannot hold your liquor."

Willie stormed back to the sofa but did not sit down. "I can. Last night was an exception. The liquor was bad, I reckon."

"I have just the thing to make you feel better. *Permanently* better." Mrs. Delancey pushed past Willie and opened the drawer of a side table. "I've joined the temperance movement."

Willie groaned.

"We meet regularly and write letters to the government demanding changes to liquor licensing laws. Our members have all signed pledges to give up drink."

"If you're going to lecture me on the perils of liquor, I'm leaving."

"Surely I don't need to lecture you. The evidence is in my vase." She waved the leaflet under Willie's nose. "Sign this pledge. You'll feel much better if you eradicate liquor from your life."

Willie backed away so quickly she almost tripped over her own feet. "I ain't signing that," she said with horror.

Mrs. Delancey shoved the leaflet into Willie's chest. Willie took the leaflet and tossed it away then rubbed her chest as if she'd been stabbed.

The footman re-entered carrying a tray with slices of cake on plates. He handed them around and we resumed our seats. When Mrs. Delancey passed a plate to Willie, she turned her face away and shook her head. She swallowed heavily but thankfully her color remained merely grey rather than green.

"Speaking of magic," Mrs. Delancey said to me while I tried to think of a way to extract more information about Sir Charles from her. "How is your work with Mr. Charbonneau progressing?"

"Slowly," I said.

"But you must have advanced. That's why you asked me

about my husband's family, isn't it? You needed a wool magician. Did you find one?"

"Er…"

"They gave up," Willie said. "They couldn't find a wool magician but they did find a jeweler who can do magic."

Mrs. Delancey gave a little gasp. "Jewelry magic," she cooed. "How lovely."

I shot a glare in Willie's direction, but she didn't notice. She looked rather pleased with herself. "Diamonds, to be exact."

Mrs. Delancey clutched her throat, as if she could feel a magical diamond necklace nestled there. "What spell are they trying to create?"

"Turning gold into diamonds."

Mrs. Delancey gasped. "Why gold?"

Willie shrugged and Mrs. Delancey turned to me for an answer. I stared back at her, utterly lost for words.

"Only something precious can be turned into a more precious thing," Willie said with authority.

Mrs. Delancey nodded in earnest. "Yes, of course. That makes sense."

"They've got a problem, though."

"Oh? What is it?"

"Willie," I warned.

"I know you don't want me to say, India," Willie said with a very smug look in her eyes. "But I think Mrs. D. can help."

"Oh yes, I'd be glad to help," Mrs. Delancey said. "Tell me what to do."

"You can donate some of your gold jewelry to India to continue the experiment. It takes rather a lot to perfect the diamond creating spell and, well, India has run out of gold."

"But Mr. Glass is wealthy, as is Mr. Charbonneau. Can't they just purchase more?"

Willie paused ever so slightly, before recovering. "Don't

you want to help with the most incredible magical break-
through of all time?"

"Yes, of course I do. Let me fetch something from my
jewelry case."

"Don't be surprised if it gets ruined in the process," Willie
said as Mrs. Delancey rose.

"Willie," I snapped. "Mrs. Delancey, we have enough
gold, thank you." I cringed. Why was I going along with this?
Was there even such a thing as diamond magic? "Willie, we
have to go."

Willie reached for the cake. "But I haven't eaten yet." She
took a large bite, only to turn violently green again. She raced
to the vase and threw up once more.

When she finished, she agreed to leave without objection.
Mrs. Delancey handed her the leaflet. Willie accepted it, much
to Mrs. Delancey's satisfaction, then wiped her mouth on it
and threw it into the vase as she passed on her way out.

I couldn't leave quickly enough. "I have never been more
embarrassed in my life," I snapped at her as we drove off.
"You threw up in a vase in front of our host!"

Willie sank into the seat and crossed her arms. "It's
Farnsworth's fault. Blame him. He made me drink a home-
made whiskey at a low-down tavern in Shoreditch. It was so
strong it was practically poison."

"First of all, no one can make you drink if you don't want
to. Secondly, why didn't you stop after a sip if it tasted so
awful?"

She answered me with a pout and turned to look out of
the window. The view of the scenery speeding past combined
with the movement of the carriage must have upset her
stomach again. She clamped a hand over her mouth.

I thumped on the carriage ceiling to let Woodall know we
needed to stop. "Do not throw up inside!"

* * *

"I AGREE WITH YOU," I said to Matt over a light luncheon served in the dining room. It was just the two of us. Cyclops was out, Duke and Aunt Letitia had gone for a walk together, and Willie had retreated to her bed as soon as we arrived home. "Willie is spending too much time with Lord Farnsworth. He's a bad influence on her."

Matt chuckled. "Usually it's the other way around."

"This isn't funny. She threw up in Mrs. Delancey's vase. Twice. It was a magical vase, too. She was very upset about it."

"Did she get angry?"

"Worse. She tried to get Willie to sign a declaration of abstinence."

Matt laughed harder.

I smiled too, despite myself. "Willie blames Lord Farnsworth for encouraging her to consume a rather poor yet lethal whiskey."

"That seems more likely than she simply drank too much. She knows when to stop," he added somberly.

I was a terrible wife. I'd forgotten Matt used to drink to excess. Because it had been some time before he met me, and he never brought it up, I'd put it from my mind. On one of the few occasions he had discussed it, he claimed he didn't know when to stop. He would recognize the signs in others, particularly someone he was as close to as Willie. I reached across the table and grasped his hand.

He squeezed. "So Farnsworth is a bad influence," he said. "What can we do about it?"

"Warning her to stay away won't work."

Matt agreed. "She needs a distraction. Someone more interesting to her than Farnsworth currently is."

"A new paramour?"

He set down his knife and fork and met my gaze. "Do you think she and Farnsworth are...together?"

C.J. ARCHER

I considered it then shook my head. "She would have told us. She's not shy about her lovers."

Matt picked up his knife and fork again and attacked the slice of beef on his plate. "That'll make it easier. We just have to find her a new lover; someone who'll take her attention away from Farnsworth."

"Or we could invite an old lover to dine with us. I know she misses the detective inspector."

"But does he miss her?"

The door opened and Cyclops entered followed by Willie, yawning. She lifted the domed cover on the platter then promptly put it back again.

"I'll eat later," she said.

Cyclops removed the cover and dragged the entire platter towards him. He tucked into beef and potatoes as if he hadn't eaten for a week.

"Doesn't Catherine feed you?" Willie asked.

"She goes home to her parents at midday. Besides, it ain't her responsibility to feed me," he all but snapped. "I've got my own home and that's right here under this roof. I ain't going nowhere." His bitter tone had the three of us exchanging glances while he wasn't looking.

"Is something wrong?" I asked.

"Catherine's parents found out that she and I are..." He waved his knife about, trying to find the right word. "That we're involved."

"And they've forbidden her to see you?"

"Not forbidden her. Not yet. They've lectured her about what it would mean to marry someone like me, someone so different."

Willie threw her hands in the air. "As if she doesn't already know!"

"They're just concerned for her," I said. "It's a good sign they haven't forbidden her from seeing you, Cyclops. It means they're not completely against you two marrying."

He didn't look convinced and, in truth, neither was I. I suspected ordering her to stay away from Cyclops was the next step, if their lectures didn't work. They had, after all, forbidden her to see me when they discovered I was a magician. Thankfully Catherine hadn't heeded their order then, and I doubted she would now and I told Cyclops so.

"I know," he said on a sigh. "But I don't want her to be estranged from her family. It'll make her unhappy."

I touched his arm. "Do you want me to talk to them?"

He shook his head. "Not yet. See if she can convince them herself, first."

"She shouldn't be the one talking to them," Matt said. "It should be you, Cyclops."

Cyclops frowned. "But they don't like me."

"They don't know you. Let them find out for themselves what a good man you are and they'll change their tune."

I agreed. Willie, however, was silent.

"What is it, Willie?" Cyclops said darkly.

"'Course I agree with Matt," she said. "I like you, and I'm real picky when it comes to letting folk be my friend. I was just wondering who told Catherine's parents about you."

"Does it matter?" he asked.

"'Course it matters. You gotta find out who did it and string 'em up."

"Cowboy justice is for the Wild West. I don't care who told them. The fact is, they know."

Willie drummed her fingers on the table and twisted her mouth to the side in thought. "One of her brothers, maybe. Not Ronnie, he's a good man and it doesn't serve his purpose. But the older one? He's jealous of Ronnie getting a shop on his own and annoyed their sister's helping him."

"He's not jealous of Catherine," I pointed out. "I don't think it was him."

"Who else would care?" Willie suddenly sat up straight and clicked her fingers. "Charity Glass! She's jealous of their

37

relationship and is mad enough to think Cyclops would care
for her if Catherine weren't around."

Matt pointed his fork at her. "You will not speak to her."

"But she's hurting one of our friends!" She waved a hand
at Cyclops.

"Leave it, Willie," Cyclops said. "Don't go stirring up
trouble."

"Trouble's already been stirred up." She rose and stormed
off.

"Don't do it, Willie," Cyclops called out.

"I'm just going to see Farnsworth," she grumbled over her
shoulder. "You folk are no fun."

Matt sighed. "The sooner you invite Brockwell over for
dinner, India, the better."

* * *

THE ARRIVAL of Mr. Bunn after lunch dampened our already
rather soggy mood further. The last time the leather magician
had called, we'd thrown him out. He'd stridently asked me to
infuse my extension magic with his to make the leather in the
shoes and boots he manufactured last longer. Like Mr. Pyke,
he saw nothing wrong with the idea.

This time, however, he was not alone. He brought a
young woman with him. Her dark brown hair was fixed high
on her head with what appeared to be two pencils poking
through the arrangement. She was petite with a sober mouth
and dark eyes that settled on me as soon as Bristow opened
the door.

Bristow had tried to shut the door immediately upon
seeing Mr. Bunn, but Mr. Bunn had inserted himself into the
gap and forced it back. Since Matt, Cyclops and I were
passing through the entrance hall, we stopped to assist the
poor butler.

"Before I shut the door in your face," Matt said to Mr.

Bunn, "I should warn you that my patience has worn very thin. We made it clear that you're not welcome here."

"What're you going to do?" the woman asked, hand on hip. "Tell Scotland Yard?"

"Nothing so conventional," Matt said icily. "Continue to pester my wife, and you will find out precisely what I'm going to do to you."

Mr. Bunn swallowed but the woman merely huffed. She sounded impressed by the warning rather than worried.

"I've only come to beg you one more time, Mrs. Glass," Mr. Bunn said. "Please, use your time spell on my magic."

"I'm sorry," I said. "But I cannot. You know why. My reasons have not changed since last we spoke."

Matt went to close the door, but Mr. Bunn blocked it again. "You have to do this! Please! My debts are mounting. I borrowed on the assumption you would use your extension spell, Mrs. Glass."

"Then you're a fool," Matt said. "Kindly leave or be forcibly moved."

The woman snorted and crossed her arms. She reminded me of Willie, a small, courageous, belligerent woman with a big mouth that tended to get her into trouble. "You think you can move both of us?" she spat.

Matt merely smiled.

Cyclops opened the door wider so they could see him better. Mr. Bunn suddenly backed away from the door, hands in the air. The woman eyed Cyclops up and down and licked her top lip. Then she too backed away, but with a bravado her companion didn't possess.

"You're being selfish, Mrs. Glass," she said. "You should be helping your own kind." She pushed past Mr. Bunn but didn't try to cross the threshold. "We magicians should stick together. You don't belong with these artless."

"I don't *belong* to anyone," I said calmly. "Not my husband, not my grandfather, and certainly not you."

CC.J. ARCHER

The woman pointed at me. "You'll regret not helping us."

Matt closed the door in their faces.

"Want me to make sure they leave the area?" Cyclops asked.

"No," Matt said, taking me in his arms. "Are you all right, India?"

"I'm fine. I'm just a little rattled." It wasn't the incident that had rattled me. At least, not this particular time. It was all the incidents together that had me worried. This was the third time Mr. Bunn had come here demanding I use my magic with his, and then there had been Mr. Pyke the other day at Fabian's. When would it end?

"I'll have Fossett answer the door with me from now on, sir," Bristow said.

"Thank you," Matt said. "Have tea brought into the sitting room, please."

Bristow bowed and headed to the back of the house while I entered the sitting room ahead of Matt and Cyclops.

"I think we should tell the police," Cyclops said. "Maybe Brockwell can send someone to Bunn's house and let him know he's being watched."

"I'll visit the inspector later," Matt said, taking my hand. "This has to stop."

"Mr. Bunn is just one magician," I said. "What about the others? That woman also knows where I live now. How many more has Bunn told?"

Matt dragged a hand over his face and settled into the sofa. For the first time in a while, he looked worried.

Duke arrived home with Aunt Letitia, and they joined us in the sitting room. We didn't tell them what had happened, and she seemed quite oblivious to our dark mood, but Duke eyed us all with suspicion. Thankfully he didn't prompt us for answers.

Willie's entry took everyone's mind off the incident with her remarkable attire: she wore a dress. Duke whooped with

40

laughter and Cyclops chuckled his deep, throaty laugh. Even Matt grinned.

"Don't any of you say a god damned word," Willie snapped, picking up her skirts to reveal her sturdy cowboy boots. She all but stomped to the fireplace where she stretched her hands to the warmth.

"You look very pretty, Willemina," Aunt Letitia said. "Are you in mourning?"

Willie looked down at her black dress and plucked at the lace sleeve. "It was all I had. My other dress has a stain on it."

"From what?" Cyclops asked. "You never wear it."

"Jasper spilled something on it." She faced us fully and thrust her hands on her hips. "Will this do?"

"For what?" I asked.

"I don't want to stand out. I want to blend into a crowd like you, India."

"India doesn't *blend* in," Matt said. "She's far too remarkable."

I suspected he was referring to my height, which was a little more than most women, but it was sweet of him to say so, and I smiled. He didn't notice. He was too busy trying not to laugh at Willie as she checked her hair in the mirror.

"You look fine," I told her. "You will blend into a crowd nicely."

"A funeral crowd," Duke muttered.

Cyclops snickered, setting Duke off again. His eyes filled with tears of laughter.

Willie spun around and glared at Cyclops. "Shut your hole. I'm doing this for you."

Cyclops's smile vanished. "Me? I never asked you to wear a dress. I like you better in man's clothes. You're less irritable in buckskins."

"I'm doing this so I can follow Charity without being noticed. I want to see where she goes, who she talks to. I reckon I'll ask her coachman if he took her to the Masons

41

C.J. ARCHER

recently, and maybe talk to the maids and see if anyone accompanied her."

Cyclops groaned. "I wish you wouldn't."

"I don't think it's a good idea," Matt said. "What if it wasn't Charity?"

"Then I'll find out for sure. If it ain't her then we can look for the culprit elsewhere." She picked up her skirts and marched out of the room.

"Have a lovely time," Aunt Letitia called out to her. Once Willie was gone, she picked up her sewing basket. "Isn't it wonderful that she's finally becoming more feminine? Don't let her excuse fool any of you. I think she's wearing a dress because she wants to, not for some scheme involving Charity."

We filled Duke and Aunt Letitia in on Cyclops's problem then we went our different ways for the remainder of the afternoon. Matt had business matters to attend to in his study while Cyclops returned to Catherine and Ronnie's shop. Duke went out again and I spent the rest of the day in Aunt Letitia's company.

Willie didn't return home that night. That wasn't too alarming. She often stayed out all night, particularly lately. Even when Lord Farnsworth showed up at breakfast, we still didn't worry. He claimed he hadn't seen her, and we assumed she was still following Charity or perhaps had decided to rendezvous with one of her old lovers.

It wasn't until a message arrived via the late morning post that we knew something was very wrong. Matt read it and swore then he handed it to me and I gasped as I read.

According to the note, Willie had been kidnapped and she would be killed unless I agreed to use my extension magic.

CHAPTER 4

I pointed to the letter in Detective Inspector Brockwell's hand. "It states that Willie will die if I don't send word to Mr. Bunn's workshop by midnight tonight that I agree to infuse his magic with an extension spell."

"So I see," he said in his usual precise monotone as he read.

"A simple yes from me is all that is required to release her."

"So the letter states."

I waited, my hands clasped in my lap, and nibbled my lower lip. Brockwell leaned back in his chair and scratched his sideburn as he re-read the note.

It was an excruciating wait. "Well?" I prompted. "What are you going to do about it?"

He set the letter down and regarded me from the other side of the desk. "First of all, I am going to urge you to do nothing. Let the police handle this."

"I tried telling Matt that, but you know what he's like. He's fetching Duke and Cyclops now but agreed to meet me here rather than hare off to Mr. Bunn's workshop and demand Willie be released."

It hadn't been easy to coax that agreement out of him, and I still worried he would take Cyclops and Duke with him to confront Mr. Bunn.

Brockwell picked up the letter again.

I balled my hands into fists and fought for patience. "You don't look worried," I said.

"I know Willie well; perhaps better than you. She won't be a victim."

"She might not have a choice. If you know her well then you would also know that she's just as likely to dig a bigger hole for herself with that sharp tongue of hers."

He set the letter down and clasped his hands on the desk. "Tell me about this Bunn character and the woman with him."

I told him all that I knew, which amounted to very little. I didn't even know what relation the woman was to Bunn, let alone her name. "She is definitely a magician though. She referred to herself as such. I assume she's another leather magician, perhaps a family member of Bunn's. Although, on second thought, they look nothing alike. He's fair while she's dark."

Finally he rose. "I'll pay Mr. Bunn's workshop a visit with some men. We'll have Willie back safely in no time."

I let out a breath. "Thank you, Inspector. It's a great comfort to know that someone who cares for her is on the case."

He pressed his lips together and opened his office door for me. He scratched his side whiskers and opened his mouth only to shut it again without speaking. I suspected he wanted to ask me something, but was perhaps too embarrassed. I decided to put him out of his misery.

"She still cares about you," I said quietly. "But she's afraid you now think her...*too* strange."

"She has an odd way of showing she cares. She called me

all sorts of things last time I saw her. Some of them I don't even know what they mean."

"That's just her way. In fact, calling you names means she cares. If she disliked you, she would probably just..." I waved my hand, not quite sure what Willie would do if she lost interest in Brockwell.

"Shoot me?" he offered.

I smiled. "I'm glad you understand her."

He followed me out of his office and escorted me back to the Yard's front desk. "Just one more question," he said before I left. "What would happen if you used your extension spell with Mr. Bunn's leather one?"

"On the surface, it would simply extend the life of his magic and make its quality last. It would mean he could gain a reputation that would see him able to increase his prices and earn more custom. But the implications could be further reaching if word got out. Other magicians would want me to repeat the exercise for them, and the artless would feel threatened. No one really knows what would happen then. I suppose the tension between the artless and magicians would boil over."

"I see." He held up the letter. "May I keep this?"

"Of course. Please do keep us informed."

Brockwell's gaze shifted. I looked behind me to see Matt, Cyclops and Duke striding up to us. Brockwell sighed. "I suspect I won't need to inform you of anything. I assume you will be coming with me to Mr. Bunn's workshop, Glass?"

"I'm glad to see you're amenable to the idea of company," Matt said. "If we work together, we can get faster results than separately."

It would seem Matt was never going to concede such an important operation to the police, and Brockwell seemed to have expected it.

We traveled at a good clip but the denser traffic in Soho slowed us down. Mr. Bunn's workshop was located very near

Soho Square, a rather upmarket precinct where the rents must have been high. No wonder he'd needed a large loan.

Thanks to Woodall's rather nerve-wracking driving, we arrived moments ahead of the police. Matt wouldn't wait and stormed into the shop. Cyclops went with him while Duke remained outside on guard.

A youth sitting on a stool behind the counter greeted us cheerfully, but his smile quickly withered beneath Matt's ferocious glare.

"Where's Bunn?" Matt growled.

"Mr. Bunn is not here at present," the lad said in an attempt at an upper-class accent. He couldn't have been more than sixteen.

I placed a hand on Matt's arm and took over the questioning. "Do you know where he is?" I asked, employing a softer tone.

"Are you Mrs. Glass?"

I was taken aback and didn't answer immediately.

Matt slammed his hands on the counter, making the lad jump. "Where is Bunn?"

"Step away, Glass," Brockwell said from the doorway. "He's just a boy."

"Old enough to answer the question," Matt growled.

The detective inspector ambled in with two constables at his heels. I drew in a steadying breath, drawing the scent of leather into my lungs. The small shop was neat, with some fine boots displayed on the counter beside a pyramid of stacked shoe polish. Women's boots of different colored leathers were displayed on pedestals in the window along with an artfully placed fan here and a pair of gloves there. It was just the sort of shop that would attract an exclusive clientele.

Brockwell introduced himself and the lad's eyes widened even further.

"I ain't done nothing wrong, sir!" He dropped the affected

accent altogether, and reverted to a Cockney one. "Mr. Bunn asked me to wait here for Mrs. Glass. He didn't tell me where he was going. I swear, I don't know where he is. Don't arrest me!"

"I'm not going to arrest you if you are honest. Tell me, how were you going to give Bunn the message that Mrs. Glass passed on to you?"

The lad pointed to a tall wrought iron candlestick in the window. "I'd light the candle after dark. If it were lit, it meant she'd said yes."

Cyclops peered out of the window.

"Do you know what she was saying yes to?" Matt asked.

The boy shook his head quickly. "I swear, I didn't. Mr. Bunn told me nothing. I just work in the shop sometimes, when Mr. Bunn goes out. Usually I run errands. He told me nothing about Mrs. Glass, just that she would come here, probably with her husband." He looked to the constables standing by the door. "He said nothing about bobbies."

"Where does Mr. Bunn live?" Brockwell asked.

The lad hesitated then pointed to the ceiling.

Brockwell signaled to his constables and they left through the door behind the counter that led through to a workshop. Cyclops followed. I caught a glimpse of the stairs leading up to the second-floor residence before the door closed again.

"Who lives with him?" Brockwell asked.

"No one," the lad said. "He lives alone."

"What about his family?"

The boy shrugged. "I don't know if he's got a family. He hasn't mentioned a wife or parents or nothing."

"Does Mr. Bunn have another workshop?" Matt asked. "Perhaps a storeroom or warehouse that he uses?"

The boy shook his head.

"Are you certain?" Brockwell said.

The lad shrugged again. "He's never sent me to fetch anything from a warehouse. Everything he needs is back there." He jerked a thumb at the door leading to the work-shop. "All deliveries come here."

"Does he ever have visitors who aren't customers?" I asked.

"Particularly women," Matt added.

"I'll ask the questions," Brockwell said. He turned to the youth. "Has a young woman called on Mr. Bunn here, but not for footwear?"

The lad lifted a shoulder. "What does she look like?"

"Small, dark hair with pencils poking out of her arrange-ment," I said.

The boy's eyes brightened. "That'd be Miss Amelia Moreton."

"What do you know about her?" Brockwell asked at the same time that Matt said, "Are they courting?"

The lad pointed at Matt. "Don't know. They didn't seem like sweethearts, if you know what I mean." He pointed to Brockwell. "I know she works at a fireworks factory in Wandsworth. Her family owns it."

"Where precisely?" Matt pressed.

The lad shrugged again.

Cyclops returned to the shopfront with the two constables trailing behind. He shook his head.

Brockwell thanked the lad and opened the door for me to exit first.

"What should I do?" the youth asked. "Light the candle or not?"

"My answer is no," I said. "For now."

"I'll be here until midnight, ma'am, in case you change your mind."

Outside, Cyclops pointed to the shops opposite. All were two levels. "To see a lit candle in the shoe shop window, he has to be stationed in one of these buildings or on the street itself."

"He might not wait for the signal himself," Matt said,

scanning the upper windows opposite. "He might be paying someone to watch and deliver him a message."

Brockwell ordered his men to search the buildings. "Not much we can do if he is paying someone."

He was right. There were people up and down the street, many of whom were just youths like the one inside the shop, who'd do anything for a few coins in their pocket. They wouldn't tell us anything unless they felt threatened.

"Then we pay a call on Miss Amelia Moreton's fireworks factory," I said.

"Fireworks!" Duke cried. "You mean to say she's an explosives magician?"

Brockwell scratched his sideburns. "I suppose she must be."

"Bloody hell. What do you reckon a fireworks spell can do, India?"

"I hate to think," I said heavily.

"Let's hope her magic is dormant," Matt said.

But we all knew it mustn't be, or Amelia Moreton wouldn't have gone to such lengths to force me to use my magic.

* * *

THE JOURNEY to Wandsworth from Soho was a rather long one, particularly with the late afternoon traffic clogging the roads. Pedestrians seemed to be as active as ants at a picnic, hurrying through the drizzling rain to catch their train or omnibus. Public and private coaches jostled for position on the approach to Westminster Bridge but once we were across, Woodall picked up the pace again.

"What would a fireworks magician want with your extension magic, India?" Duke asked as we passed Wandsworth Common. "You can't extend a firework. It goes off when it goes off."

"It depends on what her magic does, I suppose," I said. "We'll ask her when we get to the factory."

"She won't be there," Cyclops said.

Matt agreed. "She'll be in hiding, probably with Bunn, at the location where they're keeping Willie."

"Like back at the shop so they can see if the assistant lights the flame." Duke clicked his tongue. "We should have stayed to see if they showed up."

The constables had reported no sign of anyone watching the bootmaker's shop from the buildings opposite, but Brockwell had ordered both to remain behind to keep an eye out. He then left, following behind us in his own conveyance.

A steady stream of women filed out beneath a brick archway at the Moreton Explosives firework factory on Garratt Lane. They looked tired and a little dirty, but in good spirits as they chatted and walked after a ten-hour working day. I could have been one of them, working in a factory much like this one, if not for becoming Matt's assistant all those months ago. It was a rather sobering thought. If not for our chance encounter, my life would have been so different.

I smiled at him, but he was too focused on the office entrance to notice. He strode off as Brockwell alighted from his carriage.

A man sitting at a desk looked up upon our entry. He took in all of us and his eyes widened behind his spectacles. I suspected Matt's angry face alarmed him. He hurriedly stood, scraping his chair on the floorboards. "Who are you? What do you want?"

"I'm Detective Inspector Brockwell from Scotland Yard."

"Scotland Yard! Good lord."

Brockwell put up his hands. "I merely want to make some simple inquiries. Is Miss Amelia Moreton present?"

"Miss Moreton? I, uh, no. I haven't seen her all day."

"Is that unusual?" Brockwell pressed.

"She comes and goes as she sees fit. Perhaps she's at home."

The door at the back of the office opened and a short man with gray hair combed back over his bald pate filled the doorway. A thick gold watchchain disappeared into his waistcoat pocket. "Teele? What's going on? Who are these people?"

Brockwell repeated his introduction and the newcomer's bluster faded upon hearing it. The words Scotland Yard had that effect on people.

"Dear God, what's happened?" he asked.

"We want to speak to Miss Amelia Moreton in regard to a particular matter of great urgency."

"Amelia?" The man's gaze flicked to the clerk. "Teele, you may go. Mr. Brockwell, come with me."

"It's Detective Inspector Brockwell." Brockwell followed the short man through to the office and the rest of us trailed behind.

This office was as large as the outer one but lacked its utilitarian appearance. There were no filing cabinets or drawers, no open ledgers on the mahogany desk. A drinks trolley had been wheeled to within reach of the desk and a crystal tumbler half-filled with amber liquid took pride of place on the desk itself.

A family portrait hung on a wall. I recognized a younger version of Amelia with a brother and both parents. Mr. Moreton was thinner, his hair less gray, and Amelia smiled sweetly. Both had changed since they'd sat for the picture.

"Are you Mr. Moreton?" Brockwell asked.

The man lifted his chin. "Orwell Moreton. I own this factory. Who are they?"

"My name is Matthew Glass," Matt said.

Mr. Moreton's jaw dropped. "Glass?" His gaze slid to me. "Mrs. Glass?"

"Yes." I extended my hand. "I'm pleased to meet you."

His cheeks pinked. After a moment, he seemed to realize

my hand was still extended. His cheeks grew redder as he shook it. "I am very pleased to meet you too, Mrs. Glass. Very pleased indeed."

"You know who I am," I said matter-of-factly.

He glanced at Brockwell.

"You may speak freely in front of the detective inspector. He knows about magic."

Mr. Moreton angled a spare chair towards me and invited me to sit. He did not invite the others as he sat down on the chair behind the desk. "Forgive my staring, Mrs. Glass. I expected you to be rather more…" He waved his hand in my general direction then must have realized anything he said would not sound flattering. He lowered his hand and cleared his throat. "What a surprise to have you in my office. Would you like a tour of the factory? I'd be more than happy to show you how we make fireworks. Did you know that Moreton's have a regular pyrotechnic display every Friday night in the summertime here at Wandsworth Common? It's free, of course. The people enjoy it very much, particularly the children."

"Is there magic in the fireworks?" I asked.

His enthusiasm waned. He shifted uncomfortably in the chair. "Only sometimes. It would be too conspicuous if I used magic for every display. I haven't used magic for some months now, ever since the guild became suspicious and began to sniff around my factory."

"What does your magic spell do to the fireworks?"

"It doubles the explosive effect of each firework case. It makes our displays twice as thrilling as artless pyrotechnics. That's why we're the official suppliers of fireworks to several cities both here and abroad." He frowned. "What does this have to do with my daughter?"

"She kidnapped my husband's cousin."

Mr. Moreton paled.

"She came to my house yesterday with Mr. Bunn and

demanded I use my extension spell to lengthen his leather magic. I refused."

Brockwell placed the letter on the desk. "Is this her handwriting or Bunn's?"

Mr. Moreton glanced at it. "It's not Amelia's." He passed a hand over his face.

"Where can Amelia be?" Matt demanded. "Where has she taken my cousin?"

Mr. Moreton clutched the arms of his chair. "I don't know, Mr. Glass. I swear to you, I don't know. I haven't seen her today."

"She's your daughter!"

"My *grown* daughter with a mind of her own. A very strong, willful mind." Mr. Moreton leaned his elbows on the desk and buried his head in his hands. When he looked up again, he seemed to have aged ten years. "She used to be a sweet girl, but ever since learning of her magic in her late teens, she has become more...difficult. She doesn't like having to hide her magic. She doesn't understand the need for discretion and for using spells sparingly in the factory." He picked up the letter. "I wasn't aware she had become more of an activist." He put it down again and fixed a glare on Brockwell. "I blame the bootmaker. Without him, she would never have become an advocate for magical freedom. She would never have learned about you, Mrs. Glass."

"He is certainly to blame for leading her to my home," I said.

"I am very sorry for that. For all of this." He stabbed his finger on the letter. "But Bunn is to blame. This handwriting proves it. He has taken advantage of Amelia. You should be making inquiries about him."

"We have," the inspector said. "They led us here."

"You have substantial premises," Matt said, looking out of the window. "We need to search all the buildings."

Mr. Moreton looked as though he would object, but a glare

from Matt had him nodding quickly. "Of course, of course. Go ahead. The staff have all left for the day. I'd be happy to escort you."

Matt strode toward the door. "We can do it alone."

Mr. Moreton rose and hurried after him. "I prefer to show you around myself. The factory is full of explosive material, Mr. Glass. It would be unethical of me to allow an outsider to wander around unattended."

Matt may or may not have heard him. He was already out the office door.

I moved up alongside Mr. Moreton as he followed Matt. "Do you think my husband's cousin is in danger from Amelia if I refuse to use my magic?"

"My daughter is a sweet girl. She wouldn't harm anyone. I don't know Bunn, however."

A few minutes ago he'd told us she *used* to be sweet, and now he claimed she still was. Perhaps it was a father remembering his little girl with fondness, or perhaps he was right. People didn't usually go from being kind-hearted to kidnapper in a matter of a few years.

It had grown quite dark, and the two lamps lit on either side of the courtyard did little to keep the wintry evening at bay. Mr. Moreton puffed from the rapid pace as he led us into the main factory. He lit lanterns hanging by the door, and handed one each to the men, but seemed to think I didn't need one.

"You must be careful of a naked flame at all times," Mr. Moreton said as he lifted his lantern high. "The elements that make gunpowder aren't stored in here, of course, but there might be traces on the work surfaces. The girls don't always clean up very well at the end of the day. They're not the brightest creatures and don't fully understand the dangers of not tidying up."

"Perhaps if you educated them they will," Matt said.

Mr. Moreton looked as if he'd protest, but Matt walked off before he could respond.

The work benches were of little interest to us. Nothing could be hidden there. A large steam-powered crushing machine loomed silently in the middle of the room, and a faint tangy smell lingered in the air, but otherwise the factory was like any other.

Matt pointed to some barrels stacked in a corner. "What's in those?"

"Various chemicals for making different colored fire-works." Mr. Moreton pointed to the chemical symbols painted on the crates. "Strontium for red, barium for green, copper for blue, sodium for yellow and so forth."

Matt opened one, much to Mr. Moreton's distress.

Meanwhile, Cyclops and Duke were inspecting the floor. "What are you doing?" I whispered.

"Looking for a trapdoor," Duke whispered back. "If there's a storeroom underneath, Willie could be down there."

"We could just ask Mr. Moreton," I said.

"You trust him?"

I wasn't sure. He didn't seem to condone his daughter's behavior, but that could be a façade.

We inspected the factory thoroughly, moving every barrel to ensure there were no trapdoors. We headed upstairs to the mezzanine level where the foreman's office and a walkway overlooked the factory floor. There was no trace of Willie or her captors anywhere.

"Take me to the warehouse," Matt ordered.

"Of course, of course. Follow me." Mr. Moreton turned to go but stopped suddenly. "Where is the detective inspector?"

Brockwell had indeed disappeared. I hadn't noticed him slip out.

"He shouldn't have gone off alone," Mr. Moreton muttered as he hurried out of the factory. "It can be dangerous taking a naked flame near gunpowder."

"He ain't a fool," Cyclops snapped.

"But what if he trips over? What if he has a fainting spell?"

He stopped in the courtyard and scanned the buildings around it. When he spotted a flickering light through one of the windows, he strode off in that direction.

"You shouldn't wander," he scolded Brockwell when we caught up to him.

Brockwell pointed to a collection of a dozen or more stacked crates in the corner of the small warehouse. "What's in those?"

"Firework rockets. They're ready for a shipment to a customer in Southampton, along with those set pieces." Mr. Moreton pointed to a Catherine wheel and some wooden structures that looked as though they would make very large ships once put together. "Recreating sea battles with Roman candles as cannon are very popular, particularly for seafaring cities and ports."

We inspected the warehouse, moving aside every crate, and tapping the floor to search for hollow spaces. Again, we found nothing.

We returned outside to the courtyard where Matt was already striding off to the last building. "Not in there!" Mr. Moreton said, chasing after him. "That's the magazine where the elements to make the charges are stored. It's far too dangerous to go rummaging about inside."

"We have to search everywhere," Brockwell said, pushing past.

"I can assure you, there are no places for Mr. Glass's cousin to hide. Not in there; not anywhere!"

We ignored him and continued to the magazine. It was quite a large space, again packed with barrels and crates. There were far too many to check individually. It would also take some time to move them all aside.

"We use this warehouse to store the components to make

gunpowder," Mr. Moreton said. "Some contain potassium nitrate—what we used to call saltpeter—and the rest are charcoal and sulfur."

"This quantity would make a lot of black powder," Cyclops said.

"We make a lot of fireworks."

"Which crates contain the potassium nitrate?"

"The third to the left. The central third are charcoal and the right-hand third contain sulfur."

Cyclops shook his head. "Those proportions are all wrong. Fireworks are seventy-five percent potassium nitrate, fifteen percent charcoal and ten percent sulfur."

I went cold. If Willie was in one of the crates, then she must be... *Oh God.*

Mr. Moreton held his lamp higher to get a better look at Cyclops. He sniffed. "I doubt you are an expert on fireworks."

"I worked with explosives in mines back home. Sometimes we made Roman candles for fun." He picked up a crowbar and opened one of the crates on the left. "Saltpeter," he said, smelling the contents.

"Of course it is. I told you—"

"Duke, open one of the crates in the middle. I'll open one on the right."

Mr. Moreton stepped in front of Cyclops. "That's really not necessary. You can take my word, there is nothing but powders in those crates."

Duke wedged open a crate with a crowbar. The lid slid off and clattered onto the floor. "Looks like powder to me."

"See!" Mr. Moreton declared. "There's nothing of interest to you in here. Your cousin in not being kept anywhere on these premises. I've been very accommodating, Inspector, but I really must insist that you leave now. My wife is expecting me. Indeed, I'm sure my daughter is at home as we speak. Why not come with me to the house and we'll settle this nonsense."

Duke opened another crate.

Mr. Moreton tugged on his tie knot. "I'm sure Amelia will be happy to answer all your questions, Inspector. Once she knows the gravity of the situation, she'll lead you straight to Mr. Glass's cousin who no doubt will tell you it was all Mr. Bunn's idea."

"That's a heavy looking fireworks case," Duke said, peering into the crate.

Matt held the lamp over the crate. "That's not a firework case. That's a bomb."

CHAPTER 5

*M*r. Moreton took one look at the inspector and set off at a run.

Fortunately he was not the most athletic of men and Cyclops easily caught him. He escorted Mr. Moreton back to the magazine to stand before Brockwell.

"You're making explosive devices," the detective inspector stated. "Illegally."

Mr. Moreton wisely remained silent.

Matt opened another crate. "There's one in here too. Where are these going? Who is your customer?"

Mr. Moreton pressed his lips together.

"Cyclops, if you would be so kind as to escort Mr. Moreton to my conveyance and accompany us to Scotland Yard," Brockwell said. "Mr. Moreton, you are under arrest."

Duke moved to block their exit, a determined set to his jaw. "We'll overlook this is if you tell us where to find Willie."

"I cannot overlook it," Brockwell said, somewhat sadly. "Not even for Willie's sake. These bombs could be heading to the realm's enemies."

"I don't send them overseas," Mr. Moreton shot back.

"Enemies can live on English soil. Duke, I sympathize, but step aside."

"But—"

I touched Duke's arm. "The inspector's right. This must be dealt with properly. Those bombs could do great harm on a comprehensive scale."

Duke closed his eyes and sighed. He stepped aside.

Matt, however, grabbed Mr. Moreton by his jacket lapels and shook him. "Where is she?" he snarled. "Where is my cousin?"

Mr. Moreton put up his hands in surrender. "I don't know! I swear to you, I don't know where she is. Amelia tells me nothing anymore. It's that Bunn character. He's corrupting her, giving her ideas."

Matt screwed his fist into the jacket, tightening it at Mr. Moreton's throat. The firework magician's face turned a rather deep shade of red very quickly. Matt suddenly let go, shoving Mr. Moreton for good measure.

"If I find out you lied and you knew all along…"

Mr. Moreton smoothed the front of his jacket and stretched his neck out of his collar. "I think I'd like to go to Scotland Yard now, thank you, Inspector."

Cyclops escorted Mr. Moreton out. Brockwell went to follow but paused at the door. "I can rely on you to find her, Glass."

Matt nodded.

Brockwell pulled out his watch, checked the time, and returned it to his pocket. "It's six-thirty."

"I'll find her," Matt said again, gentler. "You have my word."

The problem was, where to look next? We'd searched all the buildings at the factory; Willie wasn't here.

"We could try Amelia's home," I said. "Although I doubt she took Willie somewhere where her mother could see."

"Maybe an abandoned warehouse," Duke suggested with

a shrug as we crossed the courtyard. "Or tenement. Maybe Moreton owns some places and one's vacant right now."

It was a good idea. Luckily we were in the right place to check. If Moreton kept financial records of other properties, they were most likely in his office.

We split up and checked a different filing cabinet each. It didn't take long for Matt to declare success. He slammed a thick file onto the desk and flipped through the pages.

"Moreton seems to own…" He ran his finger down the first page. "Eight different properties in addition to this factory."

Duke joined him at the desk. "It'll take some time to check them all." He leaned his knuckles on the desk and lowered his head. We won't get to all of them before midnight.

I pressed his shoulder. "Woodall is an excellent driver and the traffic will have decreased considerably."

"It's raining," he said flatly. "The slippery roads will slow the horses."

"We have to try!"

My bark startled him. "You're right. Sorry, India." He turned to the file. "Where's the closest property?"

I looked over the addresses, feeling my heart sink a little more with each one. Not only were they all on the other side of the river, they were quite spread out. We couldn't visit them all. We had to hope Willie was in one of the first three if we were to free her before midnight.

"Who are you?" came a shrill voice from the doorway.

We'd been so intent on the property list we hadn't noticed the woman arrive. She reminded me of a wounded bird, dressed as she was in all black with her gray hair poking out in unkempt strands from beneath a tall hat trimmed with crushed silk. Despite the defiant tilt of her chin, her darting gaze gave away her anxiety.

"Get out of my husband's office," she said in a trembling voice.

61

"Mrs. Moreton?" Matt said smoothly. "My name is Matthew Glass and this is my wife, India, and my associate, Duke. We're very glad to see you."

"I am *not* glad to see you." She indicated the front door. "Leave."

Beyond her stood Mr. Teele, Mr. Moreton's assistant. He must have fetched her. He cleared his throat and stepped forward. "They came with the policeman, ma'am."

Mrs. Moreton's chin lowered.

Matt took some steps toward her. "Detective Inspector Brockwell of Scotland Yard has authorized me to continue the investigation into the disappearance of my cousin in his absence."

"Where is he?"

Matt paused before answering. "He took your husband to Scotland Yard. He has some questions over some illegal devices found in one of the warehouses."

She blinked rapidly. "What sort of devices?"

"Bombs."

She gasped. "Mr. Teele? Do you know anything about this?"

"Nothing, I swear to you!" The assistant backed towards the door. "I have to leave now. My wife is expecting me home for dinner."

Mrs. Moreton watched him go and some of her fortitude seemed to leave with him. She pressed a hand to her stomach. "What should I do?"

"I suggest you contact a lawyer for your husband," Matt said. "But that isn't why we came here tonight. We're looking for my cousin. She has been kidnapped by your daughter and—"

"Amelia!"

"She sent a note demanding my wife use her magic to extend the life of Mr. Bunn's magic. If my wife refuses, she will kill my cousin."

Mrs. Moreton went very pale and slumped against the doorframe. Matt took one elbow and I grabbed the other while Duke pushed a chair closer. We directed Mrs. Moreton to sit.

"Duke, a drink for Mrs. Moreton, please," Matt said.

Duke disappeared into Mr. Moreton's office and came out with a glass of the liquor Mr. Moreton had been drinking earlier. He handed it to Mrs. Moreton who sniffed, reeled back, then sipped.

It seemed to rally her but not lift her spirits. Tears welled in her eyes. "This is awful. Just awful. I am so sorry, Mr. Glass." She lifted her distressed gaze to mine. "Mrs. Glass, you're that powerful magician, aren't you? My daughter told me about you." Her face crumpled. "I'm so sorry for this. For everything."

"It's all right," I said gently, not sure what to say. What did one say to a woman whose child had done something as despicable as kidnap and threatened to do worse?

Matt seemed to know. He crouched before Mrs. Moreton and gave her his handkerchief. "The worst can be averted if you assist us. There is still time to find my cousin. Will you help us, Mrs. Moreton? Will you set this right?"

She wiped her damp cheeks on his handkerchief. "I'll do everything in power to help, but I'm not sure I can."

Matt turned to Duke and nodded at the desk. Duke fetched the file of papers.

"My daughter frightens me," Mrs. Moreton said quietly. "Her magic is strong. Not as strong as yours, Mrs. Glass, but it comes easily to her. She can use the same spell as my husband and yet her fireworks are more spectacular than his, more colorful and varied." She accepted the file from Duke. "But her power is not the problem. It's her recklessness." She tapped the rolled-up handkerchief against her chest above her heart. "They say boys are the reckless ones, but that's not my experience. Amelia can be wild at times."

"Mrs. Moreton, can you look through that list of your husband's properties," Matt said. "I need to know which one Amelia is more likely to hide my cousin in."

Mrs. Moreton dabbed at her eyes and opened the file. Her movements were excruciatingly slow, grating on my nerves. Matt shifted his weight on his haunches, while Duke paced the room. The wait frustrated all of us.

"I think this one is without tenants," Mrs. Moreton said, pointing to an address.

Matt took the file from her and rifled through it until he found the papers he needed. "You're right. It's not. It's in a terrible state, according to this report, and requires urgent repairs before it can be leased again."

"And possibly this one," Mrs. Moreton said, pointing to another on the list. "My husband was grumbling about the cost of something or other just last week."

Matt looked through the papers again. "It appears to be tenanted."

"Then she must be at the other one," Duke said. "Let's go, Matt."

Matt rose and thanked Mrs. Moreton.

I looked back at her from the exit, a forlorn creature crying into Matt's handkerchief. She had all but lost her husband and daughter in one night, and in some ways I felt responsible. If it hadn't been for my magic, none of this would have happened.

Matt must have sensed my melancholia because he took my hand as we headed through the drizzling rain to the carriage. "Only Amelia and Bunn are responsible for their actions, no one else. And if it hadn't been for you, Moreton's secret arms business would never have been discovered." He squeezed my hand. "Now come on and let's rescue Willie."

Woodall outdid himself steering the horses through the slippery streets on the southern side of the Thames. Even so, our progress felt excruciatingly slow, particularly through the narrow, dark lanes of the East End. Whereas the West End streets were deserted of pedestrians most evenings in winter, the slums were a hive of activity by comparison. People huddled around braziers tucked away in lanes and yards. Drunks slept in doorways, while a few hardy prostitutes braved the cold to ply their trade near taverns.

We found Mr. Moreton's property at the edge of a small court. The windows were broken and the front door hung by a single hinge. Outside, men sat around a brazier, bottles in hand. They looked warily upon us as we approached, and one even spat on the ground at Matt's feet.

Matt handed the man some coins. "We're looking for the tenants of that building."

"Ain't no tenants," the man said.

"What about squatters?"

He crossed his arms.

"We're not the police," Matt said. "We're looking for my cousin. She was kidnapped and we have reason to believe she was brought here by the building's owner."

"The owner?" another man echoed. "Tell him to get a proper lock on the door and fix the windows or just bloody well fix the whole building. The children keep going in, despite our warnings, and they get hurt on the nails and broken glass. It ain't safe."

"I'll tell him," Matt said, "but I need to find my cousin first. She was kidnapped by a man and a woman. Have you seen them here?"

"Nope. You're the first stranger 'round here today."

"Can we look inside?"

The man shrugged.

Matt took one of the lanterns we'd brought with us from the factory and we entered the building along with Duke. The smell hit me like a punch to the throat. I covered my mouth with my hand but it didn't hide the stench of urine and vomit. I wanted to lift my skirts to keep the hem from touching the filth, but I didn't want to remove my hand from my mouth either.

"Watch your step," Matt warned as he nudged the toe of his boot against something on the floor. It wasn't a rolled-up rug, as I first thought, but the sleeping form of a drunkard. Going by his soft snore, he was alive.

We kept together and inspected each room, all the way up to the attic and back again. Downstairs, we tapped on floor-boards with our boots, checking for hollow spaces. We found a cellar but the stairs had rotted away. Matt thrust the lamp in as far as he could reach.

"Empty," he announced.

"The whole damn place is empty," Duke muttered. "She ain't here."

We left, thanked the men warming themselves by the brazier, and returned to the carriage where Woodall waited. He didn't look in the least ruffled at being left alone in a dangerous area.

"Anyone bother you?" Matt asked him.

"Aye, but they soon left." Woodall flipped back his great coat to reveal a pistol on his lap. "Where to now, sir?"

Matt gave him the address of the second property, the one Mrs. Moreton had thought was untenanted but paperwork showed it to be rented. "It's worth a try," Matt said as he settled back in the cabin.

"Anything's worth a try." Duke removed his gloves and blew on his hands. "It's getting late."

"It's not even nine," I said. "We have time."

I was pleased that I sounded confident. I needed to, for their sakes. They were both terribly worried. As worried as me. But I wouldn't let my fear get the better of me. Not yet when we still had a few hours left. One of us had to remain calm.

Besides, I might be required to order Woodall to drive us to Bunn's workshop at a moment's notice. It was my decision to make, and mine alone, and I would need my wits about me to make it at the right time. Too soon and we might not explore all our options in finding Willie. Too late and...well, it would be too late.

We found the second house in a better state than the first. It faced the street, not a yard, and all the windows and the front door appeared to be intact.

"I can't see a light," I said. "But the curtains appear to be shut. Perhaps someone's home."

Duke marched up to the door and tried the handle. "Locked."

Matt peered up at the second-floor windows. "Look for another way in."

"You can't break in," I hissed. "People could live here."

"I reckon it's deserted." Duke looked around. "There's someone over there. We could ask him."

"Stay here," Matt ordered Duke and me.

He strode off towards the man lounging in the doorway. The man pushed off from the door, whistled shrilly then set off at a run. Matt chased him.

Duke swore and went to run off too. "India, stay with Woodall!"

I tugged my cloak tighter at my throat and glanced at the tenement. This had to be it. Willie must be inside, and that man had whistled to alert the occupants of company. It could have even been Mr. Bunn himself.

I raced back to the carriage. "Woodall, give me your pistol."

The coachman gawped at me. "I don't think that's wise, ma'am."

"Are you prepared to leave the horses and carriage unattended and accompany me inside with the gun?"

He bit his lip.

"I didn't think so." I held out my hand. "Give me the gun."

67

"Mr. Glass won't like it."

"Mr. Glass's cousin is inside. I'm sure of it. But her captors have been warned and could very well be exiting the house via a rear entrance as we speak." I signaled for the pistol. "Hand it over immediately. That's an order."

He did. "Do you know how to use it?"

"Yes," I said, trying to remember what Matt had taught me.

The first obstacle was getting inside the tenement. I had to break the door down. Hopefully being an old house and not in use, the lock would be weak. I gathered up my skirts and kicked.

It rattled but didn't open.

I tried again and again. Each kick seemed to loosen the locking mechanism. I was about to try a fourth time when a gunshot sounded.

Glass broke and shattered on the pavement to my right.

Behind me, Woodall shouted for me to get back.

I covered my head and dashed away from the door, just as it burst open.

A woman tumbled out in a tangle of skirts and fell at my feet.

I gasped. "Willie!"

CHAPTER 6

*W*illie swore at the top of her voice. "God damned dress!"

I'd never been so happy to hear her foul language. I helped her to her feet and hugged her. She returned it briskly then grabbed my hand and dragged me to the carriage.

"They could still be inside," she said. "Stay here, India, and I'll check."

"No!" I caught her wrist. "If they're still in there, you're not going back."

Matt and Duke sprinted up to us, panting. "Willie!" Duke cried, flinging his arms around her. "Thank God."

She drew away. "There ain't no time for pretty reunions. We got to catch them before they escape." She marched off toward the house.

"Duke, stay here with India," Matt ordered, following her.

"Wait," I called out. "Take this." I handed him the gun and watched him jog after Willie. She pushed open the door and disappeared into the dark house.

I heard Matt hiss at her to slow down and be careful.

Duke and I watched on from the pavement. "She's real angry," he said.

"I would be too if I'd been abducted."

"You'd have been relieved to get away from your kidnappers. Willie wants revenge. She's got to be careful her hunger for it doesn't make her do something foolish."

We fell into silence as we waited, alert to every sound. But all I could hear was the blood pounding in my ears.

It felt like they were gone for an eternity. I resisted checking my watch in the carriage lamplight, but it didn't help my nerves when Duke began pacing. He wanted to go inside too.

I was about to tell him to join them when Willie and Matt emerged. I embraced Matt while Duke caught Willie up in his arms again. This time she returned his hug with an equally fierce one.

"They're gone," Matt announced. "Escaped via the rear exit."

Willie swore again. "I should have chased them after I fired."

"*You* fired that shot?" I asked.

"Aye, but I missed. God damned dress." She slapped at her skirt, as if she wanted to rip it off there and then. "I was running along the hallway as I fired, but these clothes got in the way and I tripped. I fell against the front door. The lock was loose and the door opened real easy. That's how I ended up on the porch."

"That was me," I said. "I kicked the door until the lock loosened. One more kick and I think it would have given away."

Willie snorted. "Sure. The lock weren't already loose or nothing like that."

I rounded on her. "A little gratitude wouldn't go astray. We've turned ourselves inside out looking for you. Coming here wasn't an accident. It's the result of several hours' investigation."

She blew out a breath and nodded. "Sorry. You're right."

She circled her arm around my waist. "Thanks for coming. But let's all be clear, I rescued myself. I didn't need help."

"Is that right?" Duke teased. "Then why didn't you get free before now?"

She shrugged. "I was waiting for the right time."

"And why was the right time now?"

"They got distracted."

"Aye, by the whistler on the street, I'd wager."

"So?"

"He whistled because he saw us. So if it hadn't been for us, they wouldn't have got distracted enough for you to escape." He settled his arm around her shoulders. "A simple thanks is all right by me. No need to gush."

She pushed his arm off and strode to the carriage. "I want to go home."

"You'll probably need a bath," I said. "This place doesn't look terribly clean."

"A bit of dirt and stink don't bother me. I just want to get out of this dress. I ain't never wearing one again. It's all Charity Glass's fault. If she hadn't told the Masons about Cyclops and Catherine, I wouldn't have had to go in disguise to get proof."

"You found out it was her?" I asked, stepping into the carriage.

"Nope, but who else could it be?" She slumped into the corner and crossed her arms, a sour look on her face. "I'm going to confront her right after I wring Bunn and Miss Moreton's necks."

"Let the judge mete out the punishment," I said.

"And let the police catch them," Matt added. "We're going to Scotland Yard before we go home. The police need to start looking for them before the trail goes cold."

"We also have some good news to give a very worried detective inspector," I said. "Cyclops too."

Willie grunted, sounding disinterested, but she sat up a little taller.

We met Cyclops at Scotland Yard as he was about to leave. He slapped Willie on the shoulder and told her she looked ridiculous. She punched him in the arm and he enveloped her in an enormous hug that almost swallowed her whole.

A constable escorted us to Brockwell's office where the inspector was filling out forms at his desk. He glanced up and dropped the pen. Ink splattered all over the paperwork.

He shot to his feet. "Willie! You're safe."

"Course I am. Don't know why you all thought I couldn't take care of myself."

"I tried to tell them you'd be fine, but they thought you needed rescuing anyway."

Matt arched his brow, but the inspector was too busy grinning at Willie to notice.

Willie fought back a smile.

"Bunn and Amelia Moreton are on the run," Matt said, picking up the dropped pen. He wrote down an address in Brockwell's notebook. "This is where they hid Willie. They fled when we arrived."

"After I escaped," Willie pointed out.

Brockwell ordered the constable to gather a team to meet with him in a few moments. The constable hurried away and Brockwell reached for his coat, hanging on the stand by the door.

"How did you get free?" he asked.

Matt told them how we'd learned of the vacant properties and the whistler on the street, and Willie filled in the rest, although her escape was far more elegant in this retelling. She didn't fall through the door and land on her behind, nor did her shot miss by accident. Apparently it was entirely done on purpose because she didn't feel like killing either of them.

"That's real good of you to spare their lives," Cyclops said. "Because they weren't going to spare yours."

"Is that so?" She thrust her hand on her hip. "They wouldn't tell me why they kidnapped me, but I guessed it was to force India to use her magic. I told them it wouldn't work, that Matt wouldn't let you use it even if you wanted to."

Matt looked at me but said nothing.

"Come with me, Willie," Brockwell said, indicating she should walk ahead of him out of the door. "I need to send some men to this address, as well as other places the fugitives are known to frequent. You might be able to tell us something about your kidnappers that will help."

"You should ask Moreton if his daughter has friends who'd hide her," Cyclops said.

"Thank you," Brockwell said wryly.

"And you should wire their descriptions to other police stations," Duke added. "They could be trying to leave London."

"I know what to do," Brockwell said over his shoulder. His strides were the most hurried I'd ever seen from the inspector. I wondered if he'd be this determined if the victim was someone other than Willie.

Willie also seemed to notice the change in Brockwell. Going by her small smile, she liked that he made a fuss.

Brockwell only allowed Willie into the meeting room with his men. The rest of us remained outside. Fortunately the meeting was brief. The constables and sergeants filed out and scattered in all directions. We waited, but Brockwell and Willie didn't emerge.

Duke went to look inside, but Cyclops caught his arm.

"Let them talk alone for a few minutes," Cyclops said. "I reckon he wants to tell her how worried he was."

"That won't work with Willie," Duke said with utter certainty. "You saw what she was like when we rescued her. She doesn't like being a victim or to have others think of her as one. If he tells her he was worried, she'll take it the wrong way."

He might be right. I hoped Brockwell had enough sense to know when to keep quiet. Dealing with Willie was a matter fraught with hazards lurking just below the surface.

I began to doubt Brockwell, and was considering entering the room myself, when the door opened. Willie emerged, that smile still in place, but this time with a gleam in her eyes too. Brockwell looked as bland as always.

We left Brockwell to lead the search for Mr. Bunn and Amelia Moreton and returned home.

"Want a drink, Willie?" Duke asked as we passed the drawing room door.

"Not until I get this damned dress off."

"Oh, Willie," Aunt Letitia said from the staircase. I hadn't seen her standing there, one hand on the balustrade, the other pressed to her stomach. "Look at your hair. It's quite wild. Honestly, if you're going to wear a dress, you ought to do it justice and keep yourself tidy."

"That's why I ain't wearing a dress ever again. It's too much trouble. Give me buckskins and a waistcoat any day over petticoats and a corset."

I was quite sure Willie wasn't wearing a corset but refrained from pointing it out in Aunt Letitia's company.

We dined without Willie, but she joined us later in the sitting room with a full plate of food. Aunt Letitia was so horrified that she was dining somewhere other than the dining room that she retired so that she didn't have to watch. We waited until she was gone before discussing the evening's events to avoid upsetting her.

Willie couldn't offer us much more information than she already had. She didn't know where Bunn and Amelia could have gone, but she did give us some insights into their character.

"They ain't courting," she said. "Or if they are, they've got a stranger relationship than me and Jasper."

"So why did Amelia go along with his scheme?" Cyclops asked.

"I don't think it was his scheme. He wanted to let me go, but Amelia refused. She reckoned the plan would work if they waited it out 'til midnight."

"So why did *he* go along with it then?" I asked.

Willie shrugged. "I think he's in awe of her. She's smart and fearless."

Duke smirked. "She sounds like your type. You should've tried to charm her, not shoot her."

"Real funny, Duke. She ain't my type at all. She's too intense. All she could talk about was magic, and how it needs to be shared, and how magicians should be able to be free to cast whatever spells they want. She sounded angry. Mr. Bunn was too, but only after she riled him up a bit."

"Do you think they'll give up now?" Matt asked.

Willie shook her head. "She won't." She settled her gaze on me. "You need to be careful, India. I reckon they might try kidnapping you, next."

I wasn't so sure. The best way to get me to do something I didn't want to do was threaten my friends or family. I would have given them what they wanted at midnight tonight if we hadn't found Willie. I had to hope they didn't know that. I looked to Matt and swallowed the lump in my throat.

Later, as I was walking up the stairs with Willie, I asked her about her private conversation with Brockwell. "What did he say to you in the meeting room? Did he tell you how worried he was?"

"Nothing like that," she said, looking horrified by the suggestion. "He told me he doesn't mind if I want to see other people, as long as I keep seeing him sometimes."

"You already knew that."

"Other *people*, India, not just other men. He says he was

shocked when he found out I liked women too, only because he's never met anyone like that." She stabbed her thumb into her chest. "I'm unique." Going by her smile, it would seem it was a description she embraced.

"He knows you well," I said gently. At her door, I gave her a brief hug. "I'm very happy to have you back, Willie. It's just not the same here without you."

"Glad to be back. And if I ever suggest wearing a dress again, shoot me."

* * *

DETECTIVE INSPECTOR BROCKWELL arrived while we were taking breakfast in the dining room. He had an uncanny habit of turning up at mealtimes during an investigation, claiming his reports needed to be given in person and precisely the time of day to coincide with an invitation to stay. Sometimes I wondered if he'd asked Mrs. Potter, our cook, for a schedule.

He piled his plate with sausage, boiled eggs, bacon and toast from the sideboard and poured himself a cup of coffee. He smacked his lips as he sat down. "Delicious."

He seemed in no hurry to give his report. Going by his tired appearance, the night had been a busy one.

Willie, however, was in no mood to wait for him to finish eating. To her credit, she did wait until he'd eaten a sausage before asking if Bunn and Amelia had been caught.

He licked sausage grease off his lips then dabbed at the corners of his mouth with exaggerated care. Next came a sip of coffee, a clearing of his throat, and another sip.

We held our breaths, waiting for him to speak, but Willie cracked before he did.

"Jasper! Have they been caught?"

"Not yet," he said, quite oblivious to the frustration he'd caused. "But I'm sure they haven't left the city. My men questioned staff at all the main railway stations and the docks, and no one matching their descriptions has been seen. We'll catch them soon, Willie. It's just a matter of time."

Brockwell left after breakfast. Willie walked him to the door where he pecked her cheek and waved goodbye, just like a husband heading off to work for the day. It was all rather domestic, yet Willie had no idea. I would not be the one to tell her.

I made Christmas decorations with Aunt Letitia after breakfast. I avoided all conversation about the kidnapping so as not to upset her, and I was grateful she didn't ask any questions about it. I wasn't even entirely sure she knew Willie had been kidnapped.

"I must write some Christmas cards this week," she said as she cut out felt angels. "Remind me to send Richard and Beatrice's to Rycroft Hall."

"They're leaving London?" I asked.

"In three days, so her letter tells me. She invited me to go with them, but I'd rather stay here with you and Matthew."

"That's very sweet of you to say, thank you. We're happy to have you. It'll be our first Christmas together."

She held up her garland of angels. "And what a wonderful time we will have in the city. I will miss the countryside, though. It's quite lovely at this time of year with the frost on the lawn. Not that I venture outside much in winter, so I suppose it doesn't really matter where I am, as long as the company is good." She pulled a face. "Being cooped up with Beatrice, Richard and Charity all day, day after day, is quite a challenge for my nerves. The house is large but not large enough."

I couldn't help my chuckle.

"India, do you really think Charity told the Masons about Catherine and Cyclops?"

"Who else can it be?" I said.

"Who indeed." She clicked her tongue. "Horrid girl. It's no wonder she hasn't found a husband."

C.J. ARCHER

Bristow entered and announced Lord Farnsworth was here. "I asked if he wanted to be taken to Mr. Glass's study, but he said he wishes to see the ladies of the house."

"Show him in then fetch Willie." I wasn't sure I could stand a dose of Lord Farnsworth with only Aunt Letitia to lean on. He seemed to prefer Willie's company anyway.

Lord Farnsworth entered and bowed. "Good morning, ladies. What a lovely day it is."

Aunt Letitia glanced at the window. "It's raining."

"Sleeting, in fact, yet lovely, nevertheless. I find any day where I am breathing to be marvelous."

"I quite agree, my lord."

I wasn't sure if Aunt Letitia was humoring him or entirely genuine. She seemed immune to his ridiculousness, but that could have been because he was a lord and she believed civility to members of the upper class was imperative for keeping the world from descending into chaos.

On the other hand, she could be civil towards him to ensure he felt welcomed enough to return frequently. It wouldn't surprise me if she had her sights set on him marrying Charity, and these little visits were her way of sowing the seeds.

Willie entered and Aunt Letitia put her decorations down and bestowed a smile on her. "Look who it is, Willemina. Aren't we fortunate to have Lord Farnsworth here this morning? Tell him how much we enjoy his company."

"We enjoy your company," Willie said, taking a seat.

I narrowed my gaze at Aunt Letitia as she smiled at Willie then turned it onto Lord Farnsworth. Neither of them noticed, but it rather knocked the wind out of my sails. If Aunt Letitia was considering *Willie* as a potential wife for Lord Farnsworth, she was going to be disappointed. It was obvious they were merely friends. I would have to warn Aunt Letitia not to try to match them. Willie's romantic life was complicated enough.

"Tell his lordship what you've been up to, Willemina," she said.

Willie froze. She glanced at me and I froze too. It would seem Aunt Letitia knew about the kidnapping after all.

"Willemina," she said tightly. "Tell him how you have been spying on Charity."

Willie and I both relaxed.

"Spying?" Lord Farnsworth cried. "For any particular reason or simply because you didn't have my company to occupy your time?"

Willie grinned, earning a nod of satisfied approval from Aunt Letitia. Good lord, she *was* considering matching them.

Willie told him about Cyclops and Catherine, and Charity's interest in Cyclops and the trouble this had caused in the past. "I'm trying to find out if it's true that she informed Catherine's family," she finished.

"Any luck?" he asked.

"Not yet."

"They're leaving for the countryside soon," I told her.

Willie was considering this news when Aunt Letitia piped up. "Willemina wore a dress."

Lord Farnsworth threw his head back and laughed.

Willie glared at Aunt Letitia, but Aunt Letitia barreled on, heedless of the fire she'd lit. "She looked very fetching in it. Very elegant indeed. Quite the sophisticated lady."

Lord Farnsworth pressed his lips together and nodded along, trying not to let another burst of laughter escape. The effort made his eyes water.

"Does anyone else think Charity would improve if she had a hobby?" I said quickly to distract everyone from the topic of Willie in a dress. "I think the reason she's so interested in Cyclops is because she considers him dangerous, even though he's very sweet."

"You mean she's bored," Lord Farnsworth said, having recovered from his laughing spell. "That could be the problem. I know I crave dangerous friendships when I'm bored. That's why I enjoy Willie's company."

Willie looked pleased. "I'm dangerous?"

"You do carry a gun. And your cutting remarks at the card table invite danger from time to time when uttered to an opponent with no sense of humor."

Willie all but preened.

"I have a proposal," Lord Farnsworth went on.

Aunt Letitia sat forward. "You do?"

"Why don't I look into the Charity problem?"

Aunt Letitia sat back with a sigh.

"What do you mean 'look into?'" I asked carefully.

"I'll question the staff, delicately of course. My rank opens doors, so it won't be difficult."

Willie screwed up her nose. "That won't work on servants. They're more likely *not* to tell you anything because you're a toff, and a dandy at that."

"A dandy?" He snorted. "I am most certainly not. I'll have you know that I can box quite well. Just because I like to wear elegant clothing and style my hair in the latest fashion does not mean I'm a dandy."

Willie gave a half-hearted apology but didn't retract her statement.

"How about a wager?" Lord Farnsworth said. "If I find out Charity was the one who told the Masons about the lovers, you have to accompany me to a night of cards."

"Agreed."

"Wearing a dress."

"And if you don't?"

"I have to wear a dress."

Aunt Letitia choked then tried to cover it by pretending to cough.

Willie smiled and thrust out her hand. "You got yourself a wager, Farnsworth."

They shook on it.

Lord Farnsworth made his excuses, his eyes gleaming from the thrilling adventure that awaited him in pursuit of the truth.

After he was gone, Aunt Letitia blocked Willie's exit from the drawing room, her brow drawn together in a severe frown.

"It was just a wager between friends, Letty," Willie said. "I couldn't refuse it."

"That is not what irritates me." Aunt Letitia poked a finger into Willie's shoulder. "I am trying to make a good match for you, and all you can do is make him laugh in a most ungentlemanly manner."

Willie gave her a blank look.

"You can't get better than Lord Farnsworth. Honestly, Willemina, at your age and with your...interesting character, you're lucky someone of his caliber has taken an interest in you."

"He ain't interested in me any more than I'm interested in him! Not for marriage, anyway."

Aunt Letitia looked put out.

Willie placed her hands on Aunt Letitia's shoulders and dipped her head to meet her gaze. She had quite a sympathetic look on her face, which surprised me. I thought she'd be cross.

"Farnsworth and I are just friends, Letty. Like me and Duke."

"Oh. Not like you and the detective inspector?"

"No, not like that."

Aunt Letitia sighed and patted Willie's hand. "That is a shame."

Willie kissed her cheek. "I know, but there ain't nothing you, me or him can do about it. I am what I am, and I like what I like. Ain't no explaining it."

Aunt Letitia moved aside and Willie passed her to leave.

"Are you sure he's interested in you as a friend and not a woman?" Aunt Letitia called out.

"I reckon he likes me as both. The two things can exist together. Men and women can be just friends without either party wanting more."

Aunt Letitia watched Willie leave then returned to the sofa and sat beside me. She picked up her garland of angels and spread her hands wide to survey her handiwork. "She is quite wrong, India. She just doesn't know it yet."

* * *

THERE WAS STILL no word from Brockwell about the where-abouts of the fugitives by mid-afternoon. I became quite restless. Since there were only so many Christmas decorations I could make without going mad, I went in search of Matt. I found him in his study, legs outstretched under the desk, contemplating the view out of the window. I took a moment to admire his handsome profile before entering.

"You look thoughtful," I said.

He took my hand and directed me to sit on his lap. His warm arm settled around my waist and he leaned into my shoulder with a sigh. "I wish they'd been caught."

"The police are doing everything they can."

"That doesn't make the wait any easier."

I pulled back to look at him properly. "You're not considering helping Brockwell, I hope."

"I doubt he'd find my assistance all that helpful. Besides, this is a task that requires manpower and feet on the ground. There's nothing I can do."

Cyclops and Duke had joined the police in the search, with Brockwell's approval, but Matt hadn't asked. I suspected he was staying home to protect the more vulnerable members of his family, namely Aunt Letitia and me.

"If we can't go in search of the fugitives, we should

address the matter that we had to set aside when Willie was kidnapped," Matt said. "What to do about Whittaker. Do we tell Barratt that it was most likely Whittaker who sent someone to rough him up?"

"I think he ought to know," I said.

Matt didn't look so sure. "Barratt will probably confront him about it and that could jeopardize our investigation into Whittaker's affairs. I don't want him knowing we're suspicious of him or he'll be more careful."

"Very well. I agree."

"On the other hand, Barratt has the resources of his newspaper at his disposal. He could get access to information we can't."

"Then we'll tell him what we know about Sir Charles but ask him not to confront him over the beating. Until we know more, he mustn't tell anyone."

"Including Louisa," he added.

"He has already asked us not to inform her about the beating, so I'm sure he'll keep this investigation into Sir Charles from her too."

"I'm not so certain. I wouldn't keep something so important from you."

I cupped his face. "But our relationship is vastly different from Oscar and Louisa's." I kissed him lightly on the lips. "Now, if you've got nothing better to do, we could visit Fabian. I'd like to continue with our flying carpet experiment. Your company would be very welcome."

"I'd only be in your way there. Why not send for him? That way I can keep working while you two cast your spells in the library."

It was a good compromise, and I got up to summon Bristow. The butler, however, was approaching the study when I entered the corridor.

"You have an excellent sense of when you're needed," I said, smiling.

He bowed. "Thank you, madam. I like to be helpful. In this instance, however, I didn't know I was required." He held out a note. "This arrived for you and Mr. Glass. I thought it might be urgent."

I thanked him and opened the letter. My gasp brought Matt rushing out of the study.

"What is it?" he asked, peering over my shoulder.

"It's from Mr. Bunn and Miss Moreton," I said. "They're demanding I use my magic on Mr. Bunn's leather or they'll blow up the Hyde Park bandstand at four." I glanced at the clock on the mantel. "That's less than an hour away."

CHAPTER 7

"*I* have to give them what they want," I said to Matt. "I have to use the extension spell on Mr. Bunn's leather one."

"No. We have to stop them." He strode off toward the stairs.

I ran to keep up. "Where are you going?"

"To tell Willie to fetch Brockwell."

"And where will you go after you've done that?"

He didn't answer.

"Matt!"

He did not turn around.

"Don't you dare go to the bandstand and try to stop them! It's far too dangerous."

"We're closer to Hyde Park than Brockwell." He raced down the stairs, shouting for Willie.

She emerged from the drawing room, scissors in one hand and paper in the other. "Stop your hollering. I'm trying to concentrate on my cutting." She held up a rather complicated looking pattern for a star.

"Bunn and Amelia are going to blow up the bandstand in Hyde Park unless we stop them," Matt told her.

"Unless I give them what they want," I countered.

"Christ," Willie muttered. "We've got to tell Jasper." She handed the scissors and pattern to me. "I'll leave now."

"Don't go all the way to the Yard," Matt said, following her down the stairs. "Go to our closest station and get them to send a telegram. It'll be quicker. The deadline is four."

"Bristow!" Willie shouted. "Bristow, we need you!"

"Matt," I said as Bristow emerged from the service area. "Stop and listen to me a moment. The letter tells me to go to the corner of Oxford and Regent Streets. My presence there will be confirmation that I've agreed to use my magic."

"I won't allow you to be manipulated."

"We don't have a choice!"

He accepted his coat from Bristow. "I think the bomb's a hoax. I don't think they plan to detonate it."

"How can you be certain?"

"They've given us the location of the bomb, and it's nowhere near the corner of Oxford and Regent Streets."

"So?"

"Amelia must be standing by the bandstand ready to detonate the bomb or defuse it, depending on your answer. Even if the detonator is controlled by a timing device, she'll need to be nearby to defuse it if you give in to their demand. Either way, Bunn would have to communicate your answer to her instantly at four. It's not possible."

"I suppose you're right."

"They've also given us an entire hour to look around the area and cordon it off so no one can go near the bandstand, including Amelia. If she tries to get close enough to detonate it, she'll be arrested. They won't risk that."

"Then if it's a hoax, why are you rushing to the bandstand now?"

He wouldn't meet my gaze which meant he wasn't entirely convinced by his own argument. "Waiting for Brockwell will take too long," he said. "If I go now, I can alert the police patrolling Hyde Park and we can clear the vicinity."

Willie hurried outside, letting in a cold blast of air. I shivered and rubbed my arms.

Matt gently grasped my shoulders and kissed my forehead. "It'll be fine."

He took his gloves and hat from Bristow then gave me another kiss.

"Be careful," I said lamely as he too stepped outside.

I tried to ignore the hammering in my heart as I watched the street from the library window, but it was no good. Indeed, it became worse as the danger Matt was potentially walking into hit me. This could be a way of luring him out and kidnapping him, forcing me to do as they wished to free him. There might not be a bomb at all. Matt would resist a kidnapping attempt and that could result in grave injuries. If he needed his magical watch to survive, no one there would know. I'd once had to place the watch into his own palm when he was unconscious. If I hadn't been there…

I jumped up from the window seat and called for Bristow. He didn't lecture me as I put on my coat and gloves, but I could see the censure in his eyes. He suspected where I was going and didn't want me to leave. I didn't have the will to reassure him when I was so wretched with fear.

"Do not let in a soul unless it's one of us," I said. "And don't let Aunt Letitia leave."

Outside the rain had stopped but the leaden sky threatened to dump more on the city at any moment. I raced to Hyde Park. Matt had a point when he said Mr. Bunn couldn't get word to Amelia before four if I turned up at the corner of Oxford and Regent Streets. The bomb had to be a hoax meant to draw Matt to Hyde Park.

A cold wind whipped across the open space. I clutched my coat tighter at my throat and ducked my head into the breeze. The weather kept the crowds away, but there were still people scattered about, strolling or riding. There was no sign of Amelia Moreton, however, as I forged on to the bandstand.

The octagonal structure was easy to see in the winter when the surrounding trees had lost their leaves. It loomed ahead, but appeared to be deserted. It wasn't until I drew closer that I spotted Matt and three constables nearby, urging people to leave the vicinity.

He looked up as I approached. "What are you doing here? Go home. It's not safe."

"I thought it might be a trap to capture you and I came to warn you." Now that I was here, the theory seemed far-fetched. Aside from a few thick tree trunks, there was nowhere for Bunn or Amelia to hide.

"I think they've abandoned the kidnapping idea," Matt said. "We've searched the immediate area and there's no one here. There is, however, a homemade bomb on the stage and there's no timing device attached. Someone has to light the fuse and run off before it explodes."

My heart lurched into my throat. "So it's not a hoax. But how will Amelia get close enough to detonate it now?" I eyed the bandstand, dozens of feet away. "Could it go off accidentally? Should we stand further back? If she used her spell on the gunpowder, the explosion could be bigger than an artless bomb of the same size."

"I've taken that into consideration and we are far enough from the bandstand to be safe, but we could do with some more constables to warn everyone. They're stretched thin."

"I'm sure reinforcements will arrive soon, but until they do, I can help."

"You can help by staying close to me. I'd send you home, but that might be too dangerous if they're nearby."

We directed some pedestrians away from the area by telling them a police matter was unfolding. They were curious but complied without complaint. Matt scanned the vicinity and spotted some fresh constables racing toward us.

"You're angry with me for coming," I said.

"We'll discuss it later," Matt said.

"You can be angry all you want, but when your life is in danger and you're not with a friend in possession of the knowledge about your watch, then I will always risk your displeasure and come with you."

"Noted," was all he said. At least it wasn't the silent treatment.

He informed the new constables of the situation and asked them to help keep people away from the bandstand.

A mere ten minutes later, Willie arrived, but it was another fifteen before Brockwell showed up. He inspected the bomb alone then rejoined us at a safe distance.

"There is no timing device attached," he said, confirming what Matt already knew. "It's not surprising, as they're notoriously unreliable."

Willie scanned the nearby trees. "So she planned on being here to light the fuse herself."

There was no sign of Amelia Moreton. She must have left upon seeing Matt and the constables.

"I sent for the bomb expert before I left the Yard," Brockwell said. "He'll dismantle it safely and take it away."

I checked my watch. "There are only eight minutes until four. When will he get here?"

"Not before four. He's coming from Greenwich."

"It's all right, India," Willie said. "The police have cleared the area. If it goes off by accident, no one will get hurt."

"Yes, but...I don't understand. Why put a bomb here at all when you can't detonate it? They must have guessed we'd come ourselves or send the police, so why tell us the location at all? Our presence foils their plan."

No one had answers, nor had I expected them to. There

was more going on here than we knew, but until Bunn and Amelia chose to reveal it to us, we'd remain in the dark.

Brockwell ordered some of his men to check as much of the park as possible for more bombs or a woman matching Amelia's description. It would be impossible to search more than the immediate vicinity before four, however.

I cradled my watch in my palm and watched the minutes and seconds tick by. They seemed to last hours. Brockwell estimated the bomb expert was still twenty minutes away, at least.

As the hour of four drew nearer, it was some comfort that the police hadn't found more bombs. Hopefully this was the only one. Brockwell assured us some police had been sent to Oxford and Regent Streets too. The usually busy shopping precinct would be even busier with Christmas gift buying, and that would make it extremely difficult to spot our villains, particularly if Bunn employed a disguise.

The more I considered it, the more I suspected this entire event was a ruse to lure Matt here. They must have abandoned the idea to kidnap him when he arrived with the police in tow. If kidnapping him *wasn't* the plan...

My mouth went dry. Aunt Letitia was home alone. I was very glad I'd given Bristow the order not to let anyone into the house. She and the servants would be quite safe as long as they kept the doors and windows locked. I expelled a measured breath.

A bone-shattering *boom* pounded the air.

Matt pushed me to the ground, shielding me with his body. Something thudded on the damp earth nearby then all fell silent, except for the ringing in my ears.

I peeked out from beneath my arms covering my head to see a jagged piece of wood sticking out of the ground not a foot away. Beyond it, in the space where the bandstand should be, was a burning pile of timber.

Matt stood and assisted me to my feet. He clasped my face

in both his hands and inspected me. "All right?" he asked. His voice was hard to hear over the ringing.

I nodded and looked for Willie. Brockwell had covered her as Matt had covered me. They were both getting to their feet, dusting themselves off and looking around. The shock on their faces probably matched mine.

The bomb had gone off yet no one had lit the fuse. Without a timing device attached, how was that possible?

Magic.

"Is anyone injured?" Brockwell shouted.

Some of his men responded, but those further away didn't hear.

We picked our way past more pieces of splintered, smoking wood but the fire kept us from getting too close.

Brockwell removed his hat and scrubbed a hand through his hair. "How was it detonated?"

"Amelia," I said darkly. "With a spell."

"But her father didn't tell us she could do that."

"You trust him after discovering he sold illegal bombs?" Matt all but scoffed.

Brockwell drew in a deep breath and let it out slowly. "We've got a problem on our hands. A very big, unpredictable problem." He looked to me. "India, you have to do as they ask."

I nodded but Matt shook his head. "This was a warning," he said. "They wanted us to know what Amelia's capable of. They knew we'd come here, see a bomb with no timer and no one to detonate it and think they'd made a mistake. They knew we'd clear the area so no one would get hurt."

"That's something, at least," I said. "It shows they're not willing to kill."

"Unless they have to," Brockwell added.

"It's likely Bunn and Amelia were watching for India at the corner of Oxford and Regent," Matt went on. "When she didn't turn up, Amelia exploded this bomb from there with her spell. I suspect they'll send another note soon, asking the same thing of India and threatening to explode another bomb. But this time they won't give us the location of the bomb, only where India should go."

"But if they're unwilling to kill or injure people, surely they'll tell us," I said lamely. But in my heart of hearts, I knew Matt was right. This bomb was the warning. The next one would be the real danger.

Matt took my hand in his. His eyes were as grim as the sky. "Until their letter arrives, we have some investigating to do. There's still a chance we can stop them from planting another bomb."

"We?" Brockwell echoed.

"You need our help, Brockwell."

The detective inspector conceded the point by not disagreeing.

The rain started again and Matt flipped up my hood for me. We walked back through Hyde Park with Willie, passing a fire engine pulled by two powerful horses on its way to put out the bandstand fire.

Bristow opened the door only after we identified ourselves. He reported that Aunt Letitia was waiting to have a light afternoon tea with us in the drawing room. She was upset that we'd all gone out and not told her.

"We're in the middle of an investigation," Matt said when she scolded him for being absent when she wanted company. "India and I have to go out again now. Willie will sit with you."

"Actually I'm going out too," Willie said. "I want to see how Farnsworth's faring."

"You should stay here," Matt warned her. "Or not go out alone."

"I ain't going to be a prisoner here."

"Why would you be a prisoner?" Aunt Letitia asked.

"No reason." Willie sighed and sat on a chair. "I s'pose I'll just have to eat all these cream puffs myself."

Matt paused, picked up a cream puff, and beckoned me to follow him as he took a bite.

His aunt clicked her tongue. "Honestly, Matthew. Your manners are so American sometimes. India, you're a good English girl. Educate him on the proper way to enjoy cream puffs—sitting down."

I eyed the cream puffs, then the door through which Matt had left, and looked to the plate of cream puffs again. I grabbed one and bustled out. The sound of Aunt Letitia's clicking tongue followed me all the way to the stairs.

* * *

THE SMALL FIGURE of Mrs. Moreton looked more forlorn than the last time we'd seen her. The lamplight cast shadows over her drawn face and her hollow eyes filled with tears. She cried when we told her what Amelia had done in Hyde Park.

"I loved that bandstand," she said. "I used to take the children to the concerts there when they were young. Amelia liked to dance to the music."

"I know this is hard for you," I said. "But what can you tell us about Amelia's magic?"

"Not much. My husband is the magician. I'm artless, as is our son. He's at the factory now, trying to keep the business running while his father is…" She swallowed. "Indisposed."

"What spells can she do?" Matt pressed.

"Just the two. One to make the fireworks more spectacular, and the other to detonate them from a distance."

"You knew about the detonation spell?"

She bit her lower lip. "I know I should have told you about it, but I didn't want her to be in any more trouble than she already was. I thought you might lock her away if you caught her and never let her out again. Some artless want to imprison magicians to stop them casting spells."

"I'm not artless," I pointed out.

"The police are, and the judges and law makers. They're the ones with the real power, not magicians. If they thought Amelia was a danger to society, they'd lock her away. Or worse."

"She proved she *is* a danger by bombing the bandstand," Matt said, not very kindly. "It's not just her own freedom she jeopardized through her actions, but that of all magicians. You should have told us."

Mrs. Moreton's head lowered beneath his glare. "I know," she whispered. "I'm sorry. I'd almost forgotten about the detonation spell. She rarely uses it. It's only needed when the fireworks don't explode in the sky. She speaks the spell from the ground. It's why our fireworks never fail here in London, because she's there."

"Not your husband?" I asked.

She shook her head. "The spell doesn't work for him. His father taught him the words, however, and he passed them on to Amelia when we realized she was quite powerful." She let out a thin wail. "I wish he never had! I wish she'd never discovered her magic. It's a curse!"

"It's not a curse," Matt said gently. "Not if she uses it with good intentions."

Mrs. Moreton didn't appear to hear him. She sniffed and dabbed at her eyes with her handkerchief.

Matt handed her the letter we'd received earlier. "Do you recognize this handwriting?"

She skimmed the note and gave a small nod. "It's hers."

He folded the note and slipped it back into his jacket pocket. "The police are looking all over the city for Amelia. Do you have any idea where she might have gone?"

She shook her head.

"Could someone be sheltering her? A relative or friend? A lover perhaps?"

She cringed.

"Please, Mrs. Moreton," I said, "if you can think of anyone, it would be most helpful."

"I don't know her new friends, the magicians who are advocating for freedom. She stopped confiding in me around the time she fell in with them." Her words faded toward the end, as if she'd run out of steam. She stared down at the floor. "How could she do this to me?"

Matt caught my eye and signaled that we should leave.

I touched Mrs. Moreton's hand, startling her. "If you think of anything, let us or the police know." I gave her a calling card and smiled sympathetically.

Outside, Matt spotted the policemen before I did, hunched in their coats, stamping their feet for warmth. They rather foolishly stood within the circle of light cast by the lamppost.

"What a horrid night for surveillance duty," I said.

Matt jogged over to one of the constables then returned after exchanging a few words. The constables moved out of the light into the darker stretches of the street. They were almost invisible in their uniforms and if I hadn't known they were there, I wouldn't have seen them.

"Apparently Brockwell has also sent men to search the untenanted house where we found Willie. I'll let him know the address of the other one. More constables are watching the fireworks factory in case Bunn and Amelia return there, either to hide or to steal gunpowder. Amelia might be able to detonate bombs, but she can't make them out of thin air. She needs gunpowder, and the factory has a warehouse full of it."

The resources of the Metropolitan Police were stretched thin. Even with so many men on the street, it would be near impossible to find Bunn and Amelia if someone was harboring them. We didn't know the names of their activist associates, nor even where to start looking.

"We could try Bunn's workshop again," I said as Matt assisted me into the carriage. "The lad might be more helpful if we impress upon him the dangers of remaining silent."

"I'm not sure he knows anything more. What if we question Moreton again?"

"Her father? Do you think he'll know her associates when her mother doesn't?"

"If she's going to talk to anyone in her family about magic, it would be the only other magician among them."

"Yes, you're right. Let's go now. Hopefully Brockwell will let us question him considering the exceptional circumstances."

Matt gave Woodall instructions then climbed in and sat beside me. We traveled quickly through the evening traffic to Scotland Yard and found Brockwell in his office, having just returned from Hyde Park. He looked more harried than I'd ever seen him, and considering he was often disheveled, that was quite a feat.

"You look like you need coffee," I said.

He glanced up from his paperwork. "Or something stronger. Got any leads for me?"

"Not yet," Matt said. "But we think we know how to get some."

He explained his theory and, to my surprise, Brockwell readily agreed to let us interrogate Mr. Moreton. "But I'll be present," he added.

He led the way through the building to the basement cells where Mr. Moreton was imprisoned. "He's being moved tomorrow to await trial," he said.

"Will he be hanged if found guilty?" I asked.

"Unlikely, unless we can prove he sent his bombs to our enemies, either here or abroad. He will go to jail for a long time, however."

The warden unlocked the cell door then locked us inside. Mr. Moreton looked terrible. His jaw was shadowed with stubble and his hair desperately needed a comb run through it. The smell wafting from him was rather pungent too, but I tried not to show my disgust.

The cell was small with only a slim barred window high up on the wall. A bed was positioned beneath it, and a bible and tin cup sat on a shelf and an empty plate on the bed.

Mr. Moreton greeted us politely but cautiously. "I would offer you a seat, Mrs. Glass, but they don't provide one," he said with a large dose of sarcasm and a glare for Brockwell.

The detective inspector ignored the jibe. "There has been a development today in the situation involving your daughter."

"You found your cousin?" he asked Matt.

"She was found yesterday in one of your properties," Matt said. "Amelia escaped along with Bunn, however."

"She's under his influence. He's a nasty character, not satisfied with the skills God gave him. He always wants more."

"You told us you hardly knew him," Matt said. "From what we can gather, it's more likely he is under *her* spell. Amelia is the driving force behind the movement. The two letters were written in her hand." The arch of his brow was intended to let Mr. Moreton know that he knew he'd lied about not recognizing Amelia's handwriting on the first note.

Mr. Moreton sat heavily on the bed. "What do you want from me?"

"We want to know who could be harboring her," Matt said. "Who are her associates?"

"I don't know."

"You must know. You would have introduced her to magicians."

"I didn't."

"Who are her friends, Mr. Moreton?"

"I told you, I don't know. Go away. I have nothing more to say."

"That's unfortunate," Matt said with an ominous tone.

"Because we're not leaving until you tell us where to look for her. We know you know something. She must have confided in you, her father, mentor and fellow magician."

Mr. Moreton lifted his chin and turned away, presenting us with an uncompromising profile.

Matt slammed his hands into Moreton's shoulders, shoving him backward on the bed into the brick wall.

The outburst had no effect on Mr. Moreton. He smoothed his hair down and cleared his throat. "I have nothing more to say. Leave or I'll call the warden."

Matt growled in frustration.

"Step back, Glass," Brockwell commanded. "Let me handle this." He cleared his throat. "Mr. Moreton, if you tell us who your daughter's associates are, I'll see that your sentence is lenient."

"I don't know her associates," he snarled.

"But you know something. I can see it in your eyes."

Mr. Moreton lowered his gaze.

It was Brockwell's turn to growl in frustration. Short of beating the information out of Mr. Moreton, we'd get nowhere, and neither Matt nor Brockwell had the stomach for that level of violence. Besides, we were trying to get information from a man that would see his daughter arrested. He wouldn't give in easily.

I had an idea that might convince him, however.

I sat beside him on the bed. "Mr. Moreton, Amelia is a powerful magician. We know she can use the spell to detonate bombs and fireworks from afar, yet it didn't work for you. I understand something of powerful magic, both its benefits and its dangers. I also know what it means to be feared and excluded because of that magic."

"Your point, Mrs. Glass?"

"My point is, your daughter is going to ruin not only herself but the rest of your family, and the business too. Once your own crime becomes public, the Moreton reputation will hang by a thread. Your son could save it and restore it to its prior glory if we suppress the fact that you are a magician. But your daughter's lack of discretion could ruin it altogether if she continues along the path she has chosen. We won't hide that she has detonated bombs from afar with a spell. Indeed, if you don't help us, we'll ensure the information is given to the press. Imagine the public's response. They'll both fear and loathe your family, and no artless will do business with Moreton's. The company will go bankrupt and your wife and son will be destitute."

He swallowed hard. "My son isn't a magician."

"It won't matter, not to the public or your customers."

He stared down at his clasped hands in his lap.

"You can't save Amelia," I said. "But you can secure your wife and son's futures if you tell us how to stop her."

He leaned his elbows on his knees and lowered his head into his hands. I glanced up at Matt and he gave me a grim smile and a nod.

With a heaving sigh, Mr. Moreton straightened. His watery eyes fixed on Brockwell. "If one of her bombs kills someone, she'll hang won't she?"

The inspector nodded. "But if we capture her before she creates the next one, she will merely serve time in jail." He did not say how long. I suspected her incarceration wouldn't be short.

"Very well," Mr. Moreton said. "I can't tell you the names of her other associates. I only know of Bunn. But I can tell you that she will need black powder to make another bomb. Are you watching my warehouse?"

Brockwell nodded.

"You must also watch other gunpowder stores in the city. If they can't get into my warehouse, they'll try elsewhere."

"Where are those stores?" Matt asked.

"I don't know. I am only aware of my own."

"There could be hundreds of places that use gunpowder!"

"In small quantities, yes, but not the amount she will need, particularly if she creates more than one bomb. Surely there can't be that many in London. Most ammunition factories and mines are in other counties, and there are very few fireworks factories here."

We left the forlorn figure of Mr. Moreton sitting on his prison bed and made our way back upstairs.

"This is going to be impossible," Brockwell grumbled. "Where do we even start?"

CHAPTER 8

*W*e met Cyclops and Duke in the reception area of Scotland Yard where they were briefing a sergeant in front of a map on the wall. "These streets here," Duke was saying as we joined them. He pointed to a sizeable area in the East End. "None of the residents claims to have seen people matching Bunn or Amelia's description."

"They could be lying," Cyclops said. "They ain't too keen on giving up information. East Enders look out for each other."

We briefed them on the day's developments and our reason for being at Scotland Yard on a cold evening. Both offered to help Brockwell search other factories and warehouses for stores of gunpowder.

"Yes, but which ones?" Brockwell said on a sigh. "Aside from ammunitions and fireworks factories, of which London has very few, where else?"

"Warehouses down at the docks," Matt said. "The gunpowder would be offloaded and stored until it can be dispersed around the country. We just need to find out who imports it."

"Most of the English supply of saltpeter comes from

India," Cyclops said. He shrugged when we all looked at him in surprise. "I just know it from my days working in mines back home. We had an Englishman come and learn a new blasting technique from us once."

Duke clicked his fingers. "Mining companies want gunpowder too. We just have to find out who imports it and stores it down at the docks. If it has to be imported then it probably comes to London before going by rail to its final destination?"

Brockwell turned to his sergeant. "Find out who imports the elements to make powder then gather as many men as you can for surveillance duties. Cyclops and Duke, may I commission your assistance?"

Brockwell strode off with Duke and Cyclops in tow amid shouted orders from the sergeant to the constables. Matt and I left them to it and returned home.

Willie had waited up for us. Once we informed her of the evening's developments, she insisted on going to Scotland Yard to help with the search. Nothing we said could convince her to stay home.

Matt and I retired to bed, but I couldn't sleep. My tossing must have kept him awake because he rolled over and snuggled me.

"They'll find them," he assured me in a sleepy voice. "This will all be over by the morning."

"And if it's not?" I turned to face him. "Matt, I think I should do as they ask. I should infuse my magic with Mr. Bunn's."

He propped himself up on his elbow. I could just make out his frown in the dark. "It won't end their harassment. It'll just be the beginning. Another magician will come to you, then another and another."

"I could ask for secrecy."

"You could ask, but would they agree? If they manipulate you once, they'll know they can manipulate you again. Even if they don't tell other magicians, what if Bunn asks you to do it a second time and third? I doubt he'll settle for one pair of boots. And who knows what Amelia is capable of. She might demand you make her explosions last longer."

I rolled onto my back and stared up at the ceiling. "I have to do *something*. If it weren't for my magic, this wouldn't have happened."

He touched my jaw and turned me to face him. I could sense rather than see his earnestness. It vibrated off him in waves. "This isn't your fault, India. Don't think like that." His thumb stroked along my jawline and up into my hair near my ear. He leaned in and gave me a kiss that contained all his frustrations and earnestness.

I reached around his neck but he drew back.

"So you'll stop blaming yourself?" he asked.

I nodded. "Just kiss me again."

He smiled and did as commanded.

Despite his expert kisses, I couldn't fully commit. My mind continued to play the scenarios over and over. Matt might be right, this could be finished by morning, but there were so many places to watch now, so many more to search, that it would most likely take days. We didn't have days. Amelia could create another bomb tomorrow if she found gunpowder.

Her father had proved that illegal weapons were being made right here in London. What if he wasn't the only one? What if there were illegal stores of gunpowder and illegal importers—ones we didn't know about but Amelia *did?*

Matt pulled away with a sigh. "Have I gone from a good kisser to a mediocre one?"

"That assumes you were a good kisser in the first place."

He playfully nipped my top lip then drew away again. He looked serious in the dim light. "So tell me what's stopping you from enjoying my company?"

"We need more resources."

"Scotland Yard has many men. Brockwell will be fine."

"His men are very conspicuous and some are not terribly bright. Amelia is smart. We have to outwit her, and that means being more secretive and invisible than her."

"Invisible?"

"We need spies, Matt, people who are good at blending in and not being seen. And we need a lot of them."

"Brockwell could approach the Home Office," he said thoughtfully. "But then he'd have to explain about Amelia detonating bombs from a distance, and that will expose the existence of magic to officials at that level."

He was right. While some craftsmen and guilds had long suspected magic existed to this day, the authorities were unaware, as far as we knew. The highest official who knew about magic was Commissioner Munro of the Metropolitan Police, Brockwell's superior. Knowing about it and believing in it were two different things, however. While his own son had been a magician, the commissioner had never truly believed its existence. Or perhaps he didn't want to believe. He let Brockwell investigate magical crimes, and never interfered. According to Brockwell, he had to edit his reports to play down the magical element and sometimes removed it altogether. If Munro wasn't prepared to believe in magic then he probably hadn't informed others of its existence. I hoped not anyway.

"I was thinking of someone less official for that reason," I said. "Someone with a network of spies at his disposal, or so we assume."

He sat bolt upright. "Coyle? India, if we ask him for a favor, we'll owe him."

I sat up too. "Technically, Scotland Yard will owe him."

"He won't make that distinction."

"He might. Think about it, Matt. We need him."

He thought about it for all of three seconds then shook his

head. "It doesn't matter. He's away on his honeymoon. We don't even know where they went."

"We could find out from his staff. The butler will know. Then we could wire him and he can set the wheels in motion from his hotel." I knelt and took Matt's face in my hands. "Sleep on it, but we can't wait too long. No later than tomorrow morning."

"But—"

"No more buts. Just kiss me again and remind me what a good kisser you are."

I felt his lips twitch with his smile. "Good?"

"Very well, you are a great kisser, Matt. An excellent one, in fact. Now prove it."

"Gladly."

* * *

WE WERE ABOUT to head out after breakfast when Lady Rycroft and Charity arrived. We tried to make our excuses, but Aunt Letitia insisted we join them in the drawing room.

"A few moments only," she all but begged. "I'm sure my sister-in-law can't stay longer than that."

Matt agreed, but I wasn't so sure. We needed to get word to Lord Coyle immediately. I was beginning to think Matt didn't want to approach him at all, despite agreeing to it before we went down to breakfast.

"This is an early visit," Aunt Letitia said as we settled into the drawing room.

"We came to tell you we've brought our departure forward," Lady Rycroft said stiffly. "We're leaving for Rycroft Hall today."

"A letter would have saved you the effort of coming all this way in person on such a cold morning."

Lady Rycroft's nostrils flared. "My daughter suggested it

would be more personable to come ourselves, but if our company is not welcome, we'll leave." She rose.

"Sit down, Beatrice," Aunt Letitia said tightly. "You and Charity are always welcome with open arms. We are happy to have you, no matter the hour, aren't we, India?"

"Of course," I said with a little less sarcasm than she employed.

Lady Rycroft sat again, her lips pursed into a thin line. Her daughter didn't seem to hear any of our conversation. She was too intent on watching the door, waiting for Cyclops to walk through it, no doubt. He had not yet come home after a night of surveillance. Hopefully if he did, Bristow had the foresight to warn him of what awaited in the drawing room so he could avoid Charity altogether.

"And will all your girls be joining you at Rycroft Hall for Christmas?" Aunt Letitia asked with exaggerated politeness.

"Charity will be there, of course."

"How fortunate you are to have one dear child always with you, Beatrice. It must be such a comfort having her as your constant companion."

Good lord, she was laying the hyperbole on so thickly one needed a saw to cut through it.

Lady Rycroft sensed it too, but politeness dictated she couldn't acknowledge it except with another round of flared nostrils and stiffening spine. "Charity is a comfort," she said without an ounce of sincerity.

At the sound of her name, Charity seemed to come alive. "Are your friends here, Matt?" she asked.

"Not at present," he said.

She crossed her arms and pouted.

"Hope can't come for Christmas," Lady Rycroft went on. "She's far too busy now that she's Lady Coyle."

"Oh?" Aunt Letitia said. "Do they plan on hosting many parties? I don't recall him being one for that sort of thing. He seems rather reclusive."

"I'm sure Hope will see that he changes." Lady Rycroft's eyes lit up when talking about her youngest daughter, and there was no tartness in her voice. "She did marry one of the most pre-eminent men in the country, so we must expect her to be far busier than the rest of us. She'll not only have parties to host, but a great many events to attend. Invitations will come pouring in, particularly once the London season gets underway. Things are always a little quiet in the city over winter, but they both insisted on staying here. Neither likes the country. They are so well suited, in that as in all things."

Beside her, Charity snorted softly.

Her mother's lips pinched. "Hope has made a great match for herself. The best she could possibly make." She patted Charity's hand. "It won't be long before she finds you a husband, dear girl. One of Lord Coyle's friends, perhaps."

"I'd rather stab myself in the eye with a fork than marry a fat old beast like that."

Lady Rycroft's face reddened. "Charity!"

Charity merely shrugged.

I bit my lip hard to stop myself smiling.

"Oh dear," Aunt Letitia said with a click of her tongue. "You'll never marry with an attitude like that."

"You mean I'll end up unmarried like you, Aunt," Charity said.

Aunt Letitia blinked hard, as if she'd been slapped.

"Don't be unkind," Lady Rycroft said mildly.

"I wasn't. I envy her. She's lucky *her* parents never forced her to marry someone like Coyle."

"We didn't force Hope. She chose Lord Coyle. He might not be Prince Charming, but she must be commended for looking beyond his exterior deficiencies and seeing the true value in a man of his standing."

Charity pulled a face, but wisely remained quiet. It wasn't an argument she could win against her mother.

"And Patience?" I asked. "Will she and Byron spend Christmas at Rycroft Hall?"

"They weren't invited," Lady Rycroft said. "We knew they'd be too busy with his children so didn't bother to send an invitation."

It would seem all was not forgiven where Patience and Byron were concerned. It was unfair, considering losing the title was not his fault. The poor man had suffered enough and now his own mother-in-law could barely bring herself to talk about him.

Then again, perhaps they were fortunate to be excluded from Christmas celebrations at the hall. They wouldn't have to be stuck with Lord and Lady Rycroft and their petulant middle daughter.

Lady Rycroft rose. "Come, Charity. We must leave. We still have to visit your sister."

"Hope?" I asked. "But they're away."

"They returned home last night."

"That was a brief honeymoon," Aunt Letitia said.

Charity smirked. "Hope wanted it that way."

Her mother glared sharply at her. "Lord Coyle is a busy man. He had business here he couldn't ignore for any length of time."

Charity rolled her eyes.

I arched my brows at Matt and he gave a small nod, although he didn't look particularly happy about what we had to do.

I subtly whispered in Aunt Letitia's ear asking her to keep Lady Rycroft and Charity talking for ten more minutes, then Matt and I made our excuses. Since our carriage was already waiting, we left immediately. Lord and Lady Coyle didn't live far away, so I didn't have long to convince Matt that this was a good idea.

"I don't like owing Coyle a favor," he responded. "Nor do I think he'll agree to us passing the buck onto the police. He knows the commissioner won't give him anything in return. He'll make sure he gets his pound of flesh from *you*, India. You're the only one who has what he wants."

He was right, but I wasn't going to admit it. We were almost there, so I simply sat quietly and stared out the window until we arrived at the Belgrave Square townhouse.

We greeted the newlyweds as civilly as possible considering our strained relationships in the past. I tried to gauge Hope's demeanor, but her easy manner was as charming as usual.

"What a lovely surprise," she said as we sat in the drawing room. "How did you know we were back?"

"Your mother paid us a visit," I said. "She'll be here soon, in fact, so we'd like to come to the point straight away."

"Oh? This isn't a social call?" Her wide blue eyes were all childlike innocence. It made her look every bit her youthful twenty-one years.

Lord Coyle, standing behind his wife, patted her shoulder. "It is never a social call with these two. They only come to me when they want something. Isn't that right, Glass?"

Hope gently chided her husband and smiled up at him. He stroked her cheek with his knuckles then took a seat opposite in one of the deep armchairs by the fire. It was all very sweet and loving. Or it would have been if Hope hadn't frozen when he touched her face, as if she were holding herself in position.

"So what do you want, Glass?" Coyle asked. "Information? I must admit I'm surprised you've come to me again after the last time. You seemed to take great exception to Mrs. Glass owing me a favor on that occasion. You must be desperate."

Out of the corner of my eye I saw Hope's sly smile.

Matt didn't rise to Lord Coyle's baiting tone, thankfully. I'd been prepared for him to say something ruthlessly cutting, or to glare sharply, at least. But he merely gave

Lord Coyle's statement a lazy flick of his fingers, dismissing it.

"Before we tell you," he said, "I need an agreement from you that you won't ask for anything more from us."

Lord Coyle's throaty chuckle ended in a rasping coughing fit. Hope rose and bent over him, patting his hand rather ineffectively until the seizure ended. It was at that point I noticed something missing. A cigar. Lord Coyle always had one either protruding from between his bulldog lips or wedged between his fingers like an extra appendage.

"Why would I do that?" Lord Coyle asked when he'd recovered and Hope was sitting once more. "I trade in information. Tell me, why would I give you something and expect nothing in return?"

"Because by asking for a favor, we will have to tell you why, and doing so will give you some information that we think you'd like to know. That will be our payment."

What was Matt doing? Lord Coyle wasn't going to be satisfied learning that a fireworks magician was threatening to bomb the city. He most likely knew about the Moreton family already. Granted, he might not be aware that Amelia could blow up gunpowder without using a timer or having someone present to detonate it, but would discovering that be something worthy to exchange for his help? I doubted he'd think so.

I glanced at Hope. She watched Matt intently, hanging on his every word. Admiration filled her eyes.

Her husband would not have noticed. He too watched Matt closely. "You want us to be square," he said.

"I do. You'll not ask for anything more of us or the police in exchange."

"The police? Now I am intrigued." He went to reach for something on the table beside him and, discovering it not there, cast a grim glance at his wife before regarding Matt once more. It seemed he missed having a cigar at hand.

"You cannot agree, Coyle," Hope said aghast. "What if the information is useless to us?"

"It won't be." Matt put up his hands. "I'm not saying there's anything you can do with the information, but gaining it through us will have the benefit of cutting out the middle-man, if nothing else."

"What middleman?" Hope asked.

Lord Coyle searched the table again. Finding it empty, he drummed his fingers on the surface and blew out a breath.

"Sir Charles Whittaker," Matt told Hope. "Your husband uses him to gather information about us. Perhaps about others, too." Matt was certainly up to something but I had no idea what.

I was as curious as Hope to find out, however.

"Mrs. Delancey gave Whittaker information about a spell India was creating with Fabian Charbonneau," Matt went on. "India had asked her for something and she told Whittaker, who put two and two together. He then informed Coyle."

Hope's lips parted but no sound came out. Her narrowed gaze slid to her husband.

Lord Coyle glared at Matt. "So you have information about your wife's spellcasting trials with Charbonneau?"

"I do. They're working on a new spell and in doing so, had a need for a particular type of magician. That magician has since done something dangerous and we need the use of your spy network to search for her before she does something more dangerous."

Lord Coyle finally stopped drumming his fingers. "Ah, my spy network. That is a big ask. Are you sure your infor-mation is worth it in exchange?"

"Of course." Matt had the easy response of a man convinced, or at least good at lying. I, however, couldn't risk it. We needed further inducement.

I sat forward a little. "By helping us, you're not only going to find out what Fabian and I are working on, you will also be helping to save lives. Please, my lord. The city needs you. Surely you're not so callous as to let people suffer knowing you could have done something to stop it."

"It isn't a matter of callousness, India," Hope said with a tone that was both sweet and sour. "It's a matter of fairness. You can't expect my husband to do something for nothing. His network cannot be bought cheaply, you understand. There's nothing like it in the country."

"I know his service is expensive," I snapped back.

"I'm glad you understand."

Lord Coyle chuckled, making his jowls shake. "Now, now, ladies. Let's not fight over this. That was a very pretty speech, Mrs. Glass. Very pretty indeed. Of course I will help."

Hope's nostrils flared, just as her mother's had done on multiple occasions earlier.

"Well then?" Lord Coyle prompted. "What do you need my spies for?"

"India and Fabian have been working with gunpowder magic," Matt said.

My breath caught in my throat. Now I understood what Matt was doing. This way we put Coyle off the scent of the real spell Fabian and I were creating.

"They wanted to create a spell that could send fireworks further into the sky and make them more spectacular," Matt went on.

"Fireworks or bombs?" Lord Coyle asked.

"Fireworks."

Lord Coyle stroked his long white moustache. "You must have enlisted the help of Moreton. He's the only fireworks magician in the country."

"His daughter," Matt went on. "She's a powerful magician, but is an activist for magicians' freedom. That passion has led her to employ some methods used by the Irish Fenians—blackmail and bombs. But her magic makes her more dangerous than the Fenians." He told them about her spell to detonate bombs from afar and her threat to blow up the bandstand in Hyde Park if India didn't use her magic with Mr. Bunn's. "She blew up the bandstand to show us what she was capable of," he finished.

"Good lord," Hope said on a breath.

Lord Coyle curled his hand into a fist on the chair arm. "She must be stopped."

"That's why we came to you," I said. "The police are searching the known storage facilities of importers of gunpowder, as well as factories around London that use it. But there are probably illegal stores they don't yet know about. We thought you would, or could find out, and have your men watch those stores."

"I'll do everything necessary."

Hope turned suddenly to face her husband fully. "Agreeing so readily, my dear? That doesn't sound like you."

"If Miss Moreton succeeds, it will be difficult to suppress her use of magic to ignite the bombs. We can't let the public get wind of it. It would be all over the newspapers and lead to the end of secrecy for magicians. That, my dear, would be a disaster."

Hope seemed to realize the motive behind Lord Coyle's quick acquiescence at the same time I did. He wanted the exact opposite of what Amelia Moreton desired. She wanted magicians to be free to wield their magic as they wished, to create the best products they could and to capitalize on their superior craftsmanship. But Coyle wanted magic to remain hidden, special, something only a few collectors like himself could afford.

In this instance, his interests aligned with ours. I couldn't tell whether it aligned with Hope's or not, or indeed if her interests were different to her husband's. Her smooth features gave nothing away.

Lord Coyle rattled off the names of businesses he suspected stored gunpowder illegally, and committed some men to surveillance duties. Brockwell was to work directly with Coyle, however, who would then give his spies the orders personally. He wouldn't divulge their identities.

We were finishing up when the butler entered and announced the arrival of Lady Rycroft and Charity. Hope sighed and Lord Coyle excused himself.

Lady Rycroft and Charity stared at us as we departed, no doubt wondering what we were doing there. We climbed into the conveyance and Matt directed Woodall to drive to Scotland Yard.

"Thank goodness he agreed," I said. "Well done on diverting him so that no one owes him anything."

"You mean lying to him." He smiled. "I can admit what I did."

"Very well, congratulations on successfully lying to him. I wonder what he'll do with the information about our fictional gunpowder spell."

He tapped his forehead. "Store it away up here along with the other bits of information he keeps. Sometimes I wonder how many he actually uses and how many simply gather dust in his mind."

I covered my knees with the blanket and snuggled closer to Matt for warmth. "Speaking of fakery, did you sense Hope was acting? The only genuine smile seemed to be the one she gave when Coyle mentioned the favor I'd once owed him."

He swayed back to look at me properly. "You seem surprised. You expected her to be happy to be married to him?"

"Not as happy as I am to be married to you, naturally."

He flashed me a grin.

"She seemed happy enough on their wedding day," I said. "I suppose I didn't expect their marriage to deteriorate so quickly."

"Ah, young love," he teased. "It burns as brightly as the sun only to quickly fade and disappear altogether at sunset."

"They are an odd couple. Both horrid people at their core, so they do have that in common."

"A solid marriage is built on common ground, so there's hope for them yet."

I chuckled and nudged his ribs with my elbow. "Did you also see her surprise when we mentioned he uses Whittaker as a source of information about us? She was annoyed he'd kept that from her. I wonder if she'll demand he divulge all his secrets the way she demanded he give up cigars."

Matt chuckled. "I envisage Coyle spending many evenings at his club in the future. He looked lost without a cigar to plug that maw."

I settled into Matt's side with a sigh. It was rare to feel relieved after speaking to Lord Coyle. Usually I felt sick with worry. But as we sped toward Scotland Yard, I finally felt as though something had gone our way. This investigation would turn a corner soon. There was no way Amelia could get her hands on more gunpowder once Brockwell set Coyle's men to watching the remaining warehouse facilities. That alleviated the immediate threat of the bombings, and it wouldn't be long before Bunn and Amelia were caught. They couldn't hide forever.

Yes, I was feeling much more positive about the situation now.

CHAPTER 9

The rest of the day and evening were blessedly quiet. Not even Lord Farnsworth called on us. Willie said he was busy trying to find out if Charity had been the one to inform the Masons about Cyclops and Catherine's relationship. Even though the family had departed London for their country estate, Lord Farnsworth's investigation was continuing.

"Is he flirting with the female staff?" I asked as we sat across from one another in the sitting room after dinner.

"No," Willie said from behind the newspaper she was reading.

"So is he paying them? Or is he employing some ruse to trick it out of them?"

"Ain't no trick and no, he ain't paying anyone."

I lowered the handkerchief I was embroidering. "Then how is he getting them to talk?"

"I can't tell you. You're too sensitive, India."

"Me! Sensitive!" I scoffed. "Good lord, Willie, I never batted an eyelid when you told me you liked women as well as men. Not once have I had a fainting spell when you shot at someone, and never have I so much as gasped at your foul language."

She folded the newspaper up and tossed it on the table beside her. "You've done all those things. That's why I ain't going to tell you. You'd be shocked. Then Matt would scold me for saying something that turned you paler than an iceberg."

"Actually, I'm intrigued now," Matt said, also lowering his newspaper. "What is Farnsworth doing that's so shocking?"

She huffed out a breath. "All right, I'll tell you. India, you asked me if he was flirting with the female staff and I said he ain't. I wasn't lying."

"I never thought you were."

"He's flirting with the coachman."

I swallowed my gasp before it escaped and waved off her statement with what I hoped was nonchalance. "Is that all? Good lord, Willie, if you think that sort of thing troubles me after everything I've learned about you, you don't know me at all."

She merely grunted. She didn't believe me.

"What did Farnsworth learn from the coachman?" Matt asked.

"Nothing, but I haven't spoken to him since this morning. He might find out more tonight. The coachman's been dismissed until the family comes back to London, so he's at a loose end. Farnsworth will use his charms to get answers."

"Charms?" Matt muttered, picking up his newspaper.

"He can be charming, can't he, India?"

I frowned. "I don't find him charming, but I can see how you might. There's a certain youthful exuberance about him. It's as if he never grew up."

"I guess so," Willie said. "But he's never had to lift a finger to get what he wants, so it's understandable he acts like an idiot sometimes. It's real lucky he's just a rogue, and not an ass too. Toffs like that make me want to pull my hair out rather than spend a minute in their company."

"It's true he has never had to work," Matt said from behind the newspaper. "But he hasn't lost a single dime of his inheritance, by all accounts. In fact, it sounds like his fortune has only increased." He peered at us over the top of the newspaper. "I'd wager he's not as idiotic as he seems."

Willie thought about this a little more and grunted a laugh. "I liked him before. Now I respect him, too."

Matt lifted the newspaper to cover his face. I heard him sigh. He was probably wishing he'd kept his mouth shut.

* * *

DUKE AND CYCLOPS returned home just before Willie, Matt and I retired for the evening. They informed us over a supper of soup and bread that Coyle's men had relieved them of their duties for the night, and Brockwell ordered them to get some rest.

"We'll return in the morning," Duke said.

"And the illegal gunpowder stores?" Matt asked from where he sat perched on the edge of the dining table. If Aunt Letitia walked in and saw him, she'd have a fit.

"Brockwell reckons he raided them all and confiscated supplies."

"He's questioning the illegal importers now," Cyclops added. "It's too early to say if any of them already sold gunpowder to the Moreton girl."

"Jasper's gonna be real tired," Willie muttered with a shake of her head.

"He's been taking naps in one of the empty holding cells," Cyclops reassured her.

"Why don't you take him something to eat tomorrow," I said. "Ask Mrs. Potter to prepare something in the morning. I'm sure she'd be happy to."

Willie screwed up her face. "We ain't courting, India. He ain't my beau."

"Taking him food doesn't mean you're courting. It means you're friends. I'd do it, but I'm busy tomorrow morning."

She considered it and shrugged. I suspected that meant she'd not only fallen for my lie about being busy but also agreed that Brockwell couldn't interpret the gesture in a manner she didn't intend. I was quite pleased with my effort and went to bed satisfied.

* * *

THE ARRIVAL of Mrs. Delancey before luncheon wasn't an unwelcome surprise. I needed a distraction from worrying about the progress of the investigation and she was as good a distraction as any. Indeed, she lifted my mood considerably, and it was all thanks to Willie. I only wished she was home to see Mrs. Delancey turn out the contents of her reticule onto one of the occasional tables in the drawing room.

I was so surprised to see her jewelry in all its exquisite glory that it was a full thirty seconds before I could speak. "Mrs. Delancey," I finally said. "Is this *all* your valuables?"

"Good lord no." She spread out the pieces so that nothing overlapped. There were emerald and diamond necklaces, pearl drop earrings, rings containing colorful gemstones, and a pair of cufflinks. They all had one thing in common. All contained gold.

I didn't quite know what to say. Tell her the truth or continue with the story Willie had invented about my fake spell?

I delayed my decision a few minutes by calling for tea. Mrs. Delancey hastily put her jewelry back in the reticule before the staff returned.

"Do you need the jewels to be removed from their gold settings first?" she asked me.

"Pardon?"

"Should I have a jeweler remove the diamonds and other gemstones from their gold settings before I give it to you?"

"Mrs. Delancey," I began. "It's very sweet of you to offer your gold for the purposes of my experiment with Fabian, but we have enough. There's no need to remove any of the gemstones. Take them home and enjoy wearing them as you always have."

She bristled. "But I insist!"

"I cannot accept."

She looked down at the bulging reticule in her lap. "But...I want more diamonds."

"Oh?"

"I want more diamonds. Gold is lovely, but not nearly as beautiful as diamonds. I adore how they sparkle in the light, don't you?" She clapped her hands lightly. "How thrilling that you've made a spell to change the form of gold into diamonds. Just think of the possibilities, India! Think of the fortune you could make."

"Ahhh..."

"Tell me, can one choose the color of the new diamond? I don't have any yellow, you see. The wife of a banking friend of my husband's has a brooch shaped like a bee set with yellow diamonds and jet. It's very pretty, but how she prattles on about its rarity. If I had a *magical* yellow diamond, it would put her in her place. She says she doesn't believe in magic, but I think she secretly does. Well, India? Can one choose the color of the new diamond?"

Bristow must have been listening on the other side of the door and realized I needed saving because he entered at that moment and asked to have a private conversation about a matter requiring my immediate attention. I exited with him and he proceeded to rattle off a list of tasks requiring *his* attention. He was just finishing when Peter the footman appeared with the tea things.

I thanked Bristow and told Peter I'd pour the tea then waited for them to leave. Those few moments with the butler had given me time to think of how best to send Mrs. Delancey on her way with the least amount of damage done. "Speaking of the spell," I began. "You didn't inform Sir Charles, did you?"

She pressed her hand to her chest, horrified. "Oh, no, India. I learned my lesson. I don't do that anymore. I would never betray your confidence more than once."

"I am pleased to hear there is a limit. But I must insist that not only do you not tell anyone, but you must also forget about the spell. It doesn't work."

"But Miss Johnson said it does."

It was yet another reminder of why I would throttle Willie when I saw her again. "We thought it worked, but a jeweler tested the diamonds and declared them to be fakes."

She accepted the teacup and saucer with a tilt of her head. "How fake?"

"Quite, quite fake. He said it was easy for an expert to tell. So Fabian and I have abandoned that experiment altogether before we ruin any more gold in vain."

She clutched her reticule tighter, a look of disappointment on her face. "Perhaps that's for the best. It would be unfortunate to lose the gold for no return. My husband is always talking about return on investment. So much so that it seems to have sunk into my head finally." She laughed as she picked up her teacup. "Well then. This will just be a nice visit with my favorite magician instead." She sipped then put the teacup down. "Do you know, we had a magical collectors club meeting while Lord Coyle was on his honeymoon."

"Oh?"

A wicked smile curved her lips. "He's not the leader, you know. We can have meetings whenever we want, with our without him."

"Who organized it?"

"Sir Charles." She leaned forward and lowered her voice. "Just between us, I think he was rather put out that Coyle didn't invite him to his wedding. Mr. Delancey and I had another invitation or we would have been there, but most of the collectors club members weren't invited. I think Sir Charles felt the slight more keenly than the others."

"Was Louisa at the meeting?" I asked.

"Yes."

"What did you talk about?"

"Not a great deal, as it happens. Louisa talked about her fiancé's magic. It was quite interesting, if not spectacular. He wasn't there, however. A shame, as he could have given us a demonstration of his floating ink. I suggested to her afterwards that he would have been an asset to her lecture. Professor Nash was there too, but he didn't say much." She stared into her teacup resting on her lap. "Indeed it was rather a strange evening."

"Because Lord Coyle wasn't there to stimulate conversation?" I asked.

"Oh, no. It was quite pleasant without him taking over all the time. No, I suspect if you ask the others, the evening wasn't strange for them. It was just me, and Mr. Delancey and Sir Charles, of course." She might have been avoiding my gaze, but I could still see her cheeks blush.

"Do you mean to say it was all rather awkward between you three because of your liaison with Sir Charles?"

She nodded.

"I didn't realize you'd told Mr. Delancey that we'd caught you giving him secrets about us."

She wagged her finger at me. "One secret, India. There should be no 's' on the end of secret. No, I did not tell Mr. Delancey. He somehow found out. I don't know who informed him." She met my gaze. "Was it you?"

"No!"

"Mr. Glass?"

"It wasn't Matt."

"Are you sure? Husbands and wives don't tell one another everything."

"We do."

She sighed. "Then who?"

That was a good question. Sir Charles himself could have done it, but I couldn't fathom a reason why he'd tell. I wouldn't put it past Lord Coyle stirring up trouble again either.

"It was most upsetting when Mr. Delancey confronted me over it," she said quietly. "He thought Sir Charles and I were having a liaison of an intimate nature, you see. It took me some time to convince him that we are merely club friends. I had to tell him everything about our rendezvous, what they were for, that sort of thing. He forbade me to see Sir Charles privately anymore, which is quite all right with me. I have no intention of seeing him outside club meetings. Why would I? We're just friends, after all. Not even friends. Mere acquaintances."

"Husbands can be jealous of other men," I said.

"Very true, India, very true." She sipped her tea. "It doesn't help that Sir Charles is a knight. I think it wouldn't matter to Mr. Delancey too much if Sir Charles was also poor, but he is quite flush these days."

"He is?" We knew Sir Charles had recently bought himself a carriage, but he lived in a small house and didn't seem all that wealthy.

"Not wealth on our scale, of course, but he has certainly come into some money recently."

"How do you know?"

"Through Mr. Delancey's banking friends, of course. He asked one of them about Sir Charles after he learned of our, er, connection. Oh, don't look at me like that, India. You know bankers share information with one another. It's simply good business sense."

"This had nothing to do with business."

She waved off my concern. "Mr. Delancey keeps such sensitive information to himself usually, but it just slipped out when he confronted me about my liaison with Sir Charles."

"When did Sir Charles get this money?" I asked.

"He deposits it in irregular intervals. Sometimes every week then there might be a pause of several weeks before he comes in again with another deposit. It's all rather intriguing, isn't it? I do love a good mystery, but unfortunately there's no way of solving this one, so my husband says. Not unless we ask Sir Charles directly, of course, but not even Mr. Delancey would do something as gauche as that."

She changed the subject and I tried to follow, but my mind kept returning to Sir Charles Whittaker and his secrets. His secret meetings with Lord Coyle, his secret knighthood, his secret job, and his secret money. Working for the government would explain his knighthood, but perhaps it was Lord Coyle who paid him. Did that mean Lord Coyle also worked for the government?

"India, are you listening?" she asked.

"Yes, of course."

"Well, is she?"

"I'm sorry, is who what?"

"Is Mr. Glass's odd little cousin here?"

"You'll have to be more specific," I said.

"Miss Johnson."

"No, I'm afraid she isn't. Did you want to see her?"

She gave a small shudder. "I wanted to know if she'd signed the vow of temperance yet."

"Oh! Not yet, I don't think. She's been very busy."

"Drinking?"

"Mostly gambling." I rather enjoyed seeing her lips purse so tightly they almost disappeared into altogether. I nearly told her Willie had also been cavorting, but thought it best not to. Mrs. Delancey might faint altogether and I didn't want her here longer than necessary.

* * *

I GREETED Matt as soon as he returned home from Scotland Yard. He'd visited Brockwell, but I was too intent on telling him what Mrs. Delancey had told me about Sir Charles's money to wait for his report.

"Well?" I finished. "Do you think Sir Charles and Lord Coyle both work for the government? And if so, why are the government spying on Fabian and me?"

I knew Matt had been pondering that question ever since learning of Sir Charles's secret knighthood. This was the first time I'd raised it, however.

"Because of your magic." His jaw went rigid. "They want to keep an eye on you both."

"In case we create a dangerous spell?"

He merely shrugged.

"Ridiculous," I muttered. "Sir Charles and Lord Coyle both know I'd never give my spells away, nor would I do anything to jeopardize lives, as Amelia Moreton is doing. It's rather insulting they think I would."

"There are other reasons they might want to keep an eye on you." He sat beside me on the sofa and placed my hand between both of his. They were deliciously warm. "It appears as though the government was aware of magic from before Fabian even came to England. They probably knew about it before you did. Perhaps they've always been aware, but kept the knowledge secret, known to a select few."

"But Commissioner Munro didn't know. He was very resistant to the notion of its existence. He still is."

"When I say select few, I'm not including Munro."

That would be a very select group indeed. "I'll speak to Lord Coyle and Sir Charles," I said. "It's time to tell them we know they're spying on me on behalf of the government—and to stop it. Or at least tell us why. I don't mind telling them what spells we're creating, I just won't be sharing those spells with them. If I make that clear, then there can be no misunderstanding and we can stop all these lies and subterfuge."

He put his arm around me and drew my head down onto his shoulder where he proceeded to gently massage the back of my neck. "You're too trusting, India." His voice rumbled through me, as silky and rich as chocolate. I sighed and sank into him. "The government might not believe you capable of protecting your spells and demand you give them up for safe-keeping," he said. "Or they might want you to create a spell they can use against their enemies."

Now I really did feel naïve. "I would refuse," I said lamely.

"There's one other possibility." His eyes darkened as his gaze drilled into me. "They might want to suppress magic altogether, as it has been suppressed for hundreds of years. Don't forget Whittaker employed violent means to encourage Barratt to stop writing his book."

I nodded weakly. "Yes, he did."

"If that's the case, the question is, what will they do if they think magic is in danger of becoming common knowledge? How far will they go to suppress magicians who want to make it public?"

I sucked in a breath between my teeth. "You subscribe to Mrs. Moreton's theory that artless officials want to imprison magicians?"

"I don't know. That's why I'm cautious, for now. We simply don't have enough information. For one thing, we don't yet know if Coyle and Whittaker are part of the same spying circle or not."

I pulled away to look at him better. "You think Whittaker

is feeding information to the government and Coyle separately?"

"It's possible he's playing two hands at once, yes. There are too many unknowns at this point to confront either of them. We need more time to investigate."

We certainly did, but what should we do? How would we get answers?

"We need to know why Whittaker was knighted," Matt said. "I want to be one hundred percent sure we're not imagining something that's not there. He might not be working for the government at all, but someone else entirely, or only Coyle. If his knighthood turns out to be for innocent reasons, that will give us an answer. I need to speak to someone who can go straight to the top. There's a peer at my uncle's club who is close to the Home Secretary. He might be able to help, but I need an introduction and the questioning has to be done subtly. I don't want to ask my uncle, even if he were still in London. But aside from him and Coyle, I don't know anyone, and I definitely can't ask Coyle."

"What about Lord Farnsworth?"

His brow creased. "You did hear me say subtle, didn't you?"

"I know he's an odd character, but he would be perfect, perhaps because he's so odd. No one would suspect him of trying to trick answers out of them. And you said yourself he's smarter than he looks."

"I said he might be. I'm not sure."

"He also has knowledge of magic and an interest in protecting magic and magicians."

Matt dragged his hand through his hair and down his face. "Very well. I'll ask him to introduce me to the Home Secretary's friend. Then I'll cross my fingers and hope I don't regret this."

CHAPTER 10

$\mathcal{M}$att and I called on Oscar Barratt that afternoon at the offices of *The Weekly Gazette* where he worked. We had intended to speak to him after learning that Sir Charles Whittaker had been the one to set the thug upon him on the day of Lord Coyle's wedding, but the business with Mr. Bunn and Amelia had since consumed us.

Before telling Oscar who was to blame, Matt began with a warning. "You must assure us you won't confront him yet."

"It was Coyle, wasn't it?" Oscar asked.

"Your assurance, Barratt."

Oscar squeezed the bridge of his nose but forgot about his swollen eye and winced in pain. "Very well, but I don't understand why I can't confront him. If I don't, he'll just bloody well do it again."

"Language," Matt growled.

Oscar gave me a sheepish look. "Sorry, India, but my nerves are stretched thin."

"It's all right," I said. "We understand. You want revenge."

"I want to make sure it doesn't happen again, and I can't see a way of doing that without confronting him." He indicated the closed door to his office. Outside, journalists, illustrators, editors and errand boys poured over the long desks on which the upcoming edition's pages were spread. "I should be out there but I worry every time I see a stranger so hide in here. I feel like a coward, but what else can I do?"

Poor Oscar. He did indeed look quite anxious beneath the bruising and swelling. I leaned forward and patted his hand, but could offer no words of comfort. He was right. Unless someone confronted Sir Charles, the danger would continue.

On the other hand…

"I have an idea," I said. "You let it be known in certain circles that you're giving up the idea of writing the book, but you continue to do it in secret."

"Or you could actually give it up," Matt said darkly.

Oscar ignored him. "That's a good idea, India."

"When people ask why, you tell them the truth," I went on. "That you were frightened off by an anonymous thug."

He nodded. "I'll have to inform Louisa of the incident after all so she can help me. She could inform the members of the club. That way Coyle will hear it."

"It wasn't Coyle," Matt said.

Oscar sat forward, frowning. "Then who was it?"

"Whittaker."

"Whittaker!" Oscar sat back heavily. "Why?"

"I'm investigating a theory," Matt said.

"What theory?"

"I can't tell you."

Oscar looked at me, but I shook my head. Our suspicions about Sir Charles being a spy for the government must remain within a small circle of trusted intimates for now. Oscar was too volatile, and he was engaged to Louisa, someone I trusted as much as I trusted Lord Coyle and Sir Charles Whittaker.

"I'm on your side, Glass," Oscar said. "Yours and India's."

"No, you're on *your* side," Matt said. "And you're too

arrogant to see the danger your book will bring down on the head of every magician."

"Or it could bring them freedom."

Matt scoffed. "You're naïve."

"And you have no faith in human nature. The public won't persecute magicians for their magic. They won't revile them. They'll celebrate them by clamoring for their wares. The only folk to be disadvantaged will be artless craftsmen. But there's no reason they can't become employees of the new factories built by magicians who will need to keep up with increased demand."

Matt's features set hard. "You're a fool if you believe all the artless craftsmen will be content to become employees of others."

Oscar shook his head.

"Matt's right," I said.

Oscar arched his brows. "You wish to continue to live in secret, India?"

"I don't live in secret. I live my life perfectly well, thank you. I simply don't tell people about my magic."

"I'm disappointed in you. Before you married, you had your own opinions and they didn't necessarily agree with his. But now that you're married, you've become like every other wife and taken on your husband's ideas when they are not your own."

Every word had my eyes opening a little more and my temper rising a little further until it finally boiled over. "That is *not* true, and how dare you assume to know my mind!"

He held up his hands in apology, but I wasn't letting him off by forgiving him. "I came to the conclusion *on my own* a few days ago, when a fireworks magician blew up a bomb without being near it to detonate it."

He frowned. "A fireworks magician? Who is it?"

"Moreton's Fireworks. Both father and daughter are magicians, but Amelia is the one who detonated the bomb when I refused to use my extension spell with her friend's magic."

"What do you mean she detonated it without being there? She didn't use a timer?"

"No."

He scrubbed a hand over his jaw and glanced at Matt.

Matt was still glowering Oscar's way. "She hasn't been caught yet," he said. "Scotland Yard are in possession of the facts and are searching for her now. She must be caught before she makes another bomb. The first one was a warning to show us what she's capable of. The next could be deadly."

"Unless I do as they ask," I said, as much to Matt as to Oscar. "Do you see the point I'm trying to make? If the public learned about Amelia and her magic, they'd be frightened. They'd wonder what the rest of us are capable of. They'll think that magic is dangerous in the wrong hands. And they'd be right to believe that."

"The Moretons are an exception," Oscar said. "The rest of us have benign magic that doesn't do much except create excellent boots or ink or watches."

"Try telling that to a frightened public," Matt said.

"I'll address it in my book," Oscar shot back.

I sighed. "Think about it, please. Consider abandoning your book altogether, not just pretending to. Its publication could have the opposite effect from what you intend and see magicians persecuted and ostracized even more."

Oscar had no reply, which was not only surprising it was a relief. I hoped that meant he would think about the implications a little more. He needed to step back from the project and see it from more sides than just his own.

"You can't print anything we just told you in your paper," Matt warned him. "The Moreton family's magic must remain a secret, even after she's caught. It's not just the public who need to remain blissfully unaware of what Amelia is capable of, but also persons who might want to use her power for their own nefarious reasons. Groups like the Fenians would like to detonate bombs without a timer. Do you understand, Barratt?"

Oscar sighed. "It disturbs my sensibilities to hide the truth, but I understand. My editor won't allow me to print anything related to magic these days, anyway. I won't tell anyone, not even Louisa." He sighed again. "I will have to tell her about Whittaker setting a thug on me, however."

"We'd prefer you didn't," Matt said.

"Do you know how difficult it has been to keep the truth from her? She still thinks it was a random attack and is insisting I tell the police. She can't understand why I won't report it."

Matt rose and held his hand out to me. "I'll blame you if she confronts Whittaker," he told Oscar.

"Ha! That's rich, coming from you. India has just scolded me for saying she's capable of forming her own ideas, and yet you think I am responsible for everything Louisa does."

Matt glared at him. "Tell her what you like, but ask her to inform the club members that you've abandoned the book idea. Make sure Whittaker hears but isn't aware that we're onto him. I want to find out what he's up to and why."

"It's obvious why he wants the book stopped. He and Coyle both want magic kept secret to protect the value of their collections."

Neither Matt nor I disabused him of that notion. We simply bade him goodbye and left.

"That went well," I said as we headed for our carriage parked around the corner on Fleet Street.

Matt eyed me sideways. "Were we in the same meeting?"

"I mean it. I think Oscar is coming around to the idea that his book ought not go ahead."

"We'll see."

* * *

WE STOPPED at Scotland Yard for an update from Brockwell, but he could tell us little more than we already knew. All known stores of gunpowder were being watched by his men and all illegal importers reported by Coyle's spies were being questioned.

"I've performed preliminary questioning myself," he said from where he sat at his desk.

I was happy to see one of our plates before him. A few crumbs were all that remained of his meal. Willie had brought him something from our kitchen after all.

"The problem is, they're all remaining tight-lipped," he went on. "I cannot be sure if their supplies are complete or if they've sold saltpeter to Amelia or Bunn. They're refusing to say."

"Have you offered to have their sentences reduced if they give you information that leads to an arrest?" Matt asked.

"It's not in my power to make such a promise. Unlike Moreton, some of them know that." Brockwell clasped his hands over his stomach. "It's very frustrating. I even considered employing more traditional methods to get them to talk."

"More traditional methods?" I prompted.

Brockwell stroked his tie and avoided my gaze. "Never mind." He handed me the plate. "Willie brought me some of your cook's cake and biscuits. Would you be so kind as to return this plate to Mrs. Potter and thank her for me?"

"Of course," I said, accepting it. "Isn't Willie coming past to pick it up?"

"She joined the others in surveillance."

"Is that wise, considering her kidnapping ordeal?"

"She informed me in no uncertain terms that she has recovered. I gathered from her tone that she would brook no arguments. I acquiesced, of course, since I am not a fool who likes to take his life into his own hands." He chuckled.

"She was very keen to feed you," I said. "She's worried about your wellbeing on such a difficult case as this."

He scratched his sideburns and fought against a smile, but it won out. "Oh, well, that's very good of her. She's got a good heart, although she doesn't like people knowing it."

"Only certain people," I said. "You being one."

He blushed.

Matt cleared his throat. "Let me know if you need my help. No matter the task, I'll be happy to do it."

"In that case, some more cake would be nice."

Matt gave him a thin smile. I tried not to laugh as we left together.

"Not the sort of help you had in mind?" I asked as we walked back to the front reception.

"No task is beneath me, not even food delivery," Matt said.

I looped my arm through his. "What are the traditional police methods he's reluctant to employ on the illegal gunpowder importers?"

"Violence."

I clutched his arm harder. "Well I'm glad he's not doing that."

* * *

FURTHER UPDATES ARRIVED the following morning when Willie, Duke and Cyclops returned for breakfast and a rest. Apparently a policeman reported a sighting of Mr. Bunn in the Bloomsbury area but a follow up search hadn't proved fruitful.

"Someone must be harboring them," Matt said.

"Another magician," I added.

He and I looked at one another. We didn't know of any but we could gather names from Lord Coyle or Oscar.

Between them they might know of a magician in the Bloomsbury area.

We prepared to leave for *The Weekly Gazette* as soon as breakfast was finished, since we were both of the opinion that Oscar was the lesser of two evils. It was Saturday but hopefully he was at the office and not at home.

I was caught by Aunt Letitia before I could escape, however. "You promised to take me shopping, India," she said, a pout in her voice.

"I'll take you when I get back," I assured her.

"When will that be?"

"Hopefully this afternoon."

She gave me an arched look. "Hopefully?"

I pecked her cheek. "Then we'll have a nice afternoon tea when we get home."

Matt pecked her other cheek. "India and I have an important investigation that needs our attention."

"Can't you take one of them?" She looked back into the dining room where Cyclops was still eating, but Duke and Willie were chatting quietly over cups of coffee.

"They're exhausted," I said. "They've been up all night helping the police."

Her lips formed a tight O. "I thought they'd been to a gambling den. I suppose I should be nice to them, then."

Matt and I were about to leave when a carriage rolled up and deposited Fabian on the pavement. He beamed when he saw me, but it quickly faded when he realized I was about to leave in our waiting carriage.

"I hoped we could work today, India," he said, the pout in his voice matching Aunt Letitia's. "It has been some time since we made the carpet fly and I am eager to continue."

"Yes," I said flatly.

He frowned and eyed Matt, who was approaching our carriage to speak to Woodall. "India, are you avoiding our work?"

"Not at all," I said, trying to keep my tone even. "We have an important investigation that requires both of us." My heart pinched and I winced a little. It was time to have a talk to him about our spell casting. But not here and now.

Matt signaled me from the carriage. "I must go," I said to Fabian.

"Wait." He caught my hand. "I have been thinking about the flying carpet. I think I know a way to make it hold a person in flight."

"Marvelous," I said then checked myself. If I was going to tell him we needed to stop our spell casting then it wouldn't do to show too much excitement for a spell we'd never get to create.

"I reinforce it with my iron," he said. "I will have to speak my flying spell into the iron supports, of course, or it will never get off the ground." He gave me a tentative, hopeful look. "Well?"

"Marvelous," I said again. "But I really must go now. We'll talk about it when this is all over."

He paused then bowed deeply over my hand. "As you wish, *ma femme incroyable*."

He waved us off from the pavement but there was no smile on his face, only a troubled frown.

"He must feel neglected," Matt said after I pointed it out to him.

"I'll spend some time with him after Amelia is caught, but I don't think he'll like what I have to say."

"Why?"

"I'm going to tell him I no longer want to create new spells with him. This experience with Mr. Bunn and Amelia has shown me the extremes some magicians are prepared to go to, and I don't like it. I don't like it at all. And then there's the government and what they're up to with Whittaker, and of course Coyle is circling." I pressed a hand to my forehead. "Fabian and I didn't really think it through when we began.

136

We selfishly forged on without a thought as to who would want these spells and what they'd be used for. I naively thought it was an innocent endeavor."

Matt put his arm around me and kissed my forehead. "Fabian will be disappointed."

"I know."

"But he'll recover."

"I know that, too." I tilted my face up and he kissed me lightly on the lips. "Will you come with me when I tell him? He's less likely to beg me to reconsider if your looming presence is there."

"Looming? Could you not have said towering instead? How you do deflate my sense of self-worth, India."

I patted his chest. "I'm merely righting it. It can get rather inflated at times, what with the way all the women look at you in the street."

He frowned. "They do?"

I punched him lightly and snuggled into him for the rest of the journey to *The Weekly Gazette's* office.

Unfortunately Oscar was not there. We sat in his office and waited, but after eighteen minutes, we considered abandoning the idea and seeking out Lord Coyle instead. It went against every grain of my being to ask his lordship yet another favor, and I certainly didn't want to see either him or his wife again unless absolutely necessary. Matt agreed and we continued to wait. Five minutes later the office door inched open.

"It's just you two," Oscar said on a breath. He opened the door and entered, but not before checking that no one had followed him.

"Are you all right?" I asked. "You seem more on edge today."

"I received this." He opened the top desk drawer and pulled out a piece of paper. In typed letters, it read:

Stop writing the book or you will be forced to stop.

I covered my gasp with my hand.

"Is this the first one you've received?" Matt asked, turning the paper over to inspect the back.

Oscar nodded. "Ever since the beating I've been expecting to encounter someone every time I go out, or every time I arrive home. I even asked a colleague to walk with me the other day, just to have company. And the day before, I caught a cab home. But this is the first letter."

"No wonder you're on edge," I said. "When did it arrive?"

"Late yesterday." He removed his hat and dragged a hand through his hair. "I have to confront Whittaker. I'm not getting any sleep with these threats hanging over my head."

"Not yet," Matt said. "Continue with the original plan and have Louisa tell the collectors club you've given up the idea of the book. That'll stop Whittaker and you'll no longer have to worry."

Oscar raked a hand through his hair again.

"Ask her to hold a meeting as soon as possible," Matt said.

Oscar slumped into the chair with a groan. "I hate this."

"Then go a step further and stop writing the damned book!"

Oscar sighed.

"Matt does have a point," I said gently. "You should think about it. In the meantime, we have a task for you. Do you know any magicians in the Bloomsbury area? We assume Amelia Moreton is being harbored by magicians, and there's been a sighting of her accomplice there."

Matt plucked the pen from the inkstand and handed it to Oscar then pushed the inkwell closer too. "A list will suffice."

"I don't need to write them down. I only know of two, and I'll come with you to question them." He stood and picked up his hat, only to pause when he saw us both staring at him. "I'm not staying here all day waiting for Whittaker's man to use my face as a punching bag again. Besides, I want to help you catch Miss Moreton. She's ruining the exemplary reputation of all magicians."

"Exemplary?" Matt muttered. "Have you forgotten Pitt, Hendry—"

"No. But the artless aren't aware they're magicians."

Matt muttered again but it was too low for me to hear. Oscar ignored him altogether as he led the way to the front door, only to pause before going out.

"After you, Glass."

"Nobody's going to charge at you," Matt said, pushing the door open.

"Not with you around, no."

"I am not your bodyguard."

An icy wind stung my cheeks and almost dislodged my hat. With one hand holding my hat in place and the other clutching a closed umbrella, I hurried toward our carriage waiting around the corner. Matt moved up alongside me and Oscar fell into step on my right.

We'd almost reached the corner when the gunshot rang out.

CHAPTER 11

*M*att pushed me into the wall and shielded me with his body. His heart thundered in my ear. My own heart beat a wild rhythm against my ribs. Neither quite drowned out the bellowed curse from Oscar, nor the shouts coming from the direction of Fleet Street. I recognized Woodall's voice.

"Sir! Sir, are you all right?"

Matt drew away and cupped my cheeks. He searched my face as I searched his. We were both unharmed, thank God. Shaken, but not injured. I released a shuddery breath.

"We're fine," Matt said, stepping out of my vision to reveal Oscar sitting on the ground.

"Oscar!" I went to his side but he seemed unharmed. "Are you shot?"

"I don't think so." He accepted Matt's offered hand and picked up his hat from the ground. "Has the shooter been caught?"

"He ran off along Fleet," Woodall said, waving in an easterly direction. "He'll be long gone by now."

"Did you get a look at his face?" Matt asked as he strode off toward Fleet Street.

Woodall hurried after him. "Sorry, sir, I didn't. He wore a cloak and his hat was pulled low. Someone else might have got a better look."

There were quite a number of men milling about, discussing the alarming event. Hopefully Woodall was right, and someone could identify the shooter.

The sound of the gunshot had brought some of Oscar's colleagues out of the *Gazette's* office. They crowded around Oscar and peppered him with questions. One even had his notepad and pencil ready. Oscar pushed past them as something on the brick wall of a neighboring building caught his attention.

"Is that the mark left by the bullet?" I asked.

He poked his finger into the divot. "I think so."

I looked back to where we had been at the time of the shooting. "His aim wasn't very good. You were walking on my right. Matt was on this side." All the blood suddenly rushed from my head to my stomach, making me feel sick and faint at the same time.

Oscar caught my elbow and gently steered me so that my back was to the wall. "Take some deep breaths." He breathed in and out too, as if his own nerves required steadying. "Good. Your color is beginning to return."

"Do you need to sit down, madam?" asked one of the journalists.

I gave them all a weak smile. "I'm all right, thank you. It just suddenly occurred to me how close we came to..." I swallowed.

Oscar studied the bullet hole again then looked toward Fleet Street. "The shooter must have been rushed. He probably fired without taking proper aim. Fleet Street's busy and a passerby would have raised the alarm before he fired if he'd taken his time."

"Why is someone shooting at you?" one of the reporters asked him.

"The real question is, why is only one person shooting at me? I'm sure my articles have annoyed more than a single person." Oscar smiled.

His colleague laughed nervously and glanced toward Fleet Street, where Matt was talking to witnesses. A constable had joined him and was taking notes.

It was some time before all the witness statements had been gathered. Oscar spent much of that time trying to avoid giving proper answers to his inquisitive colleagues. He laughed it off and claimed it was an entirely random attack. They might have believed him if not for the old bruises on his face. Clearly someone wanted to harm Oscar.

Matt pointed that fact out once the crowd had dispersed and the constable departed. "We have to part ways, Barratt. You can't come with us to question the Bloomsbury magicians. I don't want you near India. It's not personal but you're a risk at the moment."

"Can I at least get a ride home?"

"No," Matt said at the same time I said, "Of course."

"Catch a cab," Matt told him. "Or better still, stay at the *Gazette* and leave with colleagues. Being home alone is probably not wise right now."

Oscar heaved a sigh as he gazed at the *Gazette's* office. "I don't particularly want to be here now, either. Journalists ask too many questions."

"I cannot believe Sir Charles sent someone to shoot you!" I cried.

"Nor can I," Matt said heavily.

Oscar sighed again. "He must be getting more desperate. When beating me up didn't work, he had to employ more drastic measures." He rubbed the back of his neck above his collar. "Now that I think about it, it's unlikely he wanted to kill me just now. That's why the shot missed. Whittaker told the shooter to send me a warning, not kill me. Well, I consider myself warned."

"You're giving up on the book?" I asked.

"I'll give it serious consideration."

"You're taking your own life in your hands if you don't," Matt said.

Oscar sighed once more.

Matt snapped his fingers at him. "The names and addresses of the two Bloomsbury magicians, if you please. India and I'll pay them a call now."

Oscar didn't have the precise addresses, but he gave us the street name where they both lived. "The thing is, neither are open about being magicians, nor are they activists for the cause," he said.

"That doesn't mean they don't want other magicians to take up the cause," I said. "They could be quite happy to shelter Bunn and Amelia but not wish to rattle cages themselves."

"You're probably right, as usual." Oscar smiled at me. "I am sorry to drag you into my problems, India. You too, Glass."

"Kind of you to worry about me," Matt said with sarcasm dripping from every syllable. "If you're truly worried about India, you'd stop writing the damned book. She'll be harmed by it. All magicians will be." He took my hand and led me to the carriage without waiting for a response from Oscar.

I had to take brisk steps to keep up with his pace. As I stepped into the cabin, I glanced back at Oscar. He hurried back to the *Gazette's* office, casting frequent glances over his shoulder.

"Poor Oscar," I said when Matt sat beside me. "He's very anxious."

He didn't answer.

"I cannot believe Sir Charles sent someone to shoot him." It had been difficult enough to reconcile the debonair gentleman with the sort of fellow who paid thugs to beat someone up, but it was almost impossible to imagine him as the sort who paid gunmen to shoot people.

"It doesn't make sense," Matt said quietly.

"I agree. Sir Charles is a liar and probably a spy, but a killer? I don't think so."

He shook his head quickly as if shaking off his thoughts. "It's easy to kill someone when you are not doing the act itself. But that's not what I mean by it not making sense."

"Oh?"

He turned to face me. A spark lit his eyes and his face brightened. This mystery intrigued him. "Barratt received a warning in the post only yesterday. Today he was shot at. Why not give him more time to think it over then allow him to get the word out that he'd given up?"

"Perhaps it was just a warning shot, as Oscar thought."

"Then why both the message *and* the gunshot?"

I frowned as I tried to follow where Matt was leading. Then I frowned harder. He was right, it didn't make sense. If the message was the warning, why shoot at him too? "Are you saying Whittaker didn't hire the gunman?"

He nodded.

"If that's the case, then who did? And why?"

Matt's lips flattened and his eyes lost their spark. His gaze slid away.

"Matt?"

He lifted a shoulder in a half-hearted shrug.

I gasped as I finally realized what he was thinking. He didn't want to tell me because he didn't want me to worry. "Oscar wasn't the intended target, was he? We were. Either Mr. Bunn or Amelia fired that shot at us."

His thumb caressed mine through our gloves. "Not at you, India. You're too valuable to them."

I gasped again and clutched his hand. "*You.* You were the intended target. Oh God, Matt."

"It was probably just a warning shot. It missed us all."

"The shooter was rushed! He, or she, had no time to aim properly! If they did, it would be a different story. Good lord, Matt, we have to go home. You can't go strolling into their lair now. You're a sitting duck."

"They don't know we're heading to Bloomsbury so they won't be prepared."

I withdrew my hands and crossed my arms. "No."

"I'll be prepared." He reached under the seat and pulled out the pistol case from the storage compartment.

"You think that'll stop them when they could be watching our arrival from their hiding place? Matt, be sensible. This is far too dangerous. Let Brockwell deal with it."

He opened the case and inspected the pistol. "Will it make you feel better if we collect Brockwell and some constables?"

"Then will you go home?"

"No." He opened the window and shouted an order to Woodall to divert to Scotland Yard.

We traveled there in silence until Matt finally broke it when Woodall pulled into the curb. "The silent treatment won't work on me," he said. "I'm not changing my mind. I haven't done enough to help Brockwell, and I can't sit idly by and wait for them to do something. Besides, I'm more vulnerable at home than here. They won't expect us."

"I disagree," I said snippily. "You haven't been sitting idly by; you went to Hyde Park and helped the police keep the public away."

"That was nothing. I can do more. Like this."

"And anyway, I wasn't giving you the silent treatment. I was thinking about something you said earlier. If you never once thought it was Whittaker who shot at Oscar, why didn't you disabuse him of the notion? You let him believe it."

The corners of his mouth lifted. "Because now he's going to seriously consider giving up writing the book."

I clicked my tongue. "That's deceptive, Matt."

"Actually, I thought it clever."

We found Brockwell in one of the meeting rooms reading through the reports brought in by his men after their shifts. He looked up upon our entry only to immediately continue reading.

"There is no news," he said, turning a page. "I wish I could tell you more, but alas, Bunn and Miss Moreton are proving difficult to locate. I have men crawling all over Bloomsbury, so I'm certain they'll be found, sooner or later."

"We can help find them sooner." Matt picked up a pencil and wrote down the street names Oscar had given us. "There are two magicians in Bloomsbury who could be harboring them."

Brockwell had looked annoyed when Matt commandeered his pencil and paper but now he looked pleased. "Excellent work. Where did you get the names?"

"Oscar Barratt of *The Weekly Gazette*," I said. "We were visiting his place of work when we were shot at."

"Shot at!" Brockwell rose. "Did you catch the gunman?"

"Unfortunately not," Matt said. "He ran off."

"Who do you think it was?"

"Mr. Bunn or Amelia, of course," I said.

Brockwell frowned. "Why would they shoot you?"

"To harm Matt to get to me, just like they kidnapped Willie. If Matt is shot they will threaten to do it again to another of my loved ones to coerce me into using my magic."

Brockwell paced the room, his hands at his back, his gaze on the floor. He suddenly stopped in front of Matt and shook his head. "I don't think it was them."

"Why not?" Matt asked.

"Why not simply set another bomb as we assume they're going to do? Why do they have to shoot you too? It seems unnecessary when a bomb threat could prove incredibly effective."

The shooting could prove very effective too. I was already considering how to get word to Amelia and Mr. Bunn that I was prepared to do as they asked as long as they left my family alone.

"You could be right, Inspector," I said. "They haven't given me instructions. When Willie was kidnapped I was told to go to Brockwell's workshop. When the bomb was set to go off in Hyde Park I was told to show up at Oxford Street. But this time there has been no note, no demand, nothing."

"The note could be on its way," Matt said.

Brockwell narrowed his gaze. "Do you believe that, Glass?"

Matt threw his hands in the air. "I don't know, but somebody shot at us. If not Bunn and Amelia, then who? And why?"

"Perhaps Oscar was the intended target after all," I said.

"Oscar Barratt?" Brockwell snorted. "I imagine he has offended a few people who'd want to shoot at him."

"More than a few," Matt said.

They both gave appreciative grunts, bonding over their mutual dislike of Oscar.

"Shouldn't we go and question these magicians?" I asked.

"You're coming, Mrs. Glass?" Brockwell asked as he gathered his hat and coat. He may have posed the question to me, but he looked at Matt.

"Yes," I snapped. "I am."

Matt and Brockwell shared another knowing look which only irritated me more.

"Matt is my husband, not my keeper, Inspector."

"And as your husband, I'm worried about you walking into a dangerous situation," Matt shot back.

"You are walking into the same situation. I'm worried about you but I'm not telling you to leave this to the police."

He smirked. "Actually, you did."

I strode off and joined Brockwell in the corridor. "Are you riding with us, Inspector?"

"If that's agreeable to you both, yes. Scotland Yard has a

C.J. ARCHER

tight budget with little left over for transport." He signaled to two constables to join us and briefed them as we walked outside.

The constables sat with Woodall on the driver's seat while Brockwell sat in the cabin with us. He eyed my lap blanket with envy but politely refused it when I offered to share it with him.

Our first stop was not the addresses of the two magicians, but the Bloomsbury police station. The entire constabulary was out looking for Bunn and Amelia, and the sergeant on duty was little help. He didn't know the two men on Oscar's list. At least that told us the men had never been in trouble with police before.

"Be respectful," Brockwell said as we drove to the first address. "If the local constabulary don't know them, they must be good men."

"Good men who could be harboring dangerous criminals," Matt countered.

The first name on the list lived in a respectable looking row house. Mr. Carpenter was of middle age and somewhat portly with thick gray hair and a beard to match. He rolled his eyes when Brockwell introduced himself.

"Your lot have already been here asking questions," he said. "I haven't seen the people you described. I'll come to the station if I do."

"We have reason to suspect you might be harboring the fugitives."

He thrust his hands on his hips. "I bloody well am not! I haven't seen them. Good day." He went to shut the door, but both Matt and Brockwell stopped him.

Brockwell gave Matt a nod of appreciation, but Matt wouldn't have noticed. He was glaring at Mr. Carpenter.

"The two people we're searching for are magicians," Matt said.

Mr. Carpenter stilled.

148

"We know you are also a magician," Matt went on.

Mr. Carpenter lowered his hands to his sides. "That doesn't mean I'm helping them. I'd never do that."

"We need to search the premises."

"My wife won't like it." Mr. Carpenter stepped aside. "But go ahead."

His eagerness to comply was answer enough for me, but not Brockwell or Matt. I did not search the premises with them, but remained in the kitchen where Mrs. Carpenter was preparing a stew for dinner.

"Appalling," she said, chopping up potatoes with violent cuts of the knife. "We've done nothing wrong. This is an invasion of our home. They have no right coming in here and looking through our personal things. It's humiliating."

"They've got to look or we'll be suspects," Mr. Carpenter told her.

"Why?"

"Magic," he said simply.

Mrs. Carpenter eyed me and I realized I hadn't introduced myself. They might feel a little less persecuted if they knew I was a magician too. "My name is India Glass," I said. "I'm also a magician."

"Watch magic, I know," Mr. Carpenter said.

"Watch magic?" Mrs. Carpenter echoed. Some of her anger faded, thankfully, replaced with curiosity. "What can watch magic do?"

"Make time pieces keep perfect time," I said.

"I hear you can do more than that," Mr. Carpenter said. "I hear you extend the life of magic performed by other magicians."

Mrs. Carpenter lowered her knife to the table, her eyes wide. "Oh. That's wonderful. Will you extend my husband's magic?"

"No."

"But you don't even know what he does yet."

Perhaps introducing myself had been a mistake.

Mrs. Carpenter gathered up the pieces of potato and dropped them in the pot on the stove. "It's the least you can do considering you're barging in here accusing us of hiding criminals."

I sighed. "What magic do you do, Mr. Carpenter?"

"Wood. Hence the name, Carpenter." He gave a sheepish smile. "I'm a cabinet maker. I've got a workshop nearby. I was there this morning, but I close at midday on Saturdays. It's not large and I don't use my magic on anything." He eyed his wife as he said it.

She picked up her knife again and sliced through a potato with such force both halves rolled off the table.

Mr. Carpenter collected them and glared at her as he returned them to the chopping board. "There's no point using my magic at the workshop," he went on. "It doesn't last long. Barely even a week. If I had to rely on it to keep my pieces together, my business would have failed years ago. I just use it sometimes for myself. Making toys and doll house miniatures for my children when they were small, and now for the grandchildren. I've also made fruit bowls, chair legs, statues, that kind of thing." He pointed out a few pieces around the kitchen. They were all beautiful and some seemed quite intricately carved. "I like to create nice things like that. Do you understand, Mrs. Glass?"

"I do," I said. "A magician needs to use their magical craft or they become restless."

"We do."

"My husband is a hard worker, Mrs. Glass," Mrs. Carpenter said. "He's a good father and husband. It's not fair that he's being persecuted like this. Not fair at all." She drove her point home by pointing the knife at me.

"He's not being persecuted," I said.

She pointed the knife at the ceiling as the floorboards overhead creaked. "Isn't he?"

"You mentioned children," I said. "Are they all grown up now?"

"A son and daughter," Mr. Carpenter said.

"Do they work for you? Are they magicians?"

"My son works for me, but he's artless. They both are." He crossed his arms over his chest. "Are you accusing them of harboring these magicians?"

"Of course not." I was getting a little tired of the defensiveness, although that was perhaps unfair. I would have reacted the same way. "And they're fugitives, Mr. Carpenter. Let's call them what they are. Blackmailers and bombers."

"Bombers?" Mrs. Carpenter's eyes widened. "Good lord."

"One is," I said. "You didn't know?"

"We haven't been informed." She pressed a hand to her stomach. "Have they harmed anyone?"

"Not yet, but we're afraid they will next time."

"Oh my."

"Didn't the police tell you who they were looking for the first time they questioned you?" I asked.

"They refused," Mr. Carpenter said. "They reckoned we didn't need to know."

"This is terrible," Mrs. Carpenter muttered. "What horrid people."

"Now you see why we're going to such desperate lengths to find them before they can set another bomb," I said.

Mrs. Carpenter's gaze shifted to Matt and Brockwell as they entered the kitchen.

"Thank you for your co-operation," the inspector said. "We'll leave you be now."

Mr. Carpenter saw us out. "Good luck. We hope you find them. We truly do."

"Well?" I said as we trudged off through the drizzling rain, the constables following a little behind out of earshot.

"Nothing," Brockwell said. "No sign of another person or persons living there aside from those two."

We headed to the house of the next magician, a young man with a high forehead and slightly protruding front teeth by the name of Mr. Carroll. His reaction was the same as Mr. Carpenter's when Brockwell introduced himself.

"Your men have already been here asking about two fugitives," he said with a slight northern accent. "I haven't seen them then or since."

"We have reason to believe you might be harboring them," Brockwell said.

"Me? Why?"

"They're magicians, and you're a magician too."

Mr. Carroll swallowed heavily. "I—I..."

"It's quite all right," I said gently. "I'm also a magician." I put out my hand and introduced myself. Unlike Mr. Carpenter, there was no recognition at the mention of my name. "What's your magical craft, Mr. Carroll?"

He wiped his hand down his trouser leg then shook mine. "Cotton. But I don't use my magic. I'm a clerk for a bank in the city."

"Do you live alone?" Matt asked.

"I have a wife and two children." As he said it, a small child appeared beside him. She only came up to his hip and remained half-hidden behind his legs.

I bobbed down to her level. "Good morning," I said. "My name is India. What's yours?"

"Betty," she whispered.

"May we look around your house?" Brockwell asked Mr. Carroll.

"No!" Mr. Carroll bristled. "You cannot. My wife is cleaning upstairs. It would be most disruptive, not to mention unnecessary. We are not harboring anyone here."

"We need to check for ourselves," Brockwell said.

"Well you can't." Mr. Carroll crossed his arms and settled his feet apart. For a slight man facing off against four men and one woman, he did not lack courage.

"Please don't make my men force you to step aside."

Mr. Carroll swallowed but didn't back down. "Betty, go to your mother, please."

The little girl ran off. I didn't like the frightened look in her eyes.

"Step aside," Brockwell demanded.

"Just a moment," I said as cheerfully as possible. "Let's talk about this, shall we? I don't think you're fully aware of the dangers posed by the two fugitive magicians, Mr. Carroll. You see, one of them can detonate bombs from a distance."

He blinked hard.

"She has already set off one bomb. Did you hear of the destruction of the bandstand in Hyde Park?"

He paled. "I read about it. Good lord, are those the people you're searching for?"

"You can see why we need to find them urgently. They cannot be allowed to set off another bomb. No one was harmed in the bandstand event, but next time could be different."

"Yes, yes, of course." He stepped aside and watched as the two constables filed past him. "If you'd told me earlier, Inspector, I would have been more compliant."

Brockwell gave him a tight smile which he then cast on me. If he was irritated that I had given out too much information, it was too bad. If we wanted help then we needed to give something in return.

"You don't use your magic, Mr. Carroll?" I asked as the men went to search the house. We remained near the door, waiting. I could hear a woman's voice talking to the searchers upstairs. She sounded annoyed rather than alarmed.

"I'm a clerk, Mrs. Glass."

"I meant in your spare time. Do you do anything with cotton? Work with it, embroidery—"

"I do *not* embroider." He sounded disgusted. "I am a clerk for a bank. I haven't used my magic in years, since I fell out with my father. He owns a cotton mill and had no qualms about using his magic any chance he got. It brought him some close attention from the other mill owners who suspected magic still existed. I told him to stop speaking his spells. He refused and suspicion grew. All his friends deserted him, the other mill owners refused to let him into their clubs, no one would give him the time of day. No amount of talking to him worked. He's an obstinate old fool who can't see the effect his actions had on my mother—and me. When she died, I left and came to London. I found myself work, a wife, and settled down. I haven't seen my father since."

He suddenly stopped talking and pressed his lips together, as if afraid he'd said too much. No amount of coaxing would get him to talk about his magic again.

The men returned and we left after thanking Mr. Carroll.

"It's him," Brockwell said as we headed back to the carriage.

"How do you know?" I asked. "What did you find?"

"Nothing. It's just a feeling."

"You're a policeman, Inspector. Of all people, you know feelings can be misleading."

"On the contrary, Mrs. Glass. While I prefer to deal with facts, I have developed a very strong sensitivity for when someone is lying or withholding information. And my gut feeling is telling me he's doing both."

I shook my head. "He doesn't use his magic, and he's certainly not an advocate for magicians. He tried to encourage his father to stop using it but he refused. They had a falling out over it. That doesn't sound like someone who would be on the side of Amelia and Mr. Bunn, wanting magic to become public knowledge."

"With all due respect, Mrs. Glass, you haven't been dealing with witnesses and suspects for as long as I have. You can't tell when someone is lying."

He did have a point, as much as I hated admitting it. My

instincts were often wrong. "What gave you the impression he was lying?"

"He's young. Men his age are usually the type to take up a cause."

"Amelia isn't a man," I pointed out.

"His two daughters already display signs of strong magic," he went on. "We saw their embroidery in their room. It's very good."

"Far too good for children their age," Matt added.

"Like all fathers, Mr. Carroll will want his magician daughters to grow up in a world where they can be happy, free," Brockwell went on.

"Or he might want them to hide their magic to keep them safe," I countered. "Just as he wanted his father to hide his magic. I admit that I don't possess an intuition for liars, Inspector, but I spoke with Mr. Carroll for a few minutes and I think he's telling the truth. I doubt he's harboring anyone."

Brockwell climbed into the carriage after me, but Matt paused with one foot on the step. "Where to now?" he asked the inspector.

"Back to Scotland Yard," Brockwell said. "I want to find out if Carroll is associated with any other premises in the city. A room, a storage facility, anything where he could hide two people away from the family home. I can send out telegrams across the city from the telegraph service at the Yard."

It would seem my opinion of Mr. Carroll didn't matter. Perhaps if I were in Brockwell's shoes, I'd want to make sure too. "If you're doing that for Mr. Carroll, you ought to do it for Mr. Carpenter too," I said. "He owns a workshop."

He gave me a nod of approval. "I'll make inquiries about both."

"Good. I think we'll find Mr. Bunn and Amelia very soon, if we are thorough."

"That's if Carpenter or Carroll is harboring them at all," Matt muttered.

CHAPTER 12

$\mathcal{I}$t was early afternoon by the time we arrived home. Aunt Letitia's first words to me when I entered the sitting room were to ask when I was taking her shopping.

"I'm much too tired," I said, accepting the cup of tea she poured for me. "It's also miserable outside." I didn't want to alarm her and tell her about the dangers of going out while Bunn and Amelia were at large. It might set off her memory lapse episodes. "Can you wait a little longer?"

"But Christmas is soon."

"We have time."

She poured more tea into her empty cup and set the teapot down with a thud on the table. She put the cup to her lips but hardly sipped before setting that down with a loud clank in the saucer. She then proceeded to sigh repeatedly.

"Shall we create some more decorations or write cards together?" I asked.

"I've written all my cards and made enough decorations to cover all the Christmas trees from here to Greenwich. When will we get one?"

"We have dropped the ball on tree acquisition somewhat. I'll ask Bristow to arrange it."

Decorating it would keep her busy, although I hoped to be at home to help. Matt too. It was our first Christmas together, after all. It wouldn't be the same if we couldn't share the experience.

Duke arrived in time for dinner, and Willie halfway through it. Cyclops missed dinner altogether, but Mrs. Potter made sure he had something to eat while we convened in the library to discuss the day's events. Aunt Letitia had already retired to her room, but we liked the coziness of the library with its walls of books and large fireplace. There was something comforting about it on a winter's night.

"Whoever is hiding them is doing a good job of it," Duke said.

"Except for that time Bunn was spotted in Bloomsbury," Willie pointed out.

"Just because he was seen in Bloomsbury doesn't mean he's still there," Cyclops said as he cut through a slice of beef. It was so thick it was more of a slab than a slice. "If they're smart, they'll be long gone by now."

The enormity of the problem subdued our mood. The fugitives could be anywhere, either in or out of London. If they changed their appearances, we might never find them.

"At least the gunpowder stores are safe," Duke said.

Willie pointed at the doorway which had all of us turning to look. There was no one there. When we turned back, she was chewing with her mouth full and there was one less slice of beef on Cyclops's plate.

He shook his head. "I deserved to have my food stolen for falling for that."

Willie smiled as she chewed.

"How long will the gunpowder be safe?" I asked. "The police can't watch the storage facilities forever. Sooner or later the constables will need to return to other duties."

"Sooner rather than later," Duke said. "Word is the burglars, pick pockets, and lowlifes know the police resources are limited right now and they're making the most of their freedom. Crime is rife in the city."

Willie looked past us and smiled. "Well, look who's here."

I didn't fall for it this time, nor did Matt or Cyclops, also sitting with their backs to the door. Only Willie and Duke faced it.

Duke nodded a greeting. "You smelled Mrs. Potter's cooking from the Yard, Inspector?"

Cyclops circled a protective arm around his plate. "You must think I'm a fool."

"Detective Inspector Brockwell," Bristow announced.

I glanced around to see the inspector enter. He smiled back at Willie and shuffled into the library.

"Bristow, see if there's something left over from dinner for the inspector," I said.

Brockwell put up his hands. "I wouldn't dream of disturbing your cook at this hour. Your dinner is long since finished."

"Cyclops is still eating."

"But he's family."

"And so are you." I took him by the elbow and steered him to a chair. I gave Bristow a nod and he disappeared, shutting the door behind him.

Brockwell sat with a loud groan and stretched out his legs.

"You look exhausted," I said. "It's been a long day."

"A long few days. But it's nice to sit in your library, Mrs. Glass. Books are a comfort."

"Indeed they are."

Willie poured the inspector a glass of whiskey at the drinks trolley. I was about to tell her it didn't go with dinner and she should ask Bristow for wine, but Brockwell accepted gratefully. Willie squeezed his shoulder and sat again. She lifted her own drink and he saluted her with his glass.

Well, well. That was a promising sign.

"What did you find out about our two Bloomsbury magicians?" Matt asked. If he noticed the flirtatious interaction between Willie and Brockwell, he didn't care. I supposed the investigation was more important, but it made me feel warm inside.

"Aside from Mr. Carpenter's workshop, there are no other properties leased or owned by either fellow," Brockwell said as the door opened and Bristow brought in a tray with a glass of wine and a covered plate. The butler set it down and removed the covering. Brockwell's eyes lit up at the large helping of beef and potatoes.

It was some time before we could coax more information out of him. After a few minutes, he dabbed at the corner of his mouth with the napkin, sipped the wine, and picked up his knife and fork again.

"We are still looking for sites connected to them," he said before tucking in. "I'm quite certain Carroll is our man. There was something suspicious about him."

Matt agreed, but I wasn't so sure. I couldn't quite put my finger on why, however.

Cyclops finished his dinner and we watched the inspector eat, each of us lost in our own contemplations. Or so I thought.

"Is there something else?" Duke prompted the inspector with a large measure of impatience in his tone.

Brockwell shook his head.

"You could have sent a letter," Duke went on. "You didn't have to come all the way to Mayfair."

"I wanted to give Mr. and Mrs. Glass my report in person on account of their help earlier today."

Duke crossed his arms. "But you had nothing to report."

"That in itself is something."

Duke was about to say more when Willie smacked his arm. "Let the man eat in peace. He's tired and hungry and you heard India; he's family."

Duke shrugged. "I ain't making an issue of it, Willie."

But she was no longer listening to him. She was watching Brockwell enjoy his meal. "Why don't you stay the night here, Jasper?"

"No!" both Matt and I said before Brockwell could answer.

"Do you want my aunt to faint when she sees him coming down the stairs in the morning?" Matt asked.

"Letty's seen him at breakfast before."

"The answer's still no."

Willie *humphed* and slumped in the chair.

"You could always spend the night together at his home," I said. "Aunt Letitia is quite used to not seeing you at breakfast, Willie. She won't even question your absence."

The inspector shook his head as he finished his mouthful of potato. "Thank you for the suggestion, however I must decline. This case is keeping me very busy and I'm too tired to, er, entertain a guest." He cleared his throat and glanced at Willie before quickly looking away.

She merely *humphed* again.

Bristow opened the door. "I'm sorry to interrupt, but there's a constable here who wishes to speak to the detective inspector. He's in a rather agitated state. Shall I—"

One of the constables who'd accompanied us that morning in Bloomsbury barged past Bristow. "Sorry," he said to the butler under his breath. "But this is important. Sir, there's been a development at one of the gunpowder storage facilities."

Brockwell set his knife and fork down and dabbed at the corner of his mouth with his napkin. Each movement was maddeningly deliberate and slow. The constable shifted his weight from foot to foot as he waited, and finally turned to Matt when Brockwell picked up his wine glass and took a sip.

"Some gunpowder was stolen," the constable said. "Not a lot, so I'm told, but enough to make three homemade bombs."

Brockwell rose and buttoned his jacket. "Tell me on the

way how it's possible that a storage facility was broken into beneath the noses of Scotland Yard's finest."

"You can tell me too," Matt said, rising.

Cyclops, Duke and Willie also stood, so I did too.

Brockwell blocked our exit and regarded each of us in turn. "There isn't room for all of you in the conveyance. Mrs. Glass, may I respectfully suggest you remain here. Mr. Glass and Mr. Cyclops may come with me."

"Why them?" Duke snapped.

"Fine by me," Willie said. "I reckon I'll go out and find me a game of poker. Come on, Duke, it'll be more fun than investigating."

Matt pecked my forehead and strode after Brockwell and Cyclops. Willie and Duke also left. I followed them into the entrance hall and watched as they put on coats, gloves and hats, wondering if I ought to protest or not. When Bristow opened the front door and a blast of icy air swept inside, I decided staying home was quite all right with me.

I waited up for Matt and Cyclops to return but fell asleep in front of the fire in the sitting room with a book on my lap. I awoke when Matt gathered me in his arms.

"Where are you taking me?" I mumbled, half asleep.

"To bed." He angled me sideways so we could fit through the door and headed up the stairs.

I rested my head on his shoulder. "Don't hurt your back."

He chuckled. "I've wrangled a drunk Willie out of saloons many times. You're easy by comparison."

I smiled. It wasn't quite what I meant but I appreciated his attempt to make me feel as small as Willie.

By the time he lay me on the bed, I'd woken up enough to want a conversation. "What time is it?"

"Almost two."

"What happened? How did Amelia and Bunn steal the gunpowder when it was being watched by the police?"

He sat on the bed with a sigh and undid his tie. "There

was a distraction in the form of a small bleeding child asking for assistance to find his parents."

"They harmed a child!"

"The child was a decoy. He screamed then ran off, drawing the constable on duty after him."

"It was definitely a boy?"

"Pardon?"

"Are the constables certain the child was a boy?"

"I didn't ask. Why?"

"Mr. Carroll has two girls, no boys." I helped him remove his collar and set it on the bed.

"You think they used one of Carroll's girls to act as decoy for them?"

"Perhaps. Except the child wasn't a girl," I said, unfastening my cuffs.

"And Mr. Carpenter's children are grown," Matt said. "Damn. Someone other than Carpenter and Carroll is helping them." His hooded gaze watched my fingers undo my cuffs then followed them to the top button of my dress. "It could be anyone."

I paused. "Mr. Carpenter has grandchildren. He makes toys and dollhouse miniatures for them."

He lifted his gaze to mine. "Could his grownup children be harboring Amelia and Bunn with or without Carpenter senior's knowledge?"

"I'm not entirely sure. He claimed his son is artless, so it's likely his grandchildren are too. Why would his artless son help a cause he has no interest in?"

"Unless his grandchildren *are* magicians," Matt said. "It can skip a generation."

"We ought to inform Brockwell."

Matt sighed and cast a longing look at my throat just above the button I was undoing. "I'd better tell him now. It can't wait for the morning." He sighed again and picked up his collar and tie. "I'll try not to wake you when I return." He kissed me lightly on the lips then cast one more look at my throat. "Damn this investigation."

"Matt," I said as he opened the door. "Please be careful. The fact remains that someone shot at us. You may or may not have been the target, but until we know for sure…"

He pressed his fists onto the bed on either side of me and leaned in. "I'll wear a hooded cloak." He kissed me on the lips then left.

It took me an age to fall asleep, but eventually I did only to be awoken again by Matt's return. "Well?" I asked sleepily.

"I found Brockwell at home," he said, climbing into bed alongside me. "He thanked me for the information."

"And?"

"And Willie wasn't happy about the interruption."

I sat up. "Willie was there? I thought she was going out with Duke and the inspector was too tired."

"It seems Duke decided to pay a call on his merry widow after the card game and Brockwell wasn't so tired after all." He looped his arm around my waist and flipped onto his back, positioning me so that we were chest to chest. He ran his hands along my body beneath my nightgown. "We were interrupted earlier by your inconvenient cleverness," he said huskily.

"What's Brockwell doing about Mr. Carpenter the younger?" I asked.

His fingers lightly stroked my back. "Do you want to talk about that now, or…?"

"I'd like to talk about it now."

"Spoil sport. Very well. Brockwell said he'll pay Carpenter a visit first thing in the morning."

"Why not tonight?"

He shrugged. "Willie was there?"

"Good lord, this is an important investigation. I expect Brockwell to set aside his manly needs and put police work first."

He thought about it a moment then shrugged again. "I have no response that will put either Brockwell or myself in a good light, so I'll refrain from answering."

"Men," I muttered.

He grinned. "I know. We're incorrigible. And you are naked beneath that nightgown, so kiss me."

He didn't wait but lifted his head off the pillow and met my mouth halfway.

* * *

I PEEKED under the covers at a naked, sleeping Matt then tiptoed to my dressing room. I put on a simple day dress and slipped out of the bedroom just as the household clocks struck nine. I was heading to the dining room for breakfast when Willie returned home.

"I was hoping you'd bring news," I told her as she slapped her hat into Bristow's waiting hands. "Have you spoken to the inspector since he went to speak to Carpenter?"

She handed her gloves to Bristow and flung her coat over his arm. "It's only nine, India. He just left home."

"Just left! Good lord, we're in the middle of an important investigation. You shouldn't distract him."

"You seemed to want me to distract him last night," she said with a wink and a smug smile.

"Yes, but only for a short while."

She hooked her thumbs through her belt loops and rocked back on her heels. "Ain't no such thing as a short while with Jasper."

I groaned and followed her into the dining room where Aunt Letitia was sitting reading a copy of *The Ladies Journal*. "What do you mean there's no such thing as short?" she asked Willie without looking up. "You aren't tall, you know."

Willie chuckled. "Right you are, Letty." She helped herself to breakfast at the sideboard and sat with her plate and coffee cup beside Aunt Letitia. She peered over Aunt Letitia's shoulder as she bit into her toast.

Aunt Letitia pulled a face. "Do you have to do that here?"

"What? Eat? Aye, I do. It's the dining room. Do you want me to eat in bed?"

Aunt Letitia's nose wrinkled more. "Don't be vulgar."

Willie snorted. "That's the least vulgar thing I've said all morning." She stabbed a finger on the open page. "That's vulgar! Show India the picture. It's the most disgusting thing I've seen all week."

I peered over Aunt Letitia's other shoulder at the colored sketch of a fuchsia pink and lime green striped dress with ribbons in a row down the front and on the sleeves and swathes of material caught up with ribbons along the hem. "There are too many ribbons," I agreed.

"It would suit Hope," Aunt Letitia said.

"That it would," Willie said, wrinkling her nose as Aunt Letitia had done.

"She doesn't know when to stop when it comes to ribbons."

"Or old rich men."

They both giggled, and were still going when Matt entered, yawning. He went straight to the sideboard and poured coffee into one cup and a tea into another. "What's so funny?"

"Hope," I said.

"That wasn't the answer I was expecting." He set his two cups on the table and returned to the sideboard to load up a plate. "Are Cyclops and Duke here or out with the police?"

"Home, according to Bristow," I said. "And apparently Brockwell has only just left for Scotland Yard. It seems he slept in." I gave Willie a pointed glare.

She shook her head rapidly then jerked it at Aunt Letitia.

Aunt Letitia flipped the page of her journal and muttered "Oh dear." I wasn't entirely sure if the utterance was in reference to Willie's nocturnal activities or for the rather ugly dress on the page. It was covered in large tassels and was an unfortunate shade of brown.

Cyclops and Duke joined us for breakfast and we talked quietly about the investigation, being careful not to mention anything that might upset Aunt Letitia's delicate sensibilities. We couldn't avoid mentioning gunpowder, bombs or magicians altogether, however, but she remained quiet throughout the conversation while reading her journal.

Bristow entered carrying the mail on a salver. "This just arrived, madam," he said to me.

Everyone went very still and stared at the single letter.

"Open it, India," Willie said.

I drew in a deep breath and opened the letter. My heart leapt to my throat. "It's from them," I said weakly. "It's another threat."

"Read it out," Matt said.

I glanced at Aunt Letitia.

She closed her journal and rose. "I have to dress for church. Polly can accompany me this morning."

I waited until she'd gone before taking a deep breath. "It says: 'Be on platform four at Brighton Railway Station by two PM today or a bomb will be remotely detonated. Your appearance is confirmation of your acceptance of our terms, namely you will use your extension spell with Bunn's leather magic. Come alone'."

Matt had joined me as I read out the letter and peered over my shoulder. "Brighton," he echoed. "If they want you to appear in Brighton then they are probably there too, ready to detonate the bomb if you don't show. How did they get out of London?"

"Incompetent police work," Duke muttered.

"If Bunn and Amelia Moreton were in disguise they'd be impossible to spot in a crowd," Cyclops countered.

"Does it say anything else?" Willie asked. "Like where the bomb will go off?"

I shook my head. "I have to do as they say and go to Brighton."

Matt strode to the door. "Brockwell can send a telegram to the local constabulary and have them search the railway station."

I rose and raced after him, clutching the letter. "Bunn and Amelia will be expecting that and will be well and truly hidden. They want me there at two PM *today*. We don't have time to go to Scotland Yard and wait for the Brighton police to gather their forces. If they fail to find Bunn and Amelia…" I pressed a hand to my stomach. I felt sick. "Matt, I *have* to go to Brighton and I have to leave soon or I won't make it in time."

Brighton was an hour and a half journey by rail. Factoring in the time it took to get to Victoria Station here in London, as well as purchasing a ticket and waiting for the next scheduled train, there wasn't much time to spare.

"Bristow!" I called. The butler bustled out of the shadows. "Bristow, do you have a railway timetable at hand? I need to get to Brighton in a hurry."

He bowed and hurried off to the service rooms at the back of the house.

Matt snatched his coat off the hook and grabbed his hat. He opened the front door.

"Where are you going?" I asked.

"Scotland Yard. There's no time for Woodall to prepare the carriage; I'll get a hack."

"It won't work, Matt. You will reach Scotland Yard in time and they will send a wire to Brighton immediately, but what if the police fail to find Amelia and Bunn before two? By then, it'll be too late for me to get to Brighton. I have to leave immediately."

Matt swore under his breath and squeezed the bridge of his nose.

"Do both," Willie said. "You go to Scotland Yard, Matt, and me, Duke and Cyclops will go with India to Brighton. She'll be safe with us. I'll take my Colt and Cyclops has got big muscles and hard fists."

"And I've got the smarts," Duke added, tapping his forehead.

Cyclops and Willie eyed him sideways.

"I think that's a good idea," I said to Matt. I pressed the letter to his chest and leaned into him. "Take this."

He kissed me quickly and took the letter. He was about to leave when Bristow rushed toward us. "Stop!" he bellowed, brandishing a newspaper over his head. "Wait, sir. You must read this."

He handed me the newspaper and I read the headline in bold type on the front page. My heart dropped to my stomach. "Oh God," I whispered.

Matt took the newspaper. "'Train derailment on the Brighton main line kills two.'" He skimmed the article. "The line will be closed in both directions for days while they remove the wreckage."

Willie swore loudly and I felt like swearing too. We could not possibly reach Brighton before the deadline.

CHAPTER 13

"*A* coach is too slow," Duke said heavily. "Even if we traveled as fast as the horses can go, we wouldn't reach Brighton before nightfall, let alone by two."

I met Matt's worried gaze and felt the tears burn my eyes. A sense of deep hopelessness washed over me.

He cupped my cheeks in his hands and dipped his head to peer into my eyes. "You won't be going to Brighton, but you can come with me to Scotland Yard. All is not yet lost. All right?"

I nodded. At least he didn't ask me to stay home while he went. Doing nothing at this moment was not going to help my frayed nerves.

He planted a kiss on my forehead. "Bristow, help Mrs. Glass into her coat then tell Woodall to meet us at Scotland Yard. We don't have time to wait for him now."

Cyclops, Duke and Willie accompanied us to the Yard where we showed Brockwell the letter. He already knew about the train derailment.

"I'll wire Brighton now," he said, striding off down the corridor.

"And after that, we'll head to Bloomsbury," Matt said,

following. "We have to speak to Carpenter again. His children could be the connection to Bunn and Miss Moreton. Did you find out anything about them?"

"His daughter married and moved to Bristol," Brockwell said. "His son lives in Clerkenwell and works for his father at the workshop. He has no known properties of his own and leases rooms in an old building."

"Did you pay him a call?"

"First thing this morning. My men searched the premises and found no sign of Mr. Bunn or Miss Moreton. Mr. Carpenter was shocked by our intrusion and equally shocked that we thought him capable of harboring such persons."

"And you believed him?" Matt scoffed.

Brockwell didn't appear to hear him. He kept walking, his strides long and purposeful. It was the quickest I'd ever seen him move.

* * *

WE FOUND the younger Mr. Carpenter at home in Clerkenwell within walking distance of his parents' house. The tenement was in good condition compared to some, and while the area was quite poor, it was not a slum by any stretch of the imagination. The surrounding streets were relatively quiet, most people having gone to church or remained home out of the grim weather.

Mr. Carpenter opened the door and seemed to deflate upon seeing us. "I answered your questions this morning," he told Brockwell. "What do you want now?"

He was a rather non-descript man of medium height and build. His neatly combed brown hair was parted down the middle and he appeared to be trying to grow a beard, but it was a little patchy. He couldn't have been older than Matt.

"We need you to get word to Mr. Bunn or Miss Moreton immediately," Brockwell said. "There has been a train derailment and Mrs. Glass cannot reach the required destination of Brighton in time." He indicated me.

Mr. Carpenter's eyes narrowed. "What are you talking about? I've already told you, I have nothing to do with those people. Now please leave."

Matt stepped forward and Mr. Carpenter flattened himself against the wall. He stared unblinking up at Matt, a towering figure of fury. "We know you harbored them here then helped them escape the city. That's why no sign of them was found this morning when the police searched the premises. After we called on your father yesterday, you sent them away."

"To Brighton," I added testily. "Where they are now demanding I go and agree to their terms or they'll blow something up. Mr. Carpenter, you must help us. I cannot get to Brighton with the derailment!"

"What derailment?"

Willie pushed through and slapped the newspaper into Mr. Carpenter's chest. "That derailment."

Mr. Carpenter rubbed a hand over his jaw as he read then passed the newspaper back to Willie. "I told you, Inspector. This is nothing to do with me." His thin voice said otherwise.

"Mr. Carpenter!" I snapped. "A bomb will go off if I don't get to Brighton by two. Do you understand? Without the rail service, I can't reach it in time. We have to get word to them and ask them to delay the meeting."

"Or give themselves up," Matt snarled. "They'll be caught anyway but a judge might be lenient if they surrendered."

Mr. Carpenter swallowed hard.

"Son?" came a voice from the hallway behind Mr. Carpenter. "Son, who is it?" Mr. Carpenter Senior appeared only to stop dead when he saw us crowding the entrance. "My son has nothing to do with those people," he snapped at Brockwell. "He already told you this morning, Inspector. He's innocent. He'd never—"

"Enough!" Matt pointed a finger at Carpenter Junior.

"You're artless but your children are not. We know you helped Bunn and Amelia Moreton when they were in hiding and you helped them escape London yesterday."

"He did not!" Carpenter Senior replied. "Tell them, Son."

Carpenter Junior folded his arms over his chest. "I've answered the inspector's questions, now I ask you to leave. My wife and children will be home from church soon."

"Then you don't have long to answer me," Matt growled. "Not unless you want them knowing what you did."

Mr. Carpenter thrust out his chin. "This is harassment."

"What're you going to do?" Willie said, puffing out her chest. "Tell the police?"

I chewed the inside of my lip and cast a glance past the younger Carpenter to his father. He looked troubled by our presence but defiant. His son, however, looked worried beneath his bravado. More worried than an innocent man ought to look, in my opinion. I suspected Matt and Brockwell both knew it too, being far more experienced with guilty persons than me. Neither looked like they would back down without the answers we needed.

Mr. Carpenter Senior laid a hand on his son's shoulder. "You don't have to speak to them. You've done nothing wrong." To Brockwell, he said, "There is no possible way my son would harbor such dangerous people. He's an honest family man and a hard worker. He's also artless. Why would he help them?"

"He's artless but his children are not," I said. "Isn't that right?"

The elder Mr. Carpenter shrugged. "So?"

"So he thinks magicians should be able to live freely, as do Mr. Bunn and Miss Moreton. He wants magicians to share their magic so that your business can flourish even more. In time, it will be a thriving company to pass on to his children. Children who he hopes won't have to worry about persecution for their magic."

Mr. Carpenter Senior glanced at his son. When the son didn't deny the image I painted, he frowned at him.

"It's a lovely picture," I went on. "But a false one. The world isn't ready for magicians. Not when they use methods like this to get what they want. Mr. Bunn and Amelia are not setting magicians free through their actions, they're making life more difficult for us. They're giving the artless further reason to fear us, and when the world fears people there are consequences, sometimes dangerous ones. Is that the future you want for your children? I know I don't."

That stubborn chin lowered ever so slightly but didn't recede altogether. "You're overreacting, Mrs. Glass. The bomb threat is just that, a threat. I'm sure nothing will come of it."

"They blew up the bandstand at Hyde Park!"

"There was no one there, as I recall. The police cleared the area."

"Because we knew the location of the bomb in advance," Brockwell bit off through clenched teeth. "This time we do not. If Miss Moreton detonates it from some distance away, without being there herself, how does she even know if there will be innocent bystanders nearby?"

Mr. Carpenter's jaw went slack.

"Son?" his father muttered. "Son, you didn't harbor those people. Tell them you have nothing to do with this situation."

The younger Mr. Carpenter lowered his head. "I'm sorry I didn't tell you."

His father staggered backward. "What have you done?"

"I did it for my children! So they could live a good life—a *free* life. Do you think I want them living like you, hiding away in your pathetic little workshop making simple furniture for ordinary folk?"

Mr. Carpenter Senior stared at his son as if he were a stranger. "I like my workshop. I don't use magic in the pieces I create there, only in those I make for private use which are not for sale. I can't risk the other furniture makers in the guild becoming suspicious."

"Precisely! You can't risk them throwing you out."

"Some of them are my friends. I don't want them looking at me differently. I don't want them hating me for destroying their businesses. That's what would happen if I used my magic at work. You know that." He settled his hands on his son's shoulders. "You know that," he said, softer.

Mr. Carpenter Junior shook his head sadly. "You should be creating pieces of art, Father. Your work should grace the drawing rooms of palaces. But instead, you're half the man you ought to be because you preserve your best work for children. You just give it away!"

Mr. Carpenter Senior sighed. "That's what this is really about, isn't it? The money I could earn if I used magic at the workshop."

Carpenter Junior pushed his father's hands off his shoulders. "I don't want that life for my children."

"No, Son. The life you don't want for your children is a life where they grow up not being able to use their magic anywhere. That's what will happen if the bomber isn't caught in time. Her actions will expose us and ruin what freedom we currently have. Mrs. Glass is right about the fear that would ensue." He nodded at Brockwell. "Tell the inspector how to contact the fugitives so he can stop them in time."

Mr. Carpenter Junior lifted his gaze to Brockwell's but it didn't quite meet his eyes. "I'm afraid I can't help you. I admit that I harbored them here, and helped them with disguises so they could escape the city, but I don't know how to get in touch with them now. I didn't even know they were in Brighton until you mentioned it."

Willie swore. "God damn you, you son of a—"

"Willie!" I grabbed her arm as it went to sweep her coat aside. She was either about to put her hand on her hip or reach for her gun. I wasn't prepared to gamble on the former.

Matt strode back to the carriage. Cyclops and Duke followed, but Willie remained with Brockwell as he informed Mr. Carpenter that there would be consequences for his actions. When the inspector also returned to the carriage, I had to force Willie to move away from the door. She glared at the two Carpenters with as much force as she could muster before storming off. I raced after her.

"Now what?" she asked as she climbed into the cabin and sat beside me.

"We set off for Brighton in this contraption," Brockwell said, eyeing the horses dubiously. "Will they last the distance?"

Matt, still standing on the pavement, leaned his forearm on the doorframe. "We won't make it in time. We wouldn't even get there today."

"We should return to Scotland Yard," I said. "There might be a response from the Brighton police. Hopefully they've found them by now and we won't have to worry." I suspect my tone gave away the hopeless direction of my thoughts. Bunn and Amelia had escaped the police thus far; they wouldn't get caught now.

"Matt," Cyclops called out from the driver's seat. "Woodall thinks there might be another way to reach Brighton on time."

"You could catch the train to Hastings," I heard the coachman say. "Change trains in Hastings and travel to Brighton along the south coast. The whole journey uses different lines to the derailment."

"How long would that take?" Matt asked.

"Three hours, I reckon."

I checked my watch. "We have three and a half hours." I snapped the watch case closed. "Get in, Matt! Brockwell, make your way back to Scotland Yard. If the Brighton constabulary have caught them, send a wire to Victoria Station ticket office to notify us. Woodall, make haste!"

I thumped on the cabin ceiling before Matt had even closed the door. Brockwell leapt out of the way of the wheels but landed in a muddy puddle. He didn't care and raced off to find a cab back to Scotland Yard.

"That low down cur," Willie spat as we sped through the streets. "If he'd come forward yesterday, they could have been stopped from leaving the city."

"What's done is done," I said, peering out of the window. "I'm sure he regrets his actions now that he knows how perilous the situation is."

"I don't know. He didn't look like he regretted it. This is the problem with having children, India. Parents do stupid things for them. Don't have them. They'll loosen the screws in your head." She tapped her forehead.

"Thank you for the lecture," Matt growled. "But forgive us for not taking parenting advice from you."

Willie sniffed. "I'm just trying to be helpful."

"Well don't."

I frowned at Matt and rested my hand on his knee. Tension vibrated through him. I gave him a weak smile and he tried to give one back, but failed. He placed his hand over mine and squeezed. It was of little comfort.

It seemed to take an age to get to Victoria Station, but my watch said we still had time to make it to Hastings, but only if a train was leaving in the next ten minutes.

Unfortunately there wasn't one scheduled for another forty according to the attendant at the ticket booth. "Why so late?" Matt snapped at the elderly man dressed in the uniform of the London, Brighton and South Coast Railway company.

"It's Sunday, sir," the man said with strained friendliness. It must be difficult to remain cheerful in the face of a glowering Matt. "The trains aren't very frequent."

"Don't people wish to go to the seaside?" Willie asked.

"Not in winter, sir, and just before Christmas at that."

THE KIDNAPPER'S ACCOMPLICE

"Fools," she muttered. "And I ain't a sir, I'm a miss. You need new spectacles."

The attendant touched the frame of his glasses. "These ones work perfectly fine. I'm sorry for my mistake, but you *are* dressed in trousers."

Willie plucked the fabric at her thighs. "These are buckskins."

I nudged her aside and peered through the ticket booth window. "Have you received any telegrams here in the last few minutes for a Mr. or Mrs. Glass?"

"No, madam. No telegrams have arrived this morning."

"Would you mind checking, please?"

He turned around and looked at the machine behind him. It was silent. "No telegrams, ma'am."

I sighed. "Now what?" I asked Matt.

He tapped his finger on the ticket booth counter as he studied the timetable. "We need to get to Brighton by two."

"Impossible," the attendant said. "There has been a derailment on that line."

"We know," Matt said through gritted teeth. "That's why we're trying to purchase tickets to Hastings where we'll change trains and continue on to Brighton."

"It's almost an hour and a half journey from Hastings to Brighton, sir. You won't make it by two. Not with the Hastings train not departing for another..." He checked the large clock hanging from the roof by two rods of iron. "Thirty-seven minutes."

Matt's tapping fingers increased their tempo. "And there's no other way to reach Brighton by two?"

The attendant clasped his hands on the counter and gave a tight smile. "No."

"What about by canal or river?"

"No."

Matt shook his head and walked off to join Duke and

Cyclops. I watched him go with a sickening, sinking feeling. This truly was hopeless.

Willie placed her palms on the ticket booth counter. "Can you think of any way to get to Brighton by two?" she asked the attendant. "We're desperate. We'll pay for the fastest horses, the best driver."

The attendant's smile returned, tighter than ever. "Unless you can saddle up a large bird, there is no way for you to get to Brighton by two. Now, if you don't mind, *madam*, there are people over there who appear to be waiting to purchase a ticket but have been too afraid to approach the booth."

Willie swung around. "Why are they afraid? I ain't frightening. Come on, India, we better go. India? You all right? You look strange."

I shook my head, unable to form words. Only one thing occupied my mind and it was madness. Utter madness.

"You just had an idea, didn't you?" Willie grabbed my hand and dragged me toward Matt, pacing beneath the clock. She beckoned for Cyclops and Duke to join us. "Matt, talk to India," she said. "Find out what her plan is. She won't tell me."

I shook my head over and over but still did not speak.

Matt touched my chin and his frowning face came into focus. "India? What is it? What are you thinking?"

"No," I said. "No, it's not possible. It probably won't work. It's far too dangerous."

"Which is it?" Willie asked, hands on hips. "Impossible, improbable or dangerous?"

"It's a ridiculous idea. Forget about it."

"Tell me your idea," Matt said in the voice he used to coax information out of anxious or difficult women. It almost always worked. "We have no other choice. As it stands, you cannot get to Brighton by two. So any option is better than none, even if it's ridiculous. And magical."

I couldn't believe I was going to suggest it, but they were

all staring at me with earnestness. I was quite sure they would all agree it wasn't a *viable* option once they heard it.

"You know Fabian and I created a spell to make carpet rise off the floor and move," I said.

"You mean fly," Duke said.

"I suppose I do."

"But it didn't hold Charbonneau's weight," Matt said.

"India could send it to Brighton with a letter pinned to it," Cyclops suggested. "Can you direct its flight from here?"

"I don't think so," I said. "I need to see it to control its flight path. No, what I'm suggesting is even more ridiculous than that. Fabian came to me the other day with an idea to strengthen the rug by using iron as supports. If he uses his spell on them and I use my new one on the carpet, there'll be twice as much control as well as support and no one will accidentally slide off."

Matt's lips parted in a quiet gasp.

Willie let out a whoop and slapped her thigh. "You want us to ride it!"

"I told you it was ridiculous," I said.

"Sounds like fun to me."

"That's because you're mad," Duke told her. "No way I'm getting on that thing."

"Fine. You stay here and make decorations with Letty. Me and India are going on a magic carpet ride." She trotted off, only to glance over her shoulder and beckon us when she realized we lagged behind. "Well come on! There ain't no time for dawdling."

Matt took my hand and ushered me along the platform. "How confident are you it will work?"

I thought about lying, but Matt would see right through me. "Not very. But you were right. We don't have any other choice."

CHAPTER 14

abian was more excited by my idea than a little boy opening presents on Christmas morning. He spoke in English sentences peppered with French words as he ushered us into the drawing room.

"*Aidez moi*," he said, picking up one end of the sofa.

Duke took the other while Matt and Cyclops removed tables off the rug. It was an enormous Oriental, covering almost the entire floor surface. It would fit all of us.

A lump rose to my throat. If this failed...

Once the furniture was clear, Fabian directed us to roll up the carpet. "I will fetch my rods."

"You have iron rods lying around your house?" Willie asked.

"*Bien sûr*," he said, striding off. "I do not know if a moment such as this will arise, so I keep some on hand."

When he was gone, Matt eyed the roll of carpet. He shook his head. "It won't work."

"It might," I said. "But I agree, we shouldn't risk it. It's far too dangerous. We must experiment first under controlled conditions, and increase the height and distance of each flight before taking on such an enormous task."

"No, I mean we need to affix the iron rods to the carpet somehow. Simply resting the carpet on top of the rods could cause all sorts of issues. What if Charbonneau makes the rods fly at one speed but you direct the carpet to fly at another? The carpet will slip off."

The men stood around the roll, scratching their jaws, while Willie called for the butler.

"Fetch rope," she told him. "Lots of rope."

"You going to strap the rug onto the rods?" Duke asked her.

"Like a saddle on a horse."

Fabian returned carrying an iron rod in each hand. A footman followed, weighed down by an armful of them. The butler arrived with lengths of rope then the servants departed without batting an eye. They must have thought us mad.

We *were* mad to attempt something we hadn't practiced.

"We can't do this here," Matt said as Willie picked up the coil of rope. "Once the carpet is mounted on the rods, we won't get it through the window or door."

"Then let's take it outside onto the street," she said.

"Too visible."

"Where should we go?" Fabian asked.

"We need somewhere hidden away, discreet," I said.

Precious minutes ticked by as we considered the difficulty of finding an outdoor surface large enough to spread out the rug where we would not be visible to the general public. A flat roof would be perfect but finding a flat roof in London was nigh impossible, let alone one we could get access to on a Sunday.

"It's Sunday!" I said. "The shops are closed."

"There'll still be traffic along the main shopping thorough-fares," Matt said.

"But not in the laneways. I know of a wide alley off Regent Street. It provides access for deliveries to the shops along Regent so the public don't venture down it anyway, and today there won't be any deliveries either."

"And there won't be any staff wandering about," Cyclops said. He picked up one end of the rolled carpet and instructed Duke to get the other. "We'll put this on the roof of the coach."

"That'll be discreet," Willie said with a roll of her eyes.

"You got a better idea?" Cyclops shot back.

Between us we managed to take the carpet and the iron rods to the carriage. Thankfully we were in the large landau. With Duke sitting beside Woodall, and Cyclops standing on the groom's seat at the rear, they held the rug between them. It extended over the roof at both ends and the front flopped onto one of the horse's hind quarters, causing it to shy and the carriage to rock. Woodall calmed it and ordered Duke to hold the carpet higher.

Matt, Fabian, Willie and I sat in the cabin with the iron rods over our laps. The coach moved forward and it was as if a signal went off for Willie and Fabian. They couldn't stop chatting about the "thrilling" prospect of flying over the city and on to Brighton. All I could think about was hurtling to my death.

Matt simply stared out the window. We were passing a church when he suddenly turned in his seat to peer out of the rear window. "Damn it," he muttered.

"What is it?" I asked.

"Coyle and Hope were about to step into their carriage and saw us."

"They'll simply think we've bought a new rug and are taking it home."

"On a Sunday? When they know you've been working on a new spell with wool magic?"

"Tell them we purchased this rug off Fabian and are taking it home," Willie said.

"We're heading in the opposite direction," Matt pointed out.

"Then we're taking it to a charitable organization on account of it being threadbare." She clapped her hands together and rubbed them for warmth. "Don't be so negative, you two."

"I'm not negative," Matt said.

"You are. And you're in a bad mood."

"We're going to be flying through the air on a rug, Willie. It's never been done before and one false move could see us die."

I felt sick.

"It has been done in the past," Fabian said. "There are written accounts of magic carpet rides from centuries ago."

Matt's jaw hardened. "That makes me feel so much better."

"That ain't it," Willie said. "You were in a foul mood before India suggested the magic carpet."

"There's a lot at stake," I told her. "Matt is simply feeling the pressure of the urgency and scale of the matter."

We turned a corner very fast and we all had to clutch at the iron rods before they rolled off our laps. Matt opened the window and told Woodall to be careful.

Woodall said something back which I couldn't hear, and Matt closed the window. He turned to look through the rear window again.

"Coyle is following us," he said. "Woodall's trying to get rid of him."

Just as he said it, the carriage took another sharp turn, sending us all sliding to our right. Duke and Cyclops must be having a devil of a time keeping the carpet in place on the roof.

After some more dangerous driving, Matt declared we'd lost Coyle. "He knows we're up to something magical," he said, facing forward again.

C.J. ARCHER

"It won't matter because we won't tell him what it is," I said.

Fabian nodded. "He will ask me, I am sure of it, but I will not reveal anything to that pig. He cannot buy me."

"Has he tried?" I asked.

"Of course. But I cannot be bought."

"What about with something other than money?" Willie asked.

Fabian smiled. "He cannot get me what I want and even then, I would not give him a spell. India's spells are hers to sell, not mine."

"And I won't sell them," I said.

Matt gave me a firm nod and a half-hearted smile.

"So Fabian," Willie began, "what is it you want?"

"Ah, I cannot tell you. It is my secret." He winked at her and she blushed, which made him laugh.

When we finally came to a stop in the laneway, my fingers had frozen from holding onto the cold iron rods, despite my leather gloves. When I deposited the rods on the cobblestones beside the rolled up rug, I removed my gloves and blew on my hands.

Matt took them in his and rubbed. Behind him, the others set to work tying the iron rods to the base of the carpet. The lane was just wide enough for it to be laid out flat. Behind me, Woodall sat on the driver's seat and awaited instruction. With the carriage blocking the only entrance to the alley, no one could see what we were doing from Regent Street if they happened to walk past.

After a moment, Matt let my hands go. "Better?"

I nodded.

"You're nervous," he said.

"Aren't you?"

He chose not to answer, which I suspected was his masculine way of admitting he was terrified.

I put my gloves on as the others stepped back from the carpet. "It is ready," Fabian declared.

"Not quite." I crouched down and spoke the extension spell into each of the iron rods to lengthen Fabian's magic. He was a powerful iron magician and his magic lasted a long time, but I felt a little better afterward.

Fabian put out his hand to me. "Your flying carpet awaits, *madame*."

His attempt at an upper class English accent brought a smile to my lips, despite my fear. I took his hand, stepped onto the carpet and sat down. "It's like being at a picnic but without the food."

"And colder," Fabian added.

"The blanket," Matt said and jogged to the carriage.

I drew in a deep breath and looked up at the dense gray sky. We would be touching the clouds in just a few moments.

Or plummeting to our deaths.

"Fabian, tell me honestly," I said. "Do you think this will work?"

"I do, but you are frightened, *ma femme incroyable*. I understand. It is a frightening thing to fly when we do not have wings." He took my hands in his. "But it *will* work. I have controlled the flight of iron rods many times, and your magic is strong."

"But wool is not my expertise." I withdrew my hands from his and stood. "This is madness. We can't do it."

"India, do not be afraid. Trust your magic. Trust yourself. You are amazing, incredible!" He took my hands again and offered me a warm smile. "I have never met anyone with magic as strong as yours. This *will* work."

"India?" Matt said. "Have you changed your mind?"

I took the blanket he offered and clutched it to my chest. "I'll attempt this, despite my reservations. But you can't come."

He bristled. "I'm coming."

He went to step onto the rug but I put a hand to his chest. "No, Matt. I have to go, and so does Fabian, but you don't."

"You're my wife. Where you go, I go." He moved into the middle of the rug and sat down cross-legged. He put out his hand to me. "Come away from the edge."

"Matt, listen to me! I don't want you doing this! Please, get off."

"No."

"Matt! We haven't done this before! It could be a complete disaster. I will not be responsible for your death."

"If the experiment fails and I die then so will you so you won't feel any guilt."

I blew out an exasperated breath. "You're a fool. A mad, foolish idiot with not an iota of common sense. If we get out of this alive I'm going to have you committed to an asylum."

"That's a risk I'm willing to take." He stretched out his hand further. "Sit with me, India. I'll keep you warm."

Willie gave me a little shove in the back then proceeded to sit on the carpet beside Matt. "Sit down, India. We don't have time for your bickering."

"Not you too!" I cried.

She grinned. "I ain't missing this. What about you, Cyclops? You coming?"

"It won't hold me as well," he said. "I'm too heavy."

"It will hold as many as can fit," Fabian told him. "The iron rods already have my spell in them. They are strong and only require the flying spell now."

Cyclops backed up toward the carriage. "I promised Catherine I'd visit her today after church."

Willie grunted a laugh. "What about you, Duke?"

Duke also backed away. "I value my life and limbs."

"Coward."

"Is that any way to talk to the man who'll be arranging your funeral?"

Willie laughed then let out a *whoop*. "Come on India, Fabian. Do your magic and get this thing in the air."

I checked my watch. She was right. We were running out of time. But we couldn't simply take off without a test first.

"We speak our spells at the same time," Fabian said. "Ready?"

"Almost. I must concentrate or it'll fly off without any control."

"I am controlling the iron. It is not entirely in your hands."

I wasn't sure if that made me feel better or worse. I put my hands over the bulge in the rug where one of the iron rods had been strapped to the underside. The carpet was so thick I couldn't feel the warmth of Fabian's magic through it.

I drew in a deep breath and focused my attention on the rug beneath me. I ran my hands through the lush pile and imagined it rising gently off the ground and floating into the air. I went over the spell in my head, silently sounding out every syllable. The process calmed my rapidly beating heart a little.

"Ready," I said.

Matt sidled closer and put an arm around my waist and the blanket over my lap. Then he grabbed hold of the nearest rope holding the carpet raft together and gave Fabian a nod.

Fabian counted down from three then we both spoke our respective spells.

The carpet rose off the ground. The iron rods lifted together, keeping the rug flat. It held our weight easily.

Either Duke or Cyclops gasped loudly and I lost concentration. The rug sagged between the iron rods and the entire contraption suddenly plunged.

"India!" Fabian cried.

I focused on the words in the spell again and managed to regain concentration enough to lower the rug gently to the ground without incident. "I can't do it," I said. "I can't even

187

lift it over the buildings let alone fly it all the way to Brighton."

"You got to, India," Willie urged. "Or Amelia's going to set off a bomb."

"Fabian will have to do it alone."

Fabian blinked huge eyes. "I cannot, India. You know I cannot. That proved it. I need you. You are stronger than me. Your magic could do this alone if not for keeping the rug flat. Mine cannot."

I squeezed my eyes shut.

Matt's arm tightened around my waist and he drew me back against his body. "If you don't try again, you will always wonder if you could have done it," he whispered in my ear.

"But—"

"No buts." He rested his chin on my shoulder and cupped my cheek with his hand. "We all know you can do this. Now prove it to yourself."

I drew in a deep breath and let it out slowly. "All right."

Fabian gave me a flat smile and counted us down again. We spoke our spells at the same time and once again the carpet rose. And rose, and rose.

I didn't look down. I concentrated on the rug and the walls on either side of the alley. I listened to my words and focused on finding a rhythm. By the time we reached the third floor, I'd found it. The spell became a chant as rhythmic as a marching band's drumbeat. It flowed through me, out through my mouth and in again through my ears before I repeated it without pause.

"The eaves," came Matt's voice behind me, neither too loud nor too soft.

A quick glance showed me what he meant. The over-hanging eaves extended beyond the walls into the lane, narrowing it. The rug wouldn't fit.

Fabian's whispering stopped, but the rug didn't fall. We

were perfectly fine hovering there in mid-air, just below the roofline, and all because I was controlling it.

I stopped chanting too but continued to concentrate, picturing the rug moving past the eaves and higher. The carpet moved forward several feet then rose where the gap widened. It had found its own way up.

"Blimey," came Willie's murmur. "They look so small. Even Cyclops."

I didn't look but I could feel Matt leaning to one side. Then I felt him tense.

"Everything all right?" I asked.

"Shhh," he whispered. "Just concentrate."

I smiled. "It's fine, Matt. Stop worrying." Partly to be sure and partly to satisfy him, I continued to chant the spell.

"Isn't that Coyle and Hope?" Willie asked.

I stopped chanting and the rug took a sudden dip before I caught it and directed it to keep rising. It was too late to do anything about Coyle and Hope seeing us. That would be a conversation to have when we were safely home again.

The carpet kept close to the roofs, just above the chimneys. It was smokier up here, from the fireplaces lit all across the city, but the scenery was spectacular. The sea of roofs was punctured by church spires, more than I expected. In the distance, St Paul's dome squatted amid the city's financial district like a mother supervising her brood.

We floated rather than flew, drifting over the river, and silent factories, over the open expanses of green parks and the tightly packed slums, within spitting distance of each other. The city looked like a resting giant from up here, with the chimneys expelling their smoky breath and the vein-like streets stretching into the distance.

But even more remarkable was the silence. There were no shouting hawkers, no omnibus bells or train whistles, no rattling carriage wheels or *clip clop* of horses' hooves. There was nothing but the wind.

"India," Fabian said quietly. "We must go faster, yes?"

He was right. This floating, drifting pace was too slow. We'd never reach Brighton before two.

"Yes," I said.

A look came over his face of intense concentration. I could feel the iron rods wanting to move forward, to pick up the pace. It wasn't a sensation I could feel with my body, but rather with my mind. No, not my mind—my senses. My *magical* senses.

The carpet didn't respond to the iron rods, however. Not until I turned my focus onto it and pictured it speeding up. Only then did our pace quicken. Across from me, Fabian removed his hat before it blew off and gave me a nod of acknowledgement.

Matt's arm tightened around my waist.

We streaked through the air and soon left London behind. We all removed our hats and my hair soon came loose from its arrangement thanks to the wind. Matt unfolded the blanket and wrapped me in it, but I didn't feel cold. The magic kept me warm.

When I saw Willie shiver, I handed it to her.

She thanked me and flung it around her shoulders. The wind whipped at it, tugging the ends. She grinned then rose onto her knees and stretched out her arms. "Yeeehah! We're flying!"

I leaned back into Matt. "If she stands up, you take her left leg and I'll take her right."

His other arm came around me too and he gently squeezed. "Stop talking and just concentrate."

I smiled. The poor man was not enjoying this experience as much as his cousin. Or as much as me, I realized. I *was* enjoying myself. It wasn't necessarily the fact that I had made a carpet fly that gave me such a sense of satisfaction. It was the use of my magic. Using any spell at such a profoundly intense level would have fulfilled me, it just so happened to be a wool movement spell this time.

"Follow the railway to Brighton," Matt said, loud enough for both Fabian and me to hear.

I glanced down and spotted the train line on our left. I steered toward it. Fabian must have done so too because I felt no resistance from the iron beneath us.

We passed over green paddocks and small villages, over winter-bare trees and dark rivers snaking through the countryside. I spotted the tangle of carriages from the derailment and spared a thought for the victims.

We weren't as high as the clouds, but high enough so that people on the ground wouldn't have recognized a carpet flying overhead and would attribute the sighting to a large bird or a trick of the light. It was difficult to know how far we'd traveled and how far we had to go. I didn't check my watch, but I sensed over an hour had passed by the time the sea became visible in the distance. And there, nestled on the foreshore, was a large cluster of buildings. Brighton.

The carpet suddenly sagged in one section. Willie swore as she slipped into the dip and had to grab onto one of the ropes to haul herself out of it.

One of the iron rods had fallen off. No, not fallen but no longer seemed to be flying. It was merely a passenger, held in place by the ropes. Its weight was dragging on the carpet instead of supporting it.

I glanced at Fabian. Sweat beaded on his forehead and the muscles in his jaw were rigid.

"Charbonneau!" Matt barked. "What's happening?"

Fabian shook his head. He seemed unable to do more.

"He's concentrating," I told Matt.

"He needs to concentrate harder. This thing is going down."

Another dip appeared in the carpet as a second rod lost its

magic. The weight of it pulled against my magic and I struggled to keep the carpet flying, let alone flat.

"Grab onto the ropes!" Matt shouted over the wind.

We each clung to the ropes as the carpet began to sag on one side. All except Fabian. Sweat dripped from his temple. His lips moved as he spoke the spell, each iteration louder than the last. He no longer whispered it. He squeezed his eyes shut.

But his efforts weren't enough. Another rod suddenly stopped working and the carpet tilted violently. I fell backward into Matt. Thanks to his strength and grip on the ropes, we did not slide off.

Thank God Willie had heeded Matt's warning. She lay face down, her legs dangling off the edge of the carpet, but at least she still clung to the ropes.

Fabian, however, fell off.

CHAPTER 15

att released one of the ropes and lunged, catching Fabian's forearm.

I screamed. Fabian bellowed something in French. Matt shouted at him to hold on, and Willie shouted at Matt to hang onto the rope. His grip was the only thing stopping both he and Fabian plunging to their deaths in the paddocks below.

Dear god, no. The iron rods were failing one by one. Fabian was in no state to concentrate on the magic, and I couldn't keep the carpet flying without them. We were too heavy.

The rug suddenly dropped as the magic in the final rods gave way.

Willie, who'd been hauling herself back up, hadn't quite got her grip on the rope. Her light weight saw her rise off the carpet into the air, hanging onto the rope by her fingertips.

"India!" she shouted. "Land this thing!"

"I can't," I cried. "Not without Fabian."

I couldn't see more than his forearm and hand, gripping Matt. But his hand was slipping.

Matt gritted his teeth and tried to haul Fabian up, but he was too heavy, and with Matt's arms stretched as far as they could reach, he couldn't put his weight into it. He was using all his strength to merely hold onto Fabian.

But Fabian continued to slip.

Willie settled onto the rug again and tried to help Matt, but she was too far away, and I couldn't stretch enough to reach Fabian either.

The carpet continued to hurtle toward the ground.

I recited the spell, over and over, and focused hard on the woolen fibers. The carpet responded by slowing its descent, but the weight of the rods and us was too much, and it soon picked up speed again. If we continued to fall at this rate, we would hit the ground hard.

Too hard to survive.

"Matt," Willie said darkly, desperately. "Let him go."

Matt squeezed his eyes shut and growled with pain and frustration. He was at his limit.

And the ground was getting closer.

"Matt!" Willie cried. "We need to lose some weight."

Matt opened his eyes and what I saw in them turned me cold. The decision he had to make tortured him. He didn't want to be responsible for Fabian's death, but if he didn't let go, we might all die.

If he released Fabian he would always blame himself, no matter how many times he heard it was not his fault. He would forever tell himself he could have held on longer, could have found the extra strength necessary.

I couldn't let him suffer like that. Not when this journey was my idea. Fabian's death would be on my hands. And I knew I couldn't live with the guilt.

I'd started us on this path. Now I had to stop it.

I continued to chant the spell and focus on the carpet, but it didn't slow our progress. The carpet wasn't the problem, it was the iron rods. The very elements that had allowed us to take this journey were now our downfall. The magic within them was no longer working and Fabian was too exhausted and scared to have any effect.

I knew his spell. I'd heard it many times during our experimental sessions. If my magic had worked on wool, a substance that was not my expertise, then it could work on iron too.

But I'd never managed two spells at once.

I knew I could stop reciting the carpet spell and the magic would continue to work as long as I didn't entirely lose focus. I'd already done it and the magic had held.

There was no time to experiment. No time to be tentative. We had mere seconds now.

I stopped reciting the wool spell and spoke the iron one. The rods didn't respond. I concentrated on the rods in my mind's eye and repeated the spell. Our descent slowed.

But it wasn't enough. We were still falling too fast. The barren tree branches came into view alongside us. There was only time to speak the spell once more.

I shouted it into the wind and pictured the iron rods *and* the carpet carrying us forward instead of up, in the hope that would require less magic.

The rug skidded mere inches from the long grass and shot ahead. When Fabian's feet hit the ground, he pushed off and leapt onto the carpet. He fell flat on his face, still clutching Matt's forearm. Matt let go and rolled onto his back. He closed his eyes and sucked in deep breaths.

I focused on slowing down the carpet and soon we were skimming across the paddock at a more sedate pace. A safer pace.

I blew out a breath and rested a hand on Matt's chest, under his coat. His heart beat rapidly but steadily. There was no need to use his magic watch.

"India!" Willie cried. "Tree!"

I glanced up and only had time to picture the carpet

swerving to miss the large trunk. But instead of a smooth glide around it, the rug tipped. We all tumbled off and landed on the ground.

The grass cushioned my landing, but Willie's foot kicked my head and my vision momentarily blurred. When it cleared, I could see Willie sitting up and Fabian rolling over with a groan. Matt was already on his feet and approaching me. Nobody seemed too injured, thank God.

Matt knelt beside me, frowning and pale. He pushed back my hair and touched my temple. "You're bleeding." He removed his handkerchief from his pocket and dabbed at the cut.

I threw my arms around him and cried with relief. His arms circled me and held tight. He buried his face in my neck and drew in a shuddery breath.

"Wooweee!" Willie cried. "That was incredible! I can't wait to do it again."

I pulled away to glare at her. "Don't expect to fly home. I am never *ever* doing that again. If mankind was meant to fly we'd have wings."

Fabian picked himself up and dusted off his trousers, but he couldn't remove the patch of mud on his thigh. He gave up and approached us instead. He looked grave.

"Thank you, Glass. You saved my life." He shook Matt's hand, and Matt nodded back, and that was the end of that.

"The rug landed in mud," Willie said from where she stood over the crumpled structure. "Come and help me untie the rods and roll it up."

"Leave it," Matt said. "We have to get to Brighton."

We trudged through the paddock as quickly as the damp grass would allow, avoiding the cows and their deposits. The main thoroughfare into Brighton was busy but no carriages stopped for us. I could hardly blame them. Grass stains and dirt covered our clothes, we were all hatless, and if my hair looked anything like Willie's, the birds could mistake it for a nest.

Another carriage drove past at speed, ignoring Matt's appeals to stop. "There was only one occupant," he grumbled. "It had room for all of us."

I checked my watch. "Twenty-eight minutes until two."

Another carriage approached. "Leave this to me," Willie said, clapping Matt on the shoulder. She stepped into the middle of the road.

"Willie!" I cried. "It'll run you over!"

She put up her hands as if warding it off.

"That's not going to help. Move back!"

"Willie," Matt snapped. "Get off the road."

She planted her feet apart. "It'll stop."

The carriage hurtled toward her. The coachman shouted something but I couldn't hear him over the rumble of wheels. Willie shouted back. "Give us a ride into Brighton!"

The coachman pulled hard on the reins and the four horses responded. Even so, it took them several feet before they came to a complete stop, right in front of Willie. She stroked the nose of one. It snorted back at her.

"What in the devil's name are you doing?" the driver shouted.

"We're sorry for the inconvenience," I said as sweetly as possible. "But it's imperative we get to Brighton station in the next twenty-five minutes."

"Imperative?"

"It's a life and death situation."

The driver grunted. "It always is." He patted the seat beside him. "I've only got room for one."

"We all have to go," Matt said.

"I can't fit you all. Coach is full."

"I can pay you."

"It doesn't matter. I can't take money for a seat I don't have. So go on, who'll it be?"

I gathered up my skirts.

"No, India," Matt said. "We'll wait for the next one."

"And if there's no space on that one? I have to do this, Matt. It has to be me."

He thumped the side of the carriage with his palm.

I climbed up the ladder to the coachman's seat and settled beside him. "It'll be all right. All I have to do is show up on time."

"And then what? Do as they say? I don't think that's wise."

"Isn't that what we were going to do anyway if the police didn't catch them?"

He pressed his lips together.

"Matt?"

The coach rolled off, forcing Matt to step back.

I swiveled to see him. He stood there, flanked by Willie and Fabian, his head bowed. I sat forward again and stared ahead at the city of Brighton.

Matt's plan for the two PM meeting must have been different to mine. Had he been going to tell me at the last moment so I couldn't argue with him? What had he intended to do anyway? Keep me from arriving at the station and capture Mr. Bunn and Amelia instead of giving into their demands? But how? If they were watching from afar, we'd never find them.

Negotiate. It's what Matt was good at. It was also the only course open to us if the police didn't find them before two PM.

"Why do you want to go to the station?" the driver asked. "London line's closed on account of the derailment."

"I'm meeting some people, but I must get there as soon as possible."

"It's on the way to my final destination. We'll be there in fifteen minutes."

That gave me almost ten minutes before the deadline. It wasn't a lot of time but it was enough. After a discussion with the driver, who was born and bred in Brighton, I realized there was no place where Bunn and Amelia could hide yet look over the station platforms and avoid the police. The entire Brighton constabulary should be out looking for them now, thanks to Brockwell's telegram. The only way Bunn and Amelia could see me was if they stood on the platform themselves. Giving someone else instructions to do so and report on my appearance wouldn't work, as any number of women could be standing there, and I wasn't distinctive enough that a second-hand account would leave no doubts. According to the coachman, platform four serviced the London line so it should be deserted, but I still didn't think they'd rely on someone else to identify me.

That meant they had to show up themselves. They must be in disguise. It was how they had avoided detection in London, and managed to slip away to Brighton, and it must be how they planned to be on the platform to see me in person without being seen by the police.

Fifteen minutes later I thanked the driver and stepped down to the pavement. The grand station was not the bustling center it ought to be. Two constables wandered past. They looked me over and dismissed me instantly. I didn't look like the description they'd been given of Amelia. I considered telling them who I was, but I decided against it. It changed nothing, and I realized we'd been foolishly relying too heavily on a police force not trained to deal with magician criminals. Amelia could still detonate the bomb even if they captured her. They'd have to render her speechless, and I doubted they were willing to go to such drastic lengths on my suggestion.

The station master stood on the forecourt by the entrance, whistling as he rocked back on his heels. He spotted me approaching and tugged on the brim of his cap in greeting. "Sorry, ma'am, there's been a derailment on the London line," he said. "Only trains along the coast are operating today."

"I'm actually only here to meet my friends on platform four."

"That services the Main line to London. It's empty."

"May I go in and wait for them?"

He frowned. "Don't you want to wait here?"

"I have to be on that platform. It's a surprise, you see. We're playing a game where we each give one another clues to seek out the other. They follow the trail of clues from one place to the next, until they reach the final destination where I'm waiting. Today, the final destination is here. I must be on the platform or it doesn't count as a win."

"Sounds amusing," he said, smiling. "Very well, go on through."

"Thank you. Oh, and one other thing. Don't tell my friends I'm already here. It's important they think they read the clue incorrectly and don't realize they're about to win. It's all part of the game, you see. Promise you won't tell."

He saluted. "I promise."

"Not even a wink or a smile or any kind of hint whatso-ever. I have money riding on this, so I don't want them knowing I'm here. Understand?"

He looked me up and down and wrinkled his nose. "You're gambling?"

"Only between very good friends," I told him with what I hoped was a charming smile.

His nose returned to its usual state which I took to mean I'd passed his prudery assessment—but only just. I extracted another promise from him that he wouldn't tell anyone I was there, even if they asked him directly, and went through the gate.

Platform number four was deserted. I hurried along it,

scanning the vicinity. All was quiet, empty. There weren't even any guards. A train arrived at another platform that must service the coastal lines.

I took another look around before ducking into the waiting room. I removed my watch from my reticule and checked the time. Three minutes. I closed the cover but didn't put it away. I might need a weapon.

I wished I'd asked for Willie's gun.

I sat on one of the bench seats and checked my watch again, and again. Finally, at exactly two PM, I stepped out of the waiting room. An elderly couple entered through the gate ahead and spotted me at the same moment I saw them.

They approached, their gaits slow, their backs bent. No police followed them, but the station master poked his head around the gate and tugged on his cap brim. The couple didn't see.

I waited and clutched my watch tighter.

"Nice disguises," I said when they were within hearing distance.

"You made it," Mr. Bunn said with a large dose of relief. "Thank God. We thought with the derailment..." His gaze shifted to Amelia at his side.

"Did you consider that I couldn't get here on time?" I asked.

"You're resourceful," Amelia said with a lift of one shoulder. "And a powerful magician. I knew you'd find a way to get here."

Beside her, Mr. Bunn pulled out his handkerchief and dabbed his forehead. It was a cold day but the thick gray wig and false beard as well as the extra layers of clothing to bulk up his frame must be making him hot. That and the anxiety of being associated with someone like Amelia Moreton, a dangerous madwoman with the ability to blow up her home-made bombs from a distance.

He was the weak link I needed to exploit.

But I didn't want either of them knowing that I knew that. I focused on Amelia. "Please don't force me to do this. Think of the consequences."

"Are you alone?" she asked.

"Yes."

"How did you get here?"

"With great difficulty."

She waited.

"We're not here to talk about transport," I said. "You're here to get me to agree to do something I don't want to do, and I'm here to talk you out of it, so let's just get on with it, shall we?"

"You won't talk me out of detonating the bombs unless you agree to combine your magic with Mr. Bunn's." She held my gaze with the confidence of a poker player with a strong hand. The only way I could win with my weaker one was to bluff.

"Your father has been arrested for producing bombs illegally," I told her.

Her brows rose but the shock showed only on Mr. Bunn's face, not hers. "Illegal bombs!" He stared at her. "Did you know about that?"

"Of course," she said.

He stared harder. "Who did he make the bombs for?"

"I don't know."

"Where do you think illegal bombs go?" I asked him. "Not to British armed forces, that's for certain."

"Dear God, that's terrible."

"It's business," Amelia said. "Just like this is business. *Your* business, to be precise. I'm doing this for you, don't forget."

He rubbed his forehead.

"The police discovered the bombs while searching your

father's factory for you two," I told them. "You're responsible for his arrest."

Her lips twitched, but not with a smile. "He made his own bed."

"Your mother is distraught. She needs you now, but you're not there to help her through this difficult time. Indeed, she knows what you've done and are threatening to do. You're making it even harder for her. She's not coping."

"My brother is there. He's very capable in a crisis. Artless but capable. They'll get through this as well as what's to come."

"What do you think is to come?"

"The rise of magicians. With your magic mixed with others, magicians will make superior products that last forever. It won't be long before our businesses flourish, our fortunes increase, and we can use our money to influence guilds and governments. They'll be forced to favor us in policies and give us freedom from persecution. We won't have the fear of imprisonment—or worse—hanging over our heads. It's how the world works, Mrs. Glass. Money means power and influence. And to get money, we need you."

"That's an ambitious plan."

"It will take a few years, but we've got time."

"No, no," Mr. Bunn said to me. "It's just my leather you'll be using your magic with. Perhaps one day you'll change your mind and combine your magic with others', but Amelia and I agreed to stop with my leather. Didn't we, Amelia?"

She did not answer. Mr. Bunn was naive if he thought she would stop with his request. Or perhaps he was desperately hopeful.

"You won't get away with this," I said. "You can't run forever. The police will catch you eventually."

"With my magical power, I don't need to run," she said. "I'll simply threaten to detonate a bomb when the authorities get too close, perhaps even go through with it if they don't take me seriously. They'll soon learn we're serious and will stay away."

She reminded me of Willie. Arrogant and stubborn; an independent-minded woman in a man's world, and impossible to reason with. I was quite good at managing Willie now, but I wasn't at all sure I could manage Amelia. Willie had a good heart beneath the bravado. Amelia's was as cold as ice, through and through.

"You expect magicians to support your cause if you use those methods?" I said. "I know I wouldn't."

"They don't have to support my methods, just reap the rewards. I got the idea from the Fenians, a few years ago, and have been thinking about it ever since. Not all of the Irish agreed with their tactics, but the outcome would benefit all. What they did—what I am doing—is a selfless act."

"Selfless! It's the opposite. You're motivated by greed and power."

"I'm motivated by *freedom*. Freedom of expression and to be who we are, openly. You wouldn't understand, Mrs. Glass. You already have wealth and privilege. You don't need your magic to survive in business, like most of us."

There was no point arguing with her. People like her believed what they wanted to believe, saw only what they wanted to see. Those beliefs had become more robust over the years since their inception and their heaviness pushed common sense so far down that it couldn't rise, couldn't breathe. If she'd used her intelligence and conviction to find a less dangerous way, she might have brought about the changes she wanted.

But this violent method was only going to create deeper divisions that would take longer to heal. Harmony between magicians and the artless was delicately balanced. A nudge could tip it in either direction. A shove, such as Amelia's bombings, would see the harmony smashed altogether.

"Will you do it?" Mr. Bunn asked me. "Will you use your spell to extend my magic?"

"Is that what you want?" I asked.

"Of course."

"And if I don't?"

His gaze slid to his companion.

"I detonate the first bomb," Amelia said. "And if you still don't agree, I detonate a second and a third."

"Then you give me no choice."

Amelia's eyes gleamed.

Mr. Bunn looked relieved. "Thank you, Mrs. Glass. You won't regret it. I'll see that I make the most of this opportunity."

"And after I've extended Mr. Bunn's leather?" I asked Amelia. "What then?"

"That's all." Mr. Bunn swallowed.

I didn't let my gaze waver from Amelia. She merely smiled back with a slick smile that chilled me to the bone. She wouldn't stop with Mr. Bunn's leather, but he still hadn't fully realized it.

"Come with us without causing a commotion," she said. "If you alert anyone that you are being held captive, I will hurt them." She pulled her hand out of her coat pocket to reveal a small knife. "Not you," she added. "You're far too valuable to hurt. But I suspect you don't want the injury or death of another on your conscience. Indeed, it's what I've been counting on all along."

I nodded quickly, giving up on the notion of bluffing my way to victory. I'd never been very good at poker. Out of the corner of my eye, I saw Mr. Bunn's anxious look. He hadn't known about the knife.

"Where's your husband?" he asked as I walked between them along the platform. "He'd better not be hiding some-where, ready to ambush us. Amelia *will* use that knife, you know."

"I know," I said. "He remained behind."

"He let you come to Brighton on your own?"

"I left without telling him. I knew he wouldn't agree to me doing this so I had to sneak away."

I surreptitiously scanned the area, hoping he, Willie and Fabian hadn't arrived yet. It was a stroke of good luck that they'd not been able to come with me. Ambushing Amelia and Bunn was precisely something they'd do. They couldn't be far away, however. It was only a matter of time before they stopped another coach heading to Brighton.

The station master touched the brim of his hat as we passed him on the forecourt. "Enjoy the rest of your day," he said cheerfully.

I nodded back. Amelia and Mr. Bunn kept their faces averted. They wore gray wigs and padded clothing, but their skin was unmarked by the ravages of time, a certain give-away they were in disguise.

Instead of leaving the station, they steered me toward platforms one and two.

"Where are you taking me?" I asked.

"Back to London," Mr. Bunn said. "The long way, on account of—"

Amelia hissed at him and he pressed his lips together.

"Are you taking me to your workshop?" I asked. With the police watching it, they wouldn't get in undetected, even with disguises.

I was considering whether to tell them or not when Mr. Bunn said, "I have another facility where I've temporarily stored some leather I set aside for you."

"Stop talking!" Amelia growled at him.

"Why? Who's she going to tell?" Mr. Bunn looked around. "No one's following us. She came alone."

"If you believe that then you're a fool."

"I came to Brighton alone," I said. "It's not a lie."

This part of the station was busy with people desperate to

return to London, but unable to catch a direct train on the main line. They had to go via Hastings too. It would be easier for the fugitives to disappear among the crowd, but also easier for me to escape.

I did not want to escape, however. I was resolved to do as Mr. Bunn wanted to stop Amelia following through on her threat. It's what would happen afterward that worried me.

"She won't stop with your leather," I told Mr. Bunn. "She has admitted as much."

Amelia hissed at me to be quiet.

"What will you do with me after I use my magic on his leather?" I pressed.

"I want to let you go," he said, somewhat weakly. It was finally dawning on him that he'd been duped by his accomplice. Her aims didn't align with his.

"Amelia?" I prompted.

She grabbed my arm and hustled me forward.

"Are you going to keep me prisoner? Are you going to force me to infuse my extension spell into every London magician's magic? Will you stop at London?"

"That's enough talking," she snapped.

Mr. Bunn turned to me. "Amelia and I discussed this and agreed—"

"I never agreed."

"You did!"

"I said what I said to shut you up." She gritted her teeth and shoved me. "Get moving. The train will be leaving soon."

I managed to wrench myself free and rounded on her. "You're going to keep me prisoner," I said flatly.

Mr. Bunn shook his head. "Of course not. We'll release you as soon as you've finished with my leather."

"Are you sure she'll release me?" I asked without taking my gaze off her.

Amelia's lips whitened and her nostrils flared. "Get moving or I *will* detonate that bomb."

The engine of the waiting train hissed and a cloud of steam billowed around it. The whistle blew.

"Move," Amelia said.

"But Amelia," Mr. Bunn whined. "We can't keep her forever. That's kidnap!"

"*This* is kidnap."

"But keeping her indefinitely is far more serious. Once she uses her magic on my leather, we'll release her and nothing will happen," he said with conviction. "We go back to the way things were, with no one harmed and our point made. But if you keep her prisoner, her husband will harass me at my workshop. The police will arrest me for conspiring with you. It's all right for you. You can keep hiding. You don't have a business to run. I do. I can't do this forever. It was only meant to be temporary."

Her eyes flashed. She bared her teeth at him. "Get on that train with her now or I will detonate the bomb. Do you understand?"

Mr. Bunn turned white. He'd finally admitted to himself that Amelia never intended to stop with his leather. She'd tricked him, used him. If she succeeded with her plan to keep me prisoner, his life was effectively over. His plans for his future, his business, would come to nothing. Worse, he would be arrested and go to prison for a long time.

"I said get on that train." She bit off every word through her clenched jaw.

She might have been small, but she was fierce. Mr. Bunn all but cowered beneath her cold glare. He nodded quickly and withdrew three tickets from his coat pocket and held one out to me.

With the train about to depart, passengers surged toward the doors while onlookers gathered to farewell them. The crowd nearby suddenly parted and spat out two figures. They were on us before I could draw a breath.

"Do not move," Matt snarled as he grabbed Mr. Bunn by the arm.

"And you, don't speak," Willie said to Amelia. She parted her coat a little to reveal her gun. "You start that spell and I'll shoot you."

"We surrender," Mr. Bunn said quickly.

Amelia merely smiled that slick smile of hers. "Are you really going to shoot me here in broad daylight?"

Willie's smile matched Amelia's. "Start speaking the spell and find out."

Amelia didn't flinch. "I don't think you will. You don't want to kill me."

"You might want to be real sure about that before you speak."

Amelia's smile widened as she took a step forward, closing the gap between them. She and Willie looked so much alike, with their small stature, their straight spines and out-thrust chins. It was like watching two feral cats sizing each other up before a territorial battle.

Amelia took another step closer until she was toe to toe with Willie. That's when I remembered the blade.

"She has a knife!" I cried.

Willie danced out of the way just as Amelia swiped. The steel flashed and struck Willie's hand. She dropped the gun and Amelia kicked it onto the tracks near the engine. Willie removed her glove with a wince. Her hand bled from a cut across her knuckles.

Amelia's smile turned victorious.

"Willie, get back," Matt warned.

He didn't know Willie well if he thought she'd back down from a fight. She might be unarmed now, but in her mind, she could beat Amelia.

Turning belief into reality was another matter entirely, however.

Amelia's fingers adjusted their grip on the knife. "You

were supposed to come quietly." It took me a moment to realize she was speaking to me.

Before I could respond, strange words dripped from her lips. The detonation spell!

"No!" I cried. "Stop! I'm going to do what you want! I'm coming with you."

Amelia did not stop speaking. Nor did she stop moving toward Willie. She backed her up against a wall and raised the blade. Then she struck.

CHAPTER 16

I operated on a deep, overwhelming instinct and threw the watch at Amelia. It hit her hand, hard. Her recitation faltered and she dropped the knife. It clattered onto the platform and a passerby kicked it as he ran to catch the train.

Amelia and Willie stared at one another, neither advancing nor retreating. Willie's hands balled into fists at her sides and Amelia drew in a measured breath. People rushed around them and steam from the engine rolled toward them, but it was as if they were inside a bubble where nothing could reach them. They were in a world of their own.

The whistle blew.

The bubble burst.

Amelia backed away and began her chant again. Willie cursed and charged after her, but Amelia turned, still chanting, and ran.

She ran right into Mr. Bunn's hand, clutching the discarded knife.

Matt caught Amelia as she fell and removed the knife from Mr. Bunn's grip. He offered no resistance. He simply stared at the figure of his co-conspirator and started to cry.

"She was going to do it," he whispered through his tears. "She was going to kill people with her bombs."

I thought he wasn't addressing anyone in particular but then saw uniformed police circling and a man in a great coat directing them. He introduced himself as the local inspector but I instantly forgot his name. I found my brain was too addled to focus on any one thing.

"Your watch, India," Fabian said quietly. I looked up into his eyes as he held out my watch by its chain. There was concern in them, but something deeper too. Pride or wonder, perhaps. "You controlled its flight perfectly."

"I've had a lot of practice lately."

He touched my elbow. "It is over. You were very brave."

I released a long, pent-up breath and glanced at Amelia's body. I felt nothing for her. No sense of remorse or responsibility for how events played out. She'd paid the ultimate price, but she'd known the consequences of her actions. Her death had been inevitable from the moment we knew she could detonate bombs with a spell and was willing to use that magic to get what she wanted. She was too dangerous to be free. Even her mother had known it, deep down.

"Where's the bomb?" Matt's barked question roused me from my stupor. He addressed Mr. Bunn who hadn't moved. Amelia still lay slumped at his feet where Matt had laid her.

"Bombs," I said. "There's more than one."

The inspector snapped his fingers in front of Bunn's face. Mr. Bunn suddenly blinked as if he'd awoken from a sleep. He rattled off three locations, all in Brighton. The inspector clicked his fingers and a bespectacled man I hadn't noticed standing nearby carrying what appeared to be a medical bag, came forward. Mr. Bunn repeated the addresses and the man nodded once and left, accompanied by two constables and a sergeant. He must be the bomb expert.

Matt joined me and planted a warm kiss on my temple. "Are you all right?" he murmured.

"I'm fine."

"You have the cut from earlier." He indicated my fore-head. "It should be seen to before we head home."

I nodded, grateful that he was taking charge. I felt numb, like I wasn't really present but merely observing the scene from afar. Passengers came and went without getting too close, thanks to the circle of police surrounding us. Fabian had moved off to one side, and Mr. Bunn was being questioned by the inspector. I was vaguely aware of Willie peering onto the tracks where the train had been moments ago.

I was very aware of Matt, however, and gratefully leaned into him. My rock. My anchor.

He put his arm around me. "We'll stay overnight in a hotel and go home tomorrow."

"Make sure to wire the Yard and tell Brockwell to get word to Cyclops and Duke. One of them must stay in the house with Aunt Letitia. She prefers not to be alone of an evening, and having one of them there will mean she won't worry about us."

"I will."

"If we have time in the morning, I'd like to buy her a gift. I won't have another opportunity to shop without her this close to Christmas. She'll insist on coming with me to do her own gift buying."

"We'll go shopping in the morning and catch a midday train to Hastings if the direct line isn't cleared by then. We'll be home by late afternoon."

The numbness started to wear off as he talked. With it came an awareness of the cold. I rubbed my arms and shivered.

Matt removed his coat and placed it around my shoulders. He called Willie's name. She called back, but it wasn't until I saw a station guard crouch down at the spot where I'd last seen her that I realized she was on the track. The guard assisted her back onto the platform and proceeded to berate her and point aggressively at the signs ordering passengers not to walk across the tracks.

She strode off mid-lecture. "I'm ready to go," she said, patting her coat over the bulge at her waist band.

Two constables marched past with Mr. Bunn between them.

"Mrs. Glass," he began and they stopped. He did not go on, however. He looked somewhat stunned; numb, as I had been. I suspected he was overwhelmed by events too. Probably more so.

"Goodbye, Mr. Bunn," I said.

He blinked owlishly, his blue eyes brimming with tears. He looked so young and innocent. The determined, eager businessman I'd first met was nowhere in sight. "I don't know how this happened. I never meant for it to end this way. It somehow spiraled out of control." He looked down at Amelia's body. "Ever since I met her, I've felt my life was no longer my own. I was merely a pawn in her game. I was expendable."

"She was not a good person," I said.

His chin wobbled. "I wish I'd realized that earlier."

The constables marched the sorry figure away.

"What will happen to him?" I asked the inspector.

"He'll serve time but his crimes aren't hanging offences." He nodded at Amelia's body, now being placed on a stretcher. "He can argue he killed her in self-defense and that she manipulated him into agreeing to her kidnapping scheme." He shrugged. "Ordinarily, I'd ask you for statements now, but Detective Inspector Brockwell has said he will speak with you all upon your return. It's not the usual procedure but Scotland Yard always get their way." This last he muttered through a clenched jaw.

We followed him out of the station and caught a hackney cab to the Grand Hotel where we'd stayed on our honeymoon. I still felt a little shocked by the day's events, but by the time we sat down to dinner in the hotel's dining room, I was feeling a little more like myself.

The fine wine and food helped. I was starving. My stomach reminded me I hadn't eaten since breakfast with a loud growl of appreciation as the soup course was served. As much as I wanted to be alone with Matt, it was nice to have Willie's lively chatter to keep from becoming too melancholy.

"I reckon I'll take a walk on the pier tomorrow morning while you're shopping," she said. "What about you, Fabian? Want to come with me?"

"Thank you for the offer, but I will decline," he said. "I have gifts to buy too."

"Are you returning to France for Christmas?" I asked.

"I'm staying here so we can continue our experiments."

I bit the inside of my cheek. I really ought to tell him I had no intention of creating any more spells. But not yet. The discussion could wait for a more suitable time. I avoided his gaze for the rest of the soup course, however.

The conversation inevitably returned to what had transpired earlier. Willie was relieved to have got her gun back while Fabian continued to praise my accuracy when directing my watch's flight.

"Did you picture it hitting her hand in your mind?" he asked. "Or did it fly of its own accord?"

"Not its own accord," I said. "It only does that when my life is in danger. I had to direct it to save Willie."

Willie pointed her knife at me. "You know I was going to dodge out of the way of her knife at the last second, right?"

"Right," Matt said wryly.

"I was! I wasn't going to let that woman get the better of me. If Bunn hadn't killed her, I'd have done it myself."

"How? You had no weapon at that point."

"I'd have thought of something."

"I have a question for you, Glass," Fabian said. "How did

Bunn get free of you on the platform? You had captured him, yes?"

Matt helped himself to more potatoes from the platter. "He just did."

"Did you let him go on purpose, knowing he would attack Amelia?"

Matt picked up his knife and fork. "I can't know what's in someone's mind."

"But you suspected."

Matt said nothing.

Fabian opened his mouth to say more, but Willie cut in. "It doesn't matter how it happened, it just matters that it did. And good thing, too. Everything works out for the best this way—Bunn gets the blame, and since he was already going to prison, it doesn't matter that he has one more charge against his name. Jasper will be relieved he doesn't have to talk to his superiors and try to get us off the hook for causing her death."

"He will have to tell them Amelia was a magician," Matt said. "The police already know she could detonate bombs without a timing device."

"He could just tell them she made a new kind of device," Willie said. "He doesn't have to mention magic."

Matt liked that idea and raised his glass in salute to it.

Willie picked up her wine glass too and called for a toast. "To an eventful day full of surprises, and to the first humans in flight."

We all frowned at her. "You're forgetting ballooning," I said.

"Ballooning ain't flying. It's floating. India, you made the carpet go *fast*." She grinned. "One thing's for sure—flying makes you feel alive."

"Until you fall to your death."

"When the artless find a way to make proper flying machines, I'll be the first in line to buy a ticket."

"And I'll continue to use vehicles that travel on land or water. I don't care if it takes longer, at least I know I'll be more likely to reach my destination in one piece."

"You're so dull, India."

"And you are mad, Willie."

She grinned again. "You ain't going to get an argument about that from me."

* * *

WE ARRIVED BACK at Park Street the following afternoon with packages from our gift buying expedition. Aunt Letitia was not happy to be left out, and we had a devil of a time convincing her we'd gone to Brighton for the investigation and simply done some shopping as an afterthought. She finally stopped complaining when Catherine arrived. She was a pleasant diversion after the trials of the last few days.

"How is the shop coming along?" I asked.

"Wonderfully," she said. "My brother is enjoying it immensely. He loves the freedom of working for himself."

"Instead of for your father?"

"It's not so much my father as our older brother. Orwell feels as though Ronnie has gone into competition against him out of spite. He thinks Ronnie resents not being the eldest son."

"Ronnie has an entrepreneurial spirit," Cyclops added. "I doubt he would have liked working for someone else, especially a family member."

"Very true," Catherine said, bestowing a smile on him that made him dip his head shyly.

"Have your family come to terms with your relationship yet?" I asked.

They glanced at one another. "Not yet," Catherine said on a sigh. "Ronnie is very supportive, of course. Father is coming around too. It's my mother and Orwell who are the problem. He's stirring her up, telling her all sorts of ridiculous things which are feeding into her ignorance." She smiled but it was forced. "But she'll come around and Orwell can take a long walk off a short pier for all I care. He's not my guardian."

"Any idea how they found out about your relationship?" Matt asked.

She shook her head.

"I'll see if Farnsworth has learned anything from the Rycroft servants," Willie said.

Aunt Letitia set her cup down and regarded Catherine. "If you think it will help, I can speak to your parents for you and vouch for Cyclops's character. It's a shame that it's come to that, but that is the way of things. Matthew can say something too, if you like."

"That won't be necessary," Cyclops said just before Catherine spoke. From the look on her face, I suspected she was about to agree to the plan. "I can do something about the problem myself."

We all looked at him blankly, even Catherine.

"The problem of me being able to support her, not one about them accepting me," he clarified. "Work for Matt is intermittent. That's enough while I live under this roof, but I need to earn a regular wage."

"You got a job?" Willie asked. "Doing what? There ain't no mine work in London."

Aunt Letitia gasped. "You're leaving London? To work in the mines? No, Cyclops, I absolutely forbid it. You're staying here, with us, in this house." She picked up her cup. "You don't need to work. Matthew is quite well off and can support his family as well as yours."

"Aunt," Matt chided. "Let him make his own way in the world. If that means moving away then so be it."

"We can always visit them," I assured her.

Willie *humphed*. "I agree with Letty. Duke, say something

sensible. Don't be like Matt and India; say something to make him stay."

Duke got up and went to the drinks trolley. "I need something stronger if I'm going to lose my best friend."

"You won't lose him," Matt said at the same time that Willie said, "*I'm* your best friend."

Cyclops watched the conversation bandy back and forth with a small smile. Catherine looked amused too. I didn't see anything to be amused about and told them so.

"You're going to be missed," I added. "But we understand your need to make your own way, Cyclops."

"You're jumping ahead, India," Catherine said. "If you'd let Nate speak, he has something important to tell you."

Cyclops cleared his throat. At a nod of encouragement from Catherine, he said, "I have an announcement to make."

"Well it's about time," Willie declared.

"Finally," Aunt Letitia agreed. "How wonderful that you've decided to put aside your family's doubts, Catherine, and go ahead anyway. Where will the ceremony be?"

Cyclops glanced at Catherine. "It's not that."

"Oh," we all said as one.

"I'm joining the Metropolitan Police," Cyclops said. "Brockwell reckons he can have my application pushed through faster on account of my experience."

Matt was the first to get up and shake his hand. "I think it's a great idea. You'll make an excellent policeman."

"London's criminals will quake in their boots," I said, smiling.

"Finally, common sense prevails," Aunt Letitia said. "That idea of yours to run off to the mines was a ridiculous one, Cyclops. I don't know what got into you. You're far better off staying here with us."

He kissed her cheek. "I know. I'm glad Brockwell suggested it."

"Speaking of Brockwell," Matt said with a glance at me.

"We'd better report to Scotland Yard. You can stay here if you like, India."

Catherine took that as her signal to leave, even though I insisted she should stay. "I have to get back for closing," she said. "Ronnie's not all that good at counting the money."

After Catherine left, Matt and I put on coats, hats and gloves and were about to depart when Willie rushed down the staircase. "You going without me?"

"We didn't think you were coming," Matt said testily. "You disappeared."

"I had to make a short stop upstairs. Too much tea."

"Too much information." He signaled for her to put on her coat and join us in the carriage.

At Scotland Yard, she waved at the sergeant on duty at the reception desk. "We're visiting Detective Inspector Brockwell," she said breezily. "No need for an escort. We know our way."

The sergeant didn't try to stop us.

We found Brockwell surrounded by paperwork. It spread over his desk like a tablecloth. A series of cups, inkstands and books operated as paper weights to stop the sheets moving in the drafts. The substantial draft created by us opening the door saw him stretching his arms over the closest papers to hold them in place.

"Close it!" he snapped.

"I don't know how you can find anything," I said, reading one of the papers upside down. It was Mr. Bunn's statement. "It looks very disorganized."

He frowned. "There is a system."

"I'm sure there is."

Willie picked up the statement I'd been reading and scanned it. "Seems like an accurate account of the day to me. Except this bit." She pointed to a paragraph at the end. "I didn't nearly die at Amelia's hand. It was all under control. I was waiting until the last second to dodge out of the way. India's what we sharpshooters call a trigger twitcher."

"Nonsense," I said, taking a seat. "You would have died if not for my quick thinking and magical watch. Or lost an eye, at the very least."

She pressed her right eyelid. "I reckon I'd look good with a patch. Better than Cyclops."

I half expected her to say that women liked their lovers with eye patches, but thankfully she either didn't think of it or restrained in Brockwell's presence.

"Anyway," she went on, "I would not have lost an eye, or an ear, or anything. Amelia was no match for me."

Brockwell folded his hands on the papers. "Has this been going on long, Glass?"

"Off and on since we got back."

"You have my sympathies."

Willie and I both glared at Matt. He merely smiled and sat too.

"May I see Bunn's statement?" he asked.

"Yes, you may, and thanks for asking." Brockwell passed him the pages with a pointed glare for both Willie and me.

I sidled closer to Matt to read it properly. "It says he didn't know Amelia was going to blow anything up, including the bandstand," I said. "Do you think that's true?"

"We've got no one else's word for it except his," Brockwell said. "It'll be up to a jury to decide if he's telling the truth."

According to the statement, Mr. Bunn and Amelia were smuggled out of the city by Mr. Carpenter the younger, albeit reluctantly. Amelia had convinced him to do it, as she had convinced Mr. Bunn to persist with their kidnapping and bombing scheme.

"It's very vague," I said. "There's no mention of magic or me in there at all. It doesn't say what he and Amelia hoped to achieve in specific terms, and he makes it seem as though my watch hit its target thanks to a measure of luck."

"Indeed," Brockwell said, sounding pleased. "I wrote the statement myself after questioning Mr. Bunn as soon as he returned to London. I also instructed him not to mention magic to anyone else or at the trial. I think I got the point across that it wouldn't go well for him if he did."

Willie told him her idea about pretending Amelia created a special device for detonating bombs remotely, and Brockwell agreed to add it to the statement with a note that no one knew how to recreate the device that Amelia destroyed before her death.

"What cause will Bunn say he adopted?" Matt asked.

"I'll present him with some options before he leaves tomorrow. The Irish cause is perhaps the most believable, but I feel there are others that deserve to have a light shone on them."

I wasn't sure if he was presenting the light shining as a positive or negative for the cause.

"Is he here at Scotland Yard now?" Matt asked.

"Downstairs in the holding cells."

"May I speak with him?"

"What about?"

"I want to know if he and Amelia tried to shoot me outside the office of *The Weekly Gazette*."

Brockwell rose. "Come with me."

"Can't someone else take them?" Willie asked.

"Why?"

Willie winked. When Brockwell gave her a blank look, she said, "So we can be alone."

Brockwell's cheeks pinked. "Right, yes, you wanted to discuss that matter with me in private. That official police matter that we discussed, but requires further discussion. Of course, Willie, I'll be happy to."

She rolled her eyes.

Brockwell fetched a sergeant to take us to the holding cells in the basement. We found Mr. Bunn sitting alone on the narrow bed, his head in his hands. He looked up upon our arrival then lowered his head again. He groaned.

"What do you want now?" he muttered. "I've answered the inspector's questions."

"He didn't ask you this one." Matt crossed his arms and regarded Mr. Bunn until the prisoner finally looked up out of morbid curiosity. "Why did you shoot at me outside the office of *The Weekly Gazette*?"

"Shoot at you? We did no such thing!"

Matt lowered his arms and moved further into the cell. Indeed, it was more of a prowl than a walk. A beast hunting his prey. Mr. Bunn gulped and scrambled back over the bed to get further away.

"Did you want to kill me or merely injure me?" Matt growled.

"Neither! We didn't shoot at you."

"Did you hope my death would force India to agree to your scheme? Or was it intended as a warning only?"

"A warning? The bandstand bomb was a warning and the Brighton bombs were our threats. We didn't need to shoot anyone as well."

Matt's hands closed into fists.

Mr. Bunn's eyes widened. "You must believe me, sir!" His screech was so high I worried the sergeant would come. The cell door remained closed, however. "Why would I lie about it now? My life is over. I'll be hanged within days."

Matt's fists opened and he released a breath. Mr. Bunn, however, didn't relax. He looked on the verge of tears.

I stepped around Matt and thought about sitting on the bed beside Mr. Bunn but the mattress was stained and I wore a dark blue dress with cream panels. The cream would pick up any dirt it came into contact with.

"You probably won't hang," I said. "Not if you argue that Amelia forced you to do her bidding by threatening to blow up her bombs if you didn't. As to Amelia's death, you can say you were saving Willie's life. After all, it's true, and the police can vouch for you. So can we."

His chin trembled. "I'll still go to prison. I won't survive a week in there."

"You should have thought of that before you tried to manipulate India," Matt snapped.

Mr. Bunn lowered his head with a groan.

Matt put out his hand to escort me out of the cell, but I indicated I wanted another moment. "Are you being honest with us about the shooting?" I said gently. "Did you shoot at anyone outside the office of *The Weekly Gazette* on Lower Mire Lane?"

"I told you, no," Mr. Bunn whined. "We did not. I don't even know where Lower Mire Lane is."

I straightened and accepted Matt's hand. We left without saying goodbye.

"Do you believe him?" I asked as we followed the sergeant out of the holding cell area.

"I do."

"So the question is, who fired the shot? Could it have been Sir Charles Whittaker, trying to kill Oscar after all?"

"It's possible, although unlikely. If he wanted Barratt dead, he would have paid that thug to kill him in the lane, not merely beat him up. A knifing would be swift, whereas a beating takes longer. It gives more time for witnesses to intervene."

He was right. It was unlikely to have been the same person, so if Whittaker orchestrated the beating, he wasn't responsible for the shooting. So who had fired the shot?

And who had been the intended victim?

CHAPTER 17

*W*e sent a message to Oscar that we'd like to see both him and Louisa that evening. He sent a message back inviting us to dine with them at Louisa's townhouse.

Louisa's elderly great-aunt joined us for dinner so conversation remained polite but insignificant. She retired shortly afterward, assisted from the dining room by a maid. Thankfully the men declined the formalities of cigars and port so I didn't have to be alone with Louisa. I suspected Matt and Oscar were equally disinterested in spending time together without ladies present. We retreated to the drawing room and drank tea.

Oscar hardly waited for the butler to close the doors when he started. "What more have you discovered about Whittaker?"

"Nothing yet," Matt said. "We've been on an investigation."

"A magical investigation?" Louisa asked as she passed me a teacup.

"It's confidential." Matt wasn't about to tell her too much. Her enthusiasm for magic was rather intense. I suspected she would side with Mr. Bunn and Amelia if she knew they'd wanted to use my magic to further the cause to free magicians.

"The police could have dealt with that, surely," Oscar said. "The situation with Whittaker is critical. He wants me dead."

"He wants you stopped," Matt clarified. "He doesn't want your book to be published."

"He shot at me! The man wants to kill me, Glass. The beating was merely a warning; the shooting was intended to end my life."

Matt drew in a breath. "We don't know if it was Whittaker who fired that shot." He explained how it would have been easier to kill Oscar rather than set upon him the first time if Sir Charles's intention was to kill. "So it's unlikely he was the one shooting at you," Matt finished.

Oscar groaned. "You think there's someone else after me?"

Matt said nothing, despite the yawning silence. He didn't want Oscar to know he might not have been the intended victim at all, and that Matt was. He wanted Oscar to think he had more than one enemy who wished he'd stop writing his book. It was a little cruel, but less so than a beating.

Oscar was too focused on himself to think that someone else could have been the shooter's target, but Louisa worked it out.

"This is pure speculation," she said. "We don't know for certain that it was Sir Charles who sent that thug. We also don't know for certain that he shot at you, Oscar. The shooter could have been trying to kill India, for example."

"Me?" I said.

"You're becoming very well known in magical circles. If the artless who are worried about magicians becoming too powerful learn about you, they might want you out of the way so that magicians can't rally behind you."

"I am not a figure to rally behind. I'm not on anyone's side."

"The artless don't know that. You saw how the Watchmaker's Guild reacted towards you, even when you stopped owning a shop."

"That was a small minority who are no longer in the guild."

"Even so," she said simply.

Oscar shook his head. "It's too coincidental. First the beating then the shooting; I *must* be the target, and Whittaker is behind both. Glass heard the bruiser direct the driver to Hammersmith where Whittaker lives."

"Thousands of people live there." She put down her teacup and turned to him. "Oscar, you're not thinking clearly. Set aside your worries and try to look at the incidents objectively. If you were reporting on them, would you jump to the same conclusion? Would your editor let you smear Sir Charles's good name in his paper based on the evidence you have thus far? Or would you consider he's one possibility among many?"

Oscar stared into his teacup. "You're right. It's not enough evidence to prove anything. I'd need more information before slandering Sir Charles." He looked up at Matt. "So what do we do to get that evidence?"

"Nothing," Matt said. "You agree to stop writing the book, as we already discussed."

"No-o," Louisa said through a tight smile. "He agreed to make it *appear* as though he's no longer writing the book. Speaking of which, India, will you be guest of honor at a club gathering I'm holding here tomorrow night? I've already sent out invitations. Oh, and do urge Fabian to accept. I've sent him an invitation but have yet to receive a response. I think once he knows you're coming he'll attend too."

"We're going to announce that I'm giving up on the book at the gathering," Oscar said.

"Tell me you are actually giving it up," I said. "Not just

C.J. ARCHER

making it appear as though you are. It's getting far too dangerous now."

He glanced at Louisa.

"He is *not* giving it up," she said crisply. "Why go to such an extreme?"

"To keep him safe," I shot back.

"Tosh. Once everyone *thinks* he's giving up, the attempts on his life will cease. He'll be quite all right."

"You're willing to wager with his life?" Matt asked.

"It's a calculated risk, not a wager. Good lord, you are all over reacting. He is not giving up the book, and that's final. He has worked too hard for too long, and what is written so far is excellent. It's engaging and enlightening and puts magic in a favorable light. The vast majority of the public will be quite convinced of the goodness of magic after reading it."

"And the minority who aren't?" Matt asked. "The dangerous minority who'll do anything to protect their businesses from magicians? What if they take it upon themselves to protect those businesses with more beatings and shootings?"

"Then the law will punish them accordingly."

"And in the meantime, magicians like your fiancé and my wife might be dead." He suddenly rose and fastened his jacket. "You seem unperturbed by the treat, but I am not."

Louisa bristled. "Are you insinuating that I do not care for Oscar?"

"I am not insinuating."

Her nostrils flared. "I have his best interests at heart. I believe my fiancé would be happier if he was able to use his magic openly and not hide it away."

"And I happen to believe my wife would be happier if she was alive." He held his hand out to me. "Shall we, India?"

I appealed to Oscar who sat beside Louisa on the sofa, looking like he wished he was not the subject of the conversation. I quite agreed with the sentiment.

"Let's not argue about this," I told them. "We'll never agree. For now, the important thing is that Sir Charles knows Oscar is giving up the notion of writing a book on magic. To that end, I'd be happy to come to your party, Louisa."

She rang for the butler to show us out.

Once in the carriage, I snuggled into Matt. "Poor Oscar. He looked somewhat lost tonight. And not simply because of the threat to his safety. Louisa is dictating his life and I suspect he doesn't particularly like it."

Matt settled the blanket over my lap then wrapped his arm around me. "Then he should break off their engagement. Gentlemanly conduct be damned. If she won't agree to it, then he has to force her to sever the arrangement any way he can. I'd rather someone removed my heart with a blunt knife than be stuck with her for the rest of my life."

"That is quite a vivid picture. A horrid picture, but a vivid one."

"They bring out the horrid artist in me." He touched my chin, urging me to look up at him. "On the other hand you, my dear wife, bring out the best in me. Now kiss me to restore my good nature."

I sighed theatrically. "Very well. For everyone's benefit, bring those lips closer."

* * *

Matt offered to come with me to call on Fabian the following day, but I declined. I couldn't lean on his charming manner—or his forceful one—whenever I encountered a prickly situation. Besides, Fabian was my friend and colleague rather than Matt's. It would be better if I talked to him alone.

He greeted me with his customary kiss to both cheeks then invited me into the sitting room where we usually conducted our experiments. "The flying carpet was a great success, was it not?" he said with bright-eyed enthusiasm. "Very frightening too, but you directed it with much skill, India. Your magic is a wonder. I am excited to see what else you can do."

"Fabian, we need to talk."

"Sit, sit. Let us talk and have tea." He signaled to the butler to fetch refreshments. I didn't have the heart to tell him I wasn't staying long. "What shall we experiment with next?" he asked after the butler left. "I do not think flying magic is a challenge for you now, or I would suggest you try to make a book fly, or a statue. You could try with something large and heavy. Perhaps a boat."

"No, Fabian."

"I agree." He wagged a finger in the air. "No more flying objects. Then what shall we try next? Something exotic, yes? Not maps coming to life; we do not want water flowing off the pages and drowning people." He wagged his finger again. "Water! What if we make it flow uphill? We could bring water where there is drought, and turn deserts into oases."

"Wouldn't we need a water magician for that? Is there such a thing as a water magician?" I stopped myself before I became too enthused by the notion.

"Perhaps we should ask Chronos your *grand-père* for ideas," he said.

"Fabian, before we get too far ahead of ourselves, there's something I need to tell you."

He smiled. "Yes?"

"I don't want to create any more spells."

The smile wilted. His face sagged and the light left his eyes. "*Cherie*, what are you saying?"

"I know this will come as a shock, but I can't let it go on. Our spells are dangerous and I don't want to create any more."

"Dangerous? But you controlled the carpet's flight."

"That's not what I meant. I meant people want the spells and might do terrible things to get them."

"But we have promised one another not to give them away or sell them. They are safe, locked away."

"Until they are stolen, or until someone forces us to give them up. If the events with Amelia Moreton have taught me anything it's that I'm vulnerable. I have loved ones who will be threatened to force me to give up the spells."

"But she is dead. She cannot harm you again."

"There'll be others. Perhaps not tomorrow or next week, but one day. It's too risky to continue, Fabian. Come now, you must see the dangers outweigh the benefits. After all, who will benefit from a flying carpet?"

"It does not matter! It matters that you have created a new spell."

I sighed. "My decision is final. There'll be no more experimenting. I'm sorry, Fabian."

"*Non!*" He rattled off something in French. I didn't need to understand the words to know their meaning. He was angry.

"I know you've adjusted your entire life so you could come to England and work with me. That's why this was such a difficult decision to make."

"Then do not make it!" He thumped his fist on the chair arm and gave his head a violent shake.

"If you think about the consequences, you will see the dangers too," I said. "We can't keep our spells a secret forever. Not with the likes of Lord Coyle circling, waiting for us to reveal them to him."

"He is just one man. Your husband will protect you from him."

"He shouldn't have to. That's the point." I drew in a breath to calm my temper. It wouldn't do to get angry at Fabian. He was disappointed in me and was going to say things he would later regret. I mustn't take it personally.

"There will be others. Lord Coyle is a threat for now, but there will be other interested parties once word gets out."

He spoke in French again, appealing to both me and the ceiling rose. At least his tone was more frustrated than angry this time. I let him go on until he finally returned to English. He suddenly sat forward and grasped my hand. "You are born to be a spell maker, India. It is in your blood. Strong magic flows through you. If you deny it, you will suffer, like a rose starved of sunlight. Do not do this. Do not give up."

It was a little dramatic but I refrained from saying so. He was upset, and French.

"My decision is made, Fabian." I got up to leave. "It's for the best—for you, me and the wider world. We are safer if we give up spell casting."

He shot to his feet. "There is another way."

"How?"

The light had returned to his eyes and the smile to his face. "We say we are giving up but continue in secret."

My heart sank. The parallel to the conversation of the night before with Louisa and Oscar was uncanny. Matt had made his point rather vehemently there; it was my turn to make it here.

"Someone will discover the truth eventually," I said sadly. "They'll see me coming here, or see you visiting me at home. Besides, the spells themselves will exist, and that is the greatest danger. If they are stolen and used for nefarious purposes—"

"What purposes? Who will use a flying carpet spell that only you can control?"

"A wool magician might learn to control it using my spell," I said. "And what if the enemies of the country ordered that magician to fly the carpet over our cities with bombs? Indeed, our own government might not be able to resist such a tempting weapon. Imagine the destruction. I cannot stomach being the creator of such a weapon. Can you?"

He closed his eyes as if in pain and heaved a deep sigh. "This is Matt's idea, yes?"

"I'm capable of coming to the conclusion on my own without my husband influencing me."

"Of course. I am sorry, India. My mind is racing, and my heart too." He pressed his hand to his chest. "I do not know what to say."

"It's a shock."

"*Oui*, a shock."

"I hope it won't affect our friendship."

"No, no. Of course not." He took one of my hands between his and bowed over it. "We are connected. Our friendship is special because there are no two magicians like us. I will always value you, India."

"I'm relieved to hear it."

"But this decision...it affects my whole life. A future without you making spells with me...it is impossible to think about. But I must think about it."

"I know. And as your friend, I want to encourage you not to make life-changing decisions too soon. There is no urgency for you to leave London. Perhaps you'll even consider staying permanently. The city has much to offer an entrepreneurial gentleman such as yourself."

He gave me a smile that didn't reach his eyes. "I will not make sudden changes, I promise. But without you and our spells, I do not see the point in staying. It is a fine city, but it is not Paris."

"If there's anything Matt and I can do, let me know."

He bowed again. "I apologize again for my behavior just now."

"You're forgiven. You were upset."

"Ah, yes, but I suggested that Matt made the decision for you, and that is not fair. You are a strong woman and capable of making decisions alone. It is something I have always admired about you." He kissed the back of my hand. "I will see you soon, *non*?"

"No. I mean yes, you will. Tonight in fact, if you accept Louisa's invitation. She asked me to press upon you her desire to see you at her gathering."

"If you will be there then I will endure her company." He winced. "I know that is cruel to say, but she is very forceful."

"Forceful?"

"I think she still wants to marry me."

"But she's engaged to Oscar."

He merely shrugged. "She has not asked or mentioned it again since I tell her no, but…it is just a feeling I get when I am near her. Does that make sense?"

"Yes," I said quietly. "It does."

Poor Oscar.

Or perhaps not. He wasn't in love with Louisa, and knew she didn't love him in return. He knew she was marrying him for his magic and shouldn't be despondent if she tried to marry a more powerful magician instead.

Still, it would hurt his masculine pride if not his heart. No man liked to be rejected for another, even when he wasn't in love. While Oscar's reasons for marrying Louisa were equally avaricious, he didn't deserve to be treated so poorly by his fiancée.

I'd tell her as much tonight.

* * *

WILLIE INSISTED on coming to the meeting with Matt and me, even though she hadn't been invited. It was such an unthinkable thing to do that we didn't tell Aunt Letitia in case she had one of her episodes. I didn't feel all that comfortable committing such a grave social sin either, but I agreed. The more people supporting me at these events, the better. Willie said she wanted to keep an eye on everyone's reactions when Oscar announced he was giving up on the book, but I suspected she really went for the food.

Louisa put on a wonderful spread of cakes, sandwiches, and tarts, but I couldn't be tempted to eat. I was too busy trying to avoid people. At the top of my list were Hope and Lord Coyle. Fortunately Lord Farnsworth took it upon himself to engage me in conversation upon arrival.

"I'm very close to discovering who informed the Masons about your man and Miss Mason," he whispered after beckoning me to a corner of the room.

"It has taken you some time," I said.

He shushed me then glanced around. Nobody could have overheard yet he continued to whisper. "There have been developments."

"Oh? Do go on."

He tapped the side of his nose. "Not yet. I must confirm my suspicions. I'll call on you the day after tomorrow and reveal all."

"That's Christmas day."

"Is it? How extraordinary. I appear to have lost an entire two days somewhere. I blame late nights and too much fine liquor."

"Perhaps you ought not drink as much if you're losing entire days."

"My dear Mrs. Glass, I must! How else am I to get answers?"

"I don't understand."

"I must ply suspects and witnesses with the good stuff if I want them to talk. Nothing cheap." He pulled a face. "Can't stomach cheap stuff, and since I must partake too, only the best will do."

"You're getting the Rycroft servants drunk?"

"Not just them." He glanced around again then leaned in. "So the day after tomorrow?"

"It's Christmas day," I reminded him.

He frowned. "Didn't we have this conversation already? Yes, it's Christmas Day. So?"

"So don't you have to be with your family?"

"What family?" he asked, quite innocently.

"Oh. I am sorry, my lord, I thought you must have siblings or cousins or someone to dine with at Christmas."

"I'm an only child, my cousins only talk to me when they need money, my father's dead, and my mother's in an asylum near the old family pile. I hardly ever go there."

"I am sorry."

"Don't be. The servants have the run of the place and are quite happy for me to make a rare appearance to visit the tenants, look over the property, that sort of thing. They wouldn't know what to do if I showed up for Christmas and it hardly seems fair to turn the place upside down just for me."

I bit the inside of my cheek to stop myself laughing. He looked quite serious. "I meant I'm sorry about your mother. I didn't know she was in an asylum." He had once mentioned her appreciation for fairies, so I wasn't surprised, but I'd assumed she was dead.

He gave me a sympathetic look, as if I were the one whose mother was mad. "It's quite all right. No need to feel sorry for me. She doesn't even recognize me."

I wasn't sure how that made it better, but he seemed to think it did. "Would you like to join us for Christmas dinner?" I asked.

He beamed. "Oh, Mrs. Glass, that is most generous. Most generous indeed. You make me feel like one of the family." He touched the corner of his eye with his little finger, but it looked dry to me. "I heartily accept your invitation." He bowed. "Thank you."

Willie joined us, her gaze studiously ahead. "Don't look, but Hope is coming this way. Prepare yourselves."

Lord Farnsworth glanced around. "Ah, the new Lady Coyle. I say, she made a good match. Lucky girl."

"A good match!" Willie hissed. "He's ancient! If anyone made a good match, it's him."

"Yes, but being ancient and rather unhealthy, he'll be dead within a decade and she'll inherit everything, including his remarkable magical collection. That alone is worth a fortune." He plastered a smile on his face and bowed deeply as Hope drew close. "Good evening, Lady Coyle. That outfit is very becoming on you. Not everyone can wear that shade of green."

She stroked her hand across the front of her skirt as she regarded it. I wanted to congratulate Lord Farnsworth for making her feel self-conscious without even trying. It was a thing I'd never achieved.

"Now, if you'll excuse me, I must speak to Matt about something," I said.

He had been accosted by Lord Coyle at the same moment as Hope had joined us. It would seem their two-pronged attack was designed to keep us apart. Poor Matt had no one with him to divert attention elsewhere. I at least had Willie and Lord Farnsworth, although I wasn't sure how beneficial they'd be.

"Just a moment." Hope laid a hand on my arm. "I wanted to ask you about the carpet ride."

"The what?"

"Yes, the what?" Lord Farnsworth echoed.

"You know what I mean, India," she chided. "We saw you." She glanced at Lord Farnsworth. "Shall we talk somewhere quietly?"

"No, you may not," Willie said. "Whatever you think you saw is wrong. It was a trick of the light. An experiment with ropes and pulleys. Nothing more."

Hope arched her brows. "India? You were not working on

a fireworks spell as you claimed, were you? It was wool, or carpet to be precise."

There was no point trying to convince her they hadn't witnessed a magical flying carpet. It had been broad daylight and they'd been standing almost directly below us. I wasn't going to engage her further on the matter, however.

"We won't be discussing anything with you," I said. "Not about this or anything else. Good evening."

Her grip on my arm tightened. "My husband is currently discussing the very same thing with your husband. As you can imagine, he's very keen to negotiate terms to purchase the very first magical flying carpet for his collection. He'll want the original, of course, but I'm here to tell you that if you can't part with it, he'll accept another as long as it can fly too." She leaned forward and lowered her voice. "But don't tell him I said that."

I wrenched free, but before I could say anything, Willie spoke.

"If he wants to negotiate, he should talk to India. It was her experiment, not Matt's, and she's capable of saying no to Coyle just as well as Matt is. As an independent and strong woman, I'd expect you to have more respect for India than that."

Hope's spine stiffened. "This is a business matter."

"So?"

"Discussions about money are best left to the men."

Willie snorted. "I don't for a minute think you believe that. You're as capable of being as manipulative and devious in business as Coyle. You've had enough practice at the manipulative and devious part as anyone."

"Isn't that why she's here?" Lord Farnsworth pointed out. "Talking to Mrs. Glass in case Coyle's efforts fail? Or perhaps attempting to sweeten Mrs. Glass so she'll override her husband if he refuses, which he will." He nodded at Matt, looking like thunder as he spoke to Coyle. "Do you think they'll fight, Willie?"

"It won't be a contest if they do," she said. "Matt's a skilled pugilist. Although Coyle looks like he won't topple easily."

Lord Farnsworth chuckled.

"I don't care whether you or your husband want the carpet," I said to Hope. "It's been destroyed. The contraption can't be operated by anyone but me and is therefore useless."

"Not as a collector's item it's not. Once word gets out—"

"Word will not get out."

"My dear India." She bestowed a condescending smile on me. "The club members are a close-knit community. We share information."

"But not wedding invitations," Willie pointed out. She indicated Lord Farnsworth with her thumb. "Unless they're lords or ladies."

Hope stiffened again. She was spending most of this conversation as rigid as a pole. "That was my mother's stipulation." She turned to me. "The secret won't stay a secret for long. Soon you will be bombarded with requests to make magical objects fly."

My heart sank.

"However," she went on. "We will keep the spell a secret *if* you sell us the carpet. My husband will pay a good price for it."

It was my turn to stiffen. "I will not be manipulated. Go ahead and tell the world about it. And while you're spreading gossip, be sure to tell the other collectors that I won't be using the flying spell again, no matter what price is offered. Now if you'll excuse me, I'd like to be anywhere but near you."

Hope huffed, turned sharply, and walked off through the small gathering. Some of the men bowed at her while the women attempted to engage her in conversation, but she marched toward Matt and Lord Coyle without acknowledging anyone. The only person she did acknowledge was Matt. He said something stiffly to them both and strode back along the path Hope had carved. His thunderous expression had grown darker.

Hope glanced back at me over her shoulder and smiled in triumph.

What had Matt done?"

CHAPTER 18

"*A* magic carpet ride, eh?" Lord Farnsworth said. "Was it fun?"

"Sure was," Willie said, grinning. "I ain't never felt so free. You should have seen the city from up there. Everything was so small. I reckon if it had been a clearer day, we'd have seen from one side of the country to the other."

"May I join you next time?"

"There won't be a next time," I said, as I watched Matt approach. "It's too dangerous."

I didn't see Willie's face but I suspected she rolled her eyes or pulled a face because Lord Farnsworth chuckled quietly.

"So Matt," she said when he joined us. "Did Coyle offer you a vast amount of money to buy the carpet?"

"He did," Matt said. "But that's not why I accepted."

"You accepted!"

Lord Farnsworth shushed her as those nearest us glanced our way. "I say, that's not fair," he said with a pout in his voice. "I would have made a counteroffer if you'd given me a chance. A magic flying carpet would be a great asset to my collection. If I'd known you were going to sell, I would have

241

spoken up but Mrs. Glass said you weren't, so I didn't. Don't want to be in her bad books, you know."

"Why'd you sell it to them?" Willie spat.

"Leave," Matt said to Lord Farnsworth.

His lordship departed without so much as a mutter.

Matt checked to make sure no one could overhear us, then he lowered his voice. "I'm selling him an ordinary carpet. He wasn't close enough to see the pattern on the flying one and won't know the difference."

"Ohhhh," Willie said, nodding. She broke into a grin. "Good plan."

"Stop smiling," Matt snapped.

Her smile vanished and she blinked back rather forlornly. I frowned at Matt, for so many reasons.

"Let them think we're angry and disappointed at being manipulated," he went on.

"Manipulated?" I echoed. "What did Coyle say to convince you? Or pretend he convinced you?"

"He offered money, which I declined. He then offered up information in exchange."

"What kind of information?"

"Anything we want."

Good lord, that was quite a powerful bargain Matt had struck. And we didn't even have to give Coyle the real carpet in exchange. It was still lying somewhere in a paddock just outside of Brighton. He was right in that Lord Coyle would never know he had an ordinary artless one. It was a brilliant plan.

"I also made him promise the carpet must stay in his collection and not be given to any other magician to try and fly again," Matt said. "I told him it was too dangerous, but it's simply to ensure the swap is never discovered."

"Another magician will know it's fake when they touch it and feel no heat," Willie said, nodding along.

Conversations suddenly quieted as the butler announced

Fabian's arrival. Louisa swanned over to greet him and the conversations quickly resumed again. She hugged his arm and smiled up at him. He said something stiffly to her but she merely flicked dust off his jacket lapel and continued to chat, smiling the entire time.

"Christ," Willie muttered. "Here comes Mrs. Delancey. She's been asking me about signing that teetotaler agreement. I'd forgotten about it until tonight." She spotted Fabian and a determined look came over her. "Reckon I'll rescue him from Louisa." She joined them and took Fabian's other arm and tugged him away from Louisa.

Louisa frowned back but released Fabian and joined another party of guests.

"Poor Louisa didn't stand a chance," I said.

"Willie should watch herself," Matt said. "She'll make more enemies than she knows what to do with if she continues to be so aggressive."

I turned to him. "What's happened between you two?"

"Nothing."

"Don't pretend with me, Matt. Something's amiss. What is it?"

He pressed his lips together.

"Tell me, Matt, or I'll ask her."

"There's no point asking her. She thinks she did nothing wrong."

"Then tell me what it is and I can adjudicate. Matt," I snapped when he continued to refuse. "Just tell me."

He sighed. "It was something she said a few days ago in the carriage."

"Go on."

His gaze slid away. If we'd been alone, I'd have grasped his face between my hands and forced him to look at me. But I couldn't do that in public, so I merely squeezed his hand, hard.

He sighed again. "It was after Carpenter admitted to

243

helping Amelia and Bunn escape London. He claimed he'd done it so that his young magician children would have a free future. Willie said in the carriage afterward that parents are foolish where their children are concerned, and she said you shouldn't have them."

I waited, but there was no more. "So?"

"So it was a cruel thing to say to you."

"It was just a joke, Matt. She wasn't serious."

"It was insensitive considering…"

"Considering what?"

"You're not with child yet."

I took his hands in mine. It was enough to get him to look at me. Worry darkened his eyes, but I wasn't sure if it was worry for me or because we'd not yet conceived and he was troubled by the possibility we might never.

"Jokes like that don't upset me but I see that it upset you," I said gently. "It's all right to admit you're worried we can't have children, but don't get snappy at offhanded comments on my behalf."

His fingers clung to mine. "I'm not worried."

I let out a deep breath. "Neither am I. We haven't been married long and there's still time. I'm hardly Hope's age, but I'm not old either."

His features softened and I thought he might kiss me right there in front of everyone. "I know."

"And if we can't have children, we'll adopt."

He considered this then nodded. "There are many orphans in the city."

I smiled, relieved that he seemed amenable to the idea. "We'll provide a loving home to lots of orphans."

"All of them."

"I'm not sure even your vast resources can stretch to that, but we can certainly try."

He lowered his head to mine. I thought he was going to

whisper something, but he kissed the flesh near my ear. "I love you, India."

"And I love you. Now go and make your peace with Willie."

He squeezed my hands then dutifully left.

Fabian joined me and we chatted easily enough. There was no sign that he was disappointed in my decision to stop experimenting with new spells, thankfully. I was keen to speak with Louisa about her flirtations with him, but she was too busy flitting from group to group. When she did look our way, it was at Fabian. She ignored me most of the evening.

She couldn't avoid me forever, however. I was about to intercept her when Oscar called for silence. He had avoided Sir Charles Whittaker, although he had cast several glares his way. Sir Charles didn't seem to notice.

"May I have everyone's attention, please." When all the guests were looking at Oscar, he cleared his throat. "I have an announcement to make. I'm no longer writing my book on magic."

Murmurs filled the room.

Hope eyed Lord Coyle, but his lordship merely stared at Oscar as if he were looking into his mind, trying to determine if he was telling the truth or not. He must have his suspicions. Considering Oscar's vehement enthusiasm for the book in the past, everyone should have doubts. But going by the nods, most seemed to think he was telling the truth and had made the right decision.

Mr. Delancey wasn't one of them. "Why not?" he asked.

"I've lost interest," Oscar said flatly.

"You're not as fickle as that, Barratt."

Louisa moved up alongside Oscar. "It was likely to cost more to print than we would make back from sales. It was an economic decision, Mr. Delancey. I'm sure that's something you understand."

He gave her a shallow bow. "I certainly do."

Throughout the exchange, I tried to gauge Sir Charles's response. He looked at ease, as if the announcement had no effect on him. Until he cast one very quick and rather furtive glance at Lord Coyle.

Lord Coyle didn't notice, but Hope blinked back, startled. If I had to guess, I would say she had been looking for confirmation that Lord Coyle and Sir Charles were meeting in secret and exchanging information. She probably wasn't entirely sure we'd been telling the truth about them, but that glance convinced her.

I was so intent on the three of them that I failed to notice Matt trying to get my attention until Willie elbowed me and nodded at him. He arched his brows at me in question.

I nodded back. "Excuse me, everyone," I said over the quiet conversations that Oscar's announcement had given birth to. "I would also like to tell you something."

Mrs. Delancey clapped her hands in excitement. "Oh, I do hope it's what I think it is."

"That's enough of that talk," Willie snapped at her. It would seem Matt had spoken to her and Willie had taken it rather badly. "I need a drink," she muttered morosely before sinking into the shadows.

"I wanted you all to know that I'm no longer creating spells with Mr. Charbonneau."

My announcement received louder murmurs than Oscar's. He looked as disappointed in my news as the others. It was his fiancée who spoke up, however.

"Don't be absurd, India," Louisa scoffed. "You were born to create spells. It's your *raison d'être*."

"Her raisin what?" Willie asked.

"I like to think I have other purposes for being on this earth," I said snippily. "I am more than a magician, I am also a woman, a wife, friend—"

"You're a powerful magician." Louisa moved through the gathered guests to stand before me. Her lovely blue eyes focused sharply as if she were trying to drill her point into me. "You are perhaps the strongest of all those who are left. Fabian knows of no stronger in the world and he's been searching for years."

She looked to Fabian, but he merely stood there, unmoving. She bristled as she realized he already knew, and he seemed unconcerned.

"India, you have a responsibility to other magicians to expand existing spells and create new ones," she went on.

"No, I don't!"

She tilted her head to the side and regarded me as if I were simple. "Is it? If you're not going to strengthen your lineage then—"

"Pardon?" I spluttered.

"Your children by Mr. Glass will be weaker than you, if they are magicians at all. With an artless father, they might be artless too. And what if their children also marry an artless? Once you are gone, no one else will ever rise again to be as strong."

"We don't know that."

"We do. It's how magic has been eroded over the centuries. A marriage to an artless here, another there, and within generations magic is weakened. Coupled with the secrecy that had to be maintained for fear of persecution, it's no wonder spells were forgotten and some magician lineages became impotent altogether. But your magic is strong, India, and with that strength comes a responsibility to the future. If you won't have magician children then you *must* create new spells and share those spells. You alone can be the instrument that rejuvenates magic and steers it to power once more."

"That's the entire problem," I bit off. "The power. It's too easy to abuse. New spells can be stolen by those who would wish to do harm. Nobody can be trusted not to abuse that power, Louisa. Not even you."

"It is India's decision to make," Fabian said.

Louisa shook her head. "But—"

"She is right. It is for the best."

"Fabian! How can you say that? You of all people should be trying to change her mind."

"I did try," he said. "But she is determined and I must respect her decision. So must you, Louisa." He turned his glare onto Coyle. "All of you."

Louisa huffed out a breath and marched off to speak to one of the footmen. He opened the door, looked out, and spoke to someone. A moment later the doors opened wide and more footmen entered carrying trays with port and sherry glasses. They offered them to the men.

Out of the corner of my eye I saw Mrs. Delancey make a beeline for Willie as she reached for a glass. Willie quickly snatched it up and proceeded to drain it in front of Mrs. Delancey, a triumphant gleam in her eyes.

"A pretty speech, India," came Lord Coyle's deep voice. He stood next to me with Hope on his left, her hand resting lightly on his arm. "But how many in this room believe you?"

"Why wouldn't they?" I asked.

"Louisa was right, in a way. Magic may not be your *raison d'être*, but it is certainly a force within you that you cannot deny. It wants to come out."

"Nonsense. It has been less than a year since I discovered I was a magician and I never once felt like I *needed* to cast a spell, either before or since."

"You knew something was missing from your life before you discovered magic, and you felt its absence keenly. It's why you almost married Hardacre.

Something inside me recoiled at the mention of my former fiancé's name. "I had my reasons for wanting to marry him that had nothing to do with an empty void that required filling. If you don't believe that I truly am giving up spell making, then that is not my concern." I turned to go, but stopped. "Congratulations on the carpet, by the way. I'm very annoyed with Matt for agreeing to your terms. That carpet should have been destroyed immediately we'd finished with it. I hope you keep to your side of the bargain and leave it in your cupboard with your other magical pieces."

His answer was a bow.

"Of course we'll keep it locked away safely," Hope said.

They moved off to join the Delanceys and I sought out Matt, but he was having a discussion with Sir Charles so I decided to leave them alone and find out later if he'd learned anything important from him.

"I think it worked," Oscar said as he came up to me.

"What did?" I asked.

"My announcement. I think they believed I'm really giving up the book."

"Which of course you are. Aren't you, Oscar?"

He smiled and nodded.

"Your fiancée is rather upset with me," I said.

His gaze sought her out and found her by the mantel having a rather heated discussion with Fabian. "Poor Charbonneau," he said, chuckling. "I should rescue him. She's probably telling him he should have tried harder to make you change your mind about giving up. The notion horrifies her." He leaned toward me and whispered conspiratorially. "I want you to know it doesn't matter to me what you choose to do, India. I agree with Fabian. It's your choice. If you need to talk about it with an impartial friend, you know where to find me."

I thanked him. He really was a good man when he wasn't insisting on writing his book. I watched him move off to chase down a footman carrying a tray loaded with glasses.

His step seemed somewhat lighter, his shoulders straighter. The decision to give up the book agreed with him. Indeed, I'd say he was the happiest I'd seen him in a long time. It was why I actually believed he truly intended to stop.

Louisa wouldn't like it. She would berate him for it, and put enormous pressure on him to continue. Poor Oscar. He didn't deserve to be treated so cruelly by his fiancée.

When Fabian walked off on Louisa, I intercepted her. "Was that conversation about me?" I asked.

"Among other things."

"Were those other things about the book?"

She lifted her chin. "That's none of your affair."

"Or were you flirting with Fabian again?"

Her jaw dropped. "Pardon?"

"I know you've been flirting with him. Fortunately, your fiancé is oblivious." I leaned closer. "I want you to stop it. It's grossly unfair on both of them. Oscar doesn't deserve it and Fabian doesn't deserve to be put in that position either. They're honorable, decent men."

She tossed her fair curls and her eyes flashed. "I don't need to answer to you."

"Oscar and Fabian are my friends."

"Are they?" she sneered. "Then why did you let Fabian down so terribly?" She smiled ruefully at my shock. "I am not the one who ought to apologize. At least I know what I'm doing. I don't think you're aware of how much damage you've caused."

She strode off and I didn't speak to her again all evening. Not even to say goodbye when we left.

"This evening was a trial," I said as we settled into the carriage. "But at least it's over and I think most people believed me when I said I was giving up creating spells."

"They believed you, but didn't like it," Matt pointed out. "Don't expect Louisa to quietly accept it."

"Ain't nothing quiet about her," said the woman who was always the loudest in the room.

"I'm just glad we left when we did," I said.

"Me too. Mrs. Delancey was on the warpath. She told me I was going to hell if I didn't sign that teetotaler agreement. I told her if there's no liquor in heaven, I don't want to go anyway."

"I saw you talking to Sir Charles," I said to Matt. "Did you manage to learn anything about him?"

He shook his head. "He's too wily. He gave nothing away."

Willie sighed. "Tonight was a waste of time. I should have stayed home and drank whiskey in peace. Even Letty doesn't bat an eyelid now. Sometimes."

"One good thing came out of it." I smiled at her then Matt. "You two have resolved your problem."

Willie sank into the corner. "Sorry about that," she muttered. "I didn't mean to offend."

I patted her knee. "I know, and you didn't."

"It's going to be a full house when all the adopted babies arrive."

I laughed. "Let's wait and see if we conceive first."

"Can I make a request?"

"I'm quite sure that's not how it works," Matt said, trying hard not to laugh.

"Can you adopt one at a time? I need to adjust and I reckon it'll be easier on my nerves if we have one for a year or two before we get another."

"We?" Matt echoed.

"I ain't moving out. Besides, children are little and don't take up much space. I reckon we can all live together a while longer."

"You might change your mind after the first and want them close together," I said.

She screwed up her nose. "I don't partic'ly like children."

"How can you not like children?"

"I'll like *your* children," she said quickly. "Adopted or otherwise, they'll be good and well behaved. It's other people's children I don't like."

"What about your own? I'm sure you'd like them."

"Mine would be the worst behaved in the neighborhood. That's why I'm never going to be a mother. Can you imagine me bringing up children? I ain't mature enough to take care of myself let alone a smaller version of me. Nope, I'll be content to watch yours grow up. And I promise not to corrupt them until they're at least sixteen."

"Eighteen," Matt said.

She put out her hand. "Let's shake on it."

* * *

Our first Christmas altogether in the Park Street house was far from understated. While we'd been in Brighton, Duke and Cyclops had set up a tree in the drawing room, and helped Aunt Letitia decorate it, although they'd saved the star for me to place on the top. The tree's branches bowed under the weight of candles, sweets, and decorations made of glass, wax, paper and fabric. Aunt Letitia also insisted on holly in every reception room as well as the hall and dining room.

"There's no point in doing things in half measures," she said. "Not when we could all be dead tomorrow."

"Aunt," Matt chided. "Why the morbid thoughts?"

She waved off his concern. "Not morbid, merely practical." She passed him a gift from under the tree. "Now open mine."

We exchanged gifts in the morning until our luncheon guests arrived. Detective Inspector Brockwell handed me a parcel tied with a blue ribbon upon entry. "This came for you at the Yard. It's from Mr. Carroll."

"The cotton magician?" I unwrapped the paper, revealing

a small pincushion with a watch embroidered in gold thread on the top. Tiny silvery blue stars burst from the watch face and the watch's chain was arranged to form my initials. The thread seem to shimmer in the light. "It's exquisite," I said on a breath.

Matt picked up a note that had fallen from the parcel to the floor and handed it to me.

"Mr. Carroll writes that he's sorry for his crossness the other day," I read. "He has made this for me as an apology." I ran my fingers over the embroidered watch face. "It contains magical warmth."

"I knew it," Willie declared. "I knew he did the embroidery, not his daughters."

"You didn't see the embroidery at Carroll's house," Matt told her. "As I recall, Brockwell and I were the suspicious ones."

Duke sniffed. "Can't blame him for lying. Ain't no man going to admit he embroiders in his spare time."

"Cyclops is quite good at sewing," Aunt Letitia said.

Cyclops didn't look in the least embarrassed to have this pointed out in front of everyone.

We ate at midday then Matt dismissed all the servants so they could enjoy the afternoon with their own families. I wasn't sure what Mr. and Mrs. Bristow would do since they were one another's only family, but it wasn't my business to pry.

We had barely begun tucking into the mince pies, turkey, potatoes, pumpkin and myriad other vegetables when Chronos addressed me loudly from across the table. "Why are you giving up magic, India?"

"You're giving up magic?" Aunt Letitia asked. "But India, dear, how will our clocks run on time?"

"I'm not giving up magic," I assured them both. "I am giving up spell creation."

"Is that not the same thing?" she asked.

"No. Our clocks will continue to function efficiently, Aunt."

"Thank goodness for that. Punctuality is a sign of godliness."

Willie made a scoffing sound, but fortunately she was seated too far away for Aunt Letitia to hear.

"You can't give it up," Chronos went on. "It's what you were born to do."

"Nonsense," I said.

"India, you can't give it up. There's no one else to do it." He rested his elbows on the table, earning a scowl from Aunt Letitia.

"It's for the best, considering the trouble new spells cause," I said.

"Just because the flying carpet proved too dangerous, doesn't mean other spells will be. Next time, create something less..." He waved his fork in the air. "Flighty."

"Flying carpet?" Aunt Letitia echoed.

"I wish you'd included me," said Lord Farnsworth with a pout. "I think I'd rather enjoy flight."

I glared at Chronos. He merely shrugged and helped himself to another roasted potato. "It's not fair on Fabian," he muttered.

"No, no," Fabian said quickly. "I have made my peace with her decision, Chronos. Now you must too."

Chronos regarded him levelly. "My life has been dedicated to magical research and looking for magicians more powerful than myself. You can't expect me to give it all up now."

"I also have dedicated my life to magic," Fabian said with equal gravity. "If I can accept India's decision, then so can you."

Chronos grunted. "It's easier for you. You've spent fewer years than me at this. I'm old. Old people can't change like you younger ones. Isn't that right, Miss Glass?"

Aunt Letitia set down her knife and fork, her meal

completed. "I don't know why you're asking me. You're *much* older than I am."

Willie chuckled and raised her wine glass in salute.

Chronos turned back to me. "India—"

"I don't want to hear any more about it," I said. "You are here because you're my grandfather and its Christmas, but do not push our generosity too far. We can just as easily send you home before the dessert course."

"There's a dessert course?" Duke asked. "I thought since the servants had gone home, this was it." He indicated the platters with his knife. "I better save some room."

"Me too," Cyclops said, reaching for another slice of turkey.

Brockwell stood and raised his glass. "A toast, if I may. To our host and hostess, Mr. and Mrs. Glass. Thank you for your generosity."

"Hear, hear," Lord Farnsworth said before draining his glass. Willie refilled it for him from the bottle Bristow had left within her reach.

"It ain't generosity when it's family," Willie said to Brockwell. "You've been around long enough now, Jasper, that you're one of us."

The inspector's cheeks flushed. "Oh. That's very kind. Very kind, indeed." He gave us another salute with his glass.

"Am I like family?" Lord Farnsworth asked.

"You ain't been around as long as Jasper," Willie told him. "But keep showing up here like you have been and soon your face'll be as familiar to us as that ugly painting of a cow in the sitting room."

"It's not ugly," Matt said defensively. "I like cows."

Lord Farnsworth sat up a little straighter and the smile couldn't be wiped from his face for the rest of the day. Not until we adjourned to the drawing room, that is, with our stomachs full and our hearts content.

It was then that he brought up the matter of Cyclops and

Catherine. "I have discovered who told Catherine's parents," he announced from where he stood by the mantelpiece.

Cyclops had been nodding off by the hearth, but now his head jerked up and he pulled his outstretched legs in. "Was it Charity?"

"No. It wasn't Lord or Lady Rycroft or any of their offspring."

"Then who?" I asked.

"A fellow by the name of Abercrombie."

"Abercrombie!" cried several voices at once.

I groaned. "I loathe that man."

"You know of him?" Lord Farnsworth asked.

"He's the former master of the Watchmaker's Guild," I said. "He made my life miserable until he was ousted from the position a few months ago."

"Why does he want to ruin my life?" Cyclops asked.

"Because you're associated with me," I said.

"And he doesn't want a watchmaking family like the Masons to become connected to India," Matt added. "That would be my guess."

"I reckon he just likes stirring up trouble," Willie said. "I don't reckon it's personal. Being a prick is just his business."

Aunt Letitia shot her a glare. "That word is vulgar."

"We should confront Abercrombie," Duke said. "Tell him to leave Cyclops alone."

Cyclops shook his head. "There ain't no point. It'll only make things worse. Besides, Catherine is working on her parents, bit by bit. Maybe it was a good thing they learned about us. It was time anyway."

I gave him a sympathetic smile. "I'm glad you feel that way. Everything will be fine, you'll see. Mr. Mason will be satisfied that you can support his daughter on your police wages, and Mrs. Mason will set aside her prejudices once she gets to know you."

Willie folded her arms over her chest. "I like Duke's idea

better. We should visit Abercrombie and rough him up a little."

"I did not just hear that," Brockwell said, arching his brows at her.

Lord Farnsworth pushed off from the mantel and approached Willie where she sat in one of the armchairs. "You lost the wager, Willie. You have to wear a dress next time we go out."

"I did not lose it! You did."

His lower lip protruded as he tried to recall the conversation. After a moment, he wagged his finger at her. "I said if I find out who told the Masons, I win the bet."

"No, the bet was if you found out *Charity* told the Masons, you win. Charity didn't do it, so I win." She gave him a triumphant smile. "I can't wait to see you in a dress. Something with lots of bows on it. And it's got to be pink."

"But that's not fair. I was under the impression I had to discover the villain's identity. Otherwise I would have stopped after I learned it wasn't Charity."

"Did you find that out long before learning about Abercrombie?"

"No, the same time."

Willie threw her hands in the air. "Then why all the fuss? You lost, Farnsworth. I expect payment early in the new year."

He sighed. "Very well. But I can't wear a pink dress. There's far too much ginger in my hair for pink. Pick any other color."

Willie rubbed her hands together. "I can't wait."

Brockwell came up to Lord Farnsworth to shake his hand. "A great piece of detective work, my lord. Have you ever considered consulting for Scotland Yard? We could do with a peer's help from time to time on the non-magical side of things. Crime isn't the exclusive domain of the lower classes."

"You mean work?" Lord Farnsworth looked as though he'd smelled something rotten. "I couldn't possibly."

"The notion of getting paid to undertake endeavors is a vulgar one to people like us," Aunt Letitia explained in her kindest voice to the inspector. "Matthew was brought up as an American, so he is an exception. But to Lord Farnsworth and his ilk, working is quite out of the question."

Brockwell nodded slowly. "I see. Thank you for enlightening me, Miss Glass. I understand perfectly now." To Lord Farnsworth, he said, "We wouldn't have to pay you."

Lord Farnsworth brightened. "Oh? That puts a different light on it entirely. I'd be happy to consult for Scotland Yard on criminal matters pertaining to the peerage. You may call on me any time, discreetly of course. Can't have people I know seeing the police come to my door. How embarrassing."

I covered my mouth with my hand to hide my laughter. But Matt noticed. He winked at me then grinned.

Later, when our guests had gone home and the rest of the household retired for the evening, I curled up with Matt in bed. "What do you think of our first Christmas together?" I asked.

"Unique. Entertaining. Delicious." He drew me on top of him and pushed my hair back from my face. "And more wonderful than I dreamed it would be."

I smiled. "It was, wasn't it? Even Chronos behaved himself after he got his frustrations off his chest."

"We have quite an unruly brood already," he said. "Are you sure adding children to the mix is a wise idea?"

"Quite sure. We need more normal people in this household to restore the balance."

He laughed. "You'd better kiss me, Mrs. Glass, then we'll try to make a baby together."

Available from 2nd March 2021:
THE TOYMAKER'S CURSE
The 11th Glass and Steele novel

READ on for a description of MURDER AT THE MAYFAIR HOTEL, the first book in the Cleopatra Fox Mysteries, a new series by C.J. Archer. **Available from December 1st 2020.**

MURDER AT THE MAYFAIR HOTEL

It was the most fashionable place to stay in London, until murder made a reservation. Solve the puzzle in this new mystery from USA Today bestselling author of the Glass and Steele series.

December 1899. After the death of her beloved grandmother, Cleopatra Fox moves into the luxury hotel owned by her estranged uncle in the hopes of putting hardship and loneliness behind her. But the poisoning of a guest throws her new life, and the hotel, into chaos.

Cleo quickly realizes no one can be trusted, not Scotland Yard and especially not the hotel's charming assistant manager. With the New Year's Eve ball approaching fast and the hotel's reputation hanging by a thread, Cleo must find the killer before the ball, and the hotel itself, are ruined. But catching a murderer proves just as difficult as navigating the hotel's hierarchy and the peculiarities of her family.

Can Cleo find the killer before the new century begins? Or will someone get away with murder?

Available from December 1st 2020.

GET A FREE SHORT STORY

I wrote a short story for the Glass and Steele series that is set before THE WATCHMAKER'S DAUGHTER. Titled THE TRAITOR'S GAMBLE it features Matt and his friends in the Wild West town of Broken Creek. It contains spoilers from THE WATCHMAKER'S DAUGHTER, so you must read that first. The best part is, the short story is FREE, but only to my newsletter subscribers. So subscribe now via my website if you haven't already.

A MESSAGE FROM THE AUTHOR

I hope you enjoyed reading THE KIDNAPPER'S ACCOMPLICE as much as I enjoyed writing it. As an independent author, getting the word out about my book is vital to its success, so if you liked this book please consider telling your friends and writing a review at the store where you purchased it. If you would like to be contacted when I release a new book, subscribe to my newsletter at http://cjarcher.com/contact-cj/newsletter/. You will only be contacted when I have a new book out.

ALSO BY C.J. ARCHER

SERIES WITH 2 OR MORE BOOKS

Cleopatra Fox Mysteries

After The Rift

Glass and Steele

The Ministry of Curiosities Series

The Emily Chambers Spirit Medium Trilogy

The 1st Freak House Trilogy

The 2nd Freak House Trilogy

The 3rd Freak House Trilogy

The Assassins Guild Series

Lord Hawkesbury's Players Series

Witch Born

SINGLE TITLES NOT IN A SERIES

Courting His Countess

Surrender

Redemption

The Mercenary's Price

ABOUT THE AUTHOR

C.J. Archer has loved history and books for as long as she can remember and feels fortunate that she found a way to combine the two. She spent her early childhood in the dramatic beauty of outback Queensland, Australia, but now lives in suburban Melbourne with her husband, two children and a mischievous black & white cat named Coco.

Subscribe to C.J.'s newsletter through her website to be notified when she releases a new book, as well as get access to exclusive content and subscriber-only giveaways. Her website also contains up to date details on all her books: http://cjarcher.com She loves to hear from readers. You can contact her through email cj@cjarcher.com or follow her on social media to get the latest updates on her books:

9 780648 214991